The Chateau

- A novel by Rambaro Pellegrino -

Acknowledgements

I would like to thank the team at Hutchinson Publishers who made this book a reality for me: Aaron Wilson, Paul Hayden, James Horn, Hailey Stone and Adam Anderson.

Contents

Prologue 1

Marcus 4

Beginning of Education 23

In Battle With Tilly 42

A Thorough Reading of the Indian Book 64

Conversations With the Priest 85

John McAllister 108

The Terrible Routine of the New Platen Press 120

Marcus' First Visit to the Chateau 131

A Crash Course in Gothic 154

Vampires... 165

Sub-Operations 176

Everything is Science 195

A Further Exploration of the Vampire Book 209

Marcus Forges a Plan 240

The White Death 259

Bertus' Long-Awaited Formula 274

The Gulden Gazette 285

Mother Takes Marcus Aside in the Small Side Room 291

Glancebury's Hidden Secret 295

Epilogue 310

The Chateau

Knowledge is power, and power must know introspection…

- The Count -

Prologue

Ingland was a country as people only knew from stories and sagas. A prosperous, thriving, and also strong nation that had established itself high in the northwest on the world map. There was also a small community in Ingland called Glancebury. A former miners' village that now flourished on cattle breeding, on the dairy trade, and on some other crafts. This small town of Glancebury, named after the surrounding rolling hills where the sunlight always seemed to shine upon, was situated in a diocese, and also in a shire, which was strange since a duke was the head of the province. However, there were more things strange to this small village…

We draw the beginning of the 19th century, although it seemed as if Glancebury had been halted for at least a hundred years. There were no paved roads around the village. Journalistic news reached the area only sparingly. And most of its inhabitants struggled to keep their heads above water.

This also applied to the Pritchard family. An honest and hard-working family that had focused on everyday farm life. They went back for many generations, who had always set foot on the swampy clay soil that the country was rich in, and who had always worked this wild ground with diligence. The Pritchards were not miners; they were farmers, they had always been, even though they never really seemed to fit in. Even though this 'living off the land' was anything but easy, there seemed to be something else brewing within their surroundings that managed to make life just a bit more unbearable...

Ingland was a country with lots of power. It was no different than other influential countries eager to maintain their power through domination. A war began; the production of the coal mines increased tenfold, and so it came to a day when the Glancebury mine was completely depleted.

A war had been fought, victory had been secured, and so the rest of the remaining troops trickled into the nation again. Yet, since then, a different wind seemed to blow over the country, over the province of Lancastershire, and also over the small town lying in the middle of it. Glancebury was originally a mining town, it always had been, but since the waging of the aforementioned war and thus the depletion of coal, its inhabitants had to find another source of income. It was clear that one day, Glancebury would no longer be a mining village. Peace had returned to the country; the soldiers had returned to their homes; the miners had to look elsewhere for their salvation; and the farmers?

Well, the farmers did what they had always been doing: toiling on the land to provide the nation with new physical strength through their crops and cattle. New recovered energy that might be used to start a new war again, although that didn't seem to be the case for the time being.

Strangely enough, something else seemed to be going on in and around the village. It was some type of curse. Some dared to claim that this was a punishment because of a war that should never have been fought in the first place. According to others, the returning troops had brought this problem with them, carrying it on the lapels of their brownish-green coats and scattering it across their homeland that they initially had tried to protect, even though this was almost never said out loud. Worryingly, it seemed as if Glancebury was the only place in the entire duchy that was affected by this.

Be that as it may, where this problem exactly stemmed from was debatable; something wasn't right, and it was most certain...

The Pritchard family had its own problems and did not concern itself with such matters. Their main task was to put food on the table for their two young children, as well as for the environment that ate from their land and used the milk that their cows daily produced...

The story about the war was a piece of history that Marcus, the eldest son of the Pritchard family, had often heard from his father, who, of course, had received this from his own father, Marcus' granddad. And even though Marcus was quietly happy that he hadn't grown up in a miner's family, farm life, on the other hand, wasn't exactly a bed of roses either. Nevertheless, he was quite content with his life, satisfied with the parental home in which he grew up, and also happy with community life in which he regularly immersed himself. A peaceful story, one might add, but every story has its dark side.

This news about the 'curse' had spread through the nation like wildfire. The fire finally subsided. But to this day... Up until the day young Marcus gets out of bed early to help his father milk the cows, this fire seems to continue to smoulder within this small community...

Marcus

Swallows flew above the farmlands, over the fields, and along the tower of the only church that Glancebury held, and they then often saw people walking. To these winged creatures, these strange characters were only dots who walked back and forth furiously and seemed to forage like they did, only on the ground. They regularly flew above the fields of the Pritchard family, and when that happened, they often saw an even smaller dot walking. This almost insignificant character usually walked reluctantly across the yard simply because that was expected of him. This little strange creature who walked upright, produced strange sounds, and sometimes looked up to admire his winged observers was Marcus. A descendant of the Pritchard family tree who would walk across the farmyard to go to the cowshed almost every morning, just as he was told…

Marcus' father, Bertus, was up much earlier; two hours before he opened his eyes, stretched out, and washed the snot out of his eyes with the cold water his mother had already prepared for him in a tin bucket. He walked across the yard, occasionally looked up, tried to look beyond the horizon, felt the climate with the peasant blood that flowed within, and could only conclude that it was going to be another calm day. A calm day indeed, although it remained to be seen how his father's mood was going to be.

Bertus had wrapped a leather belt around his waist at least an hour ago, and the milking stool that was now dangling behind his butt made it look like he himself had a wooden udder. He had just sat down in front of the last cow when he saw his only son enter the barn...

'Marcus!' he exclaimed enthusiastically. 'Good to have you back! You know the tune, don't you? The barn has to be swept, the straw has to be refreshed again, and maybe you could take a look at the pig barn afterwards? Just to gauge whether things are still going well there. But take it easy, son. This morning is going without a hitch. I'm going as fast as lightning! The ladies,' Bertus gave a tap on the butt of the last cow that had to be milked, 'are behaving exemplary this morning! I'll probably finish much earlier!'

Marcus nodded somewhat laconically. He was already going to the storeroom to fetch a wooden broom and a pitchfork when he heard Bertus say, 'Take it easy, Marcus,' for the second time. 'We're not in a hurry this morning. Just do your chores. Do them with the zeal with which you always do them. And then we can have breakfast afterwards. Later in the afternoon, we will see if there is anything else on the program.'

That afternoon, Marcus sat in front of the window while staring into the distance. There wasn't much to do; his father didn't seem to be needing him. Otherwise, he would have called.

Marcus sat down thinking for a while, musing and daydreaming. Three things that were in line with one another, that were quite similar, and that he was strangely adept at. It was a character trait that was a big part of him, that suited him. It was also a game that he often evoked in order to escape reality, perhaps, and thus visit worlds in which he would probably never take a single step in a physical sense.

Marcus was the eldest child of his parents and he loved village life like nothing else. He loved all the various noises that came up sullenly about half-past five in the morning and which, at eight o'clock in the evening, fell silent again. He was a farmer's son. And even though he could certainly appreciate the work in the fields, he also realised more and more that his heart seemed to be asking for something else. He didn't know what that was exactly, but he was determined to find out. Perhaps the veiled cries of his heart had something to do with the peaks of Light Town, whose lights could be seen flickering on the horizon on a clear night, a spectacle of the largest city in Lancastershire. The place where it all happened; where all the news poured in, was packaged into bundles of messages, which were then flung back into the country for a single penny, or two, of course.

Light Town was so huge that the lion's share of the national news originated from there. Marcus often looked up from the windowsill of his parents' farmhouse, gazing over the family fields and over the farmlands and large tracts of forest that lay beyond to see if he could catch a glimpse of the nation's biggest city. But no matter how sharply he zoomed in, and no matter how narrow he held his eyelids, he simply could not see this city during daytime. After all, he had never been able to do so before. And even though he continued to think this was a funny game, he sometimes could get a slight headache from it.

Marcus often daydreamed, mused, and tried to listen to his cries from the heart. He didn't have a concrete life plan in mind, yet he kind of did at the same time. He had a deeply cherished wish, an ever-encroaching passion that seemed to feed his enthusiasm more and more, even though this picture of the future was so far away from him that it remained an illusion at the same time.

Marcus regularly fantasised about a career at the Light Town Post. They would even call him Sir Pritchard, and of female attention, he would have no shortage. Damsels would even throw themselves at his feet. And perhaps he would see a real carriage for once. Perhaps even own one!

Marcus slid his finger over the old and dusty windowsill so that a line, an almost imaginary itinerary, was created. Which route should he take to get there? It probably won't be a straight line like this one. After all, there were so many possibilities to choose from that it sometimes made him dizzy. It was almost as if life wanted to be discovered, as if it wanted to be invented, while it, at the same time, knew perfectly well what its possibilities were...

At times, Marcus wondered if he was actually living in the right time, although he always, and quickly, tried to ignore such thoughts since they were somewhat foolish. His grandfather, who unfortunately passed away four years ago, had mentioned that multiple times. He was a man of the old book but mentally sharper than the entire arsenal of that of the tawny owl, including its beak, claws, and sight. He just seemed to know more, even though he chose to stay simple for the most part. He had taught his grandson that foolish thoughts were inevitable from time to time but that one should not linger on them for too long because, at some point, they could take over a person and even shape someone's appearance accordingly.

I'll have to be careful that doesn't happen to me, Marcus

thought for a moment, after which he quickly wiped away the line on the windowsill. His friends in the village and all the other young children from the area didn't seem to care about these sorts of things. They didn't seem to concern themselves with this kind of stuff, but Marcus was very adamant about it. One day, he would visit Light Town, walk around there, take everything in, and finally make this city his own.

At the crack of dawn, we take the cows off the land. We milk them one by one by hand. We throw the barn door open again. We let the cows free. And at noontime, we bring the cows back to the barn so that the next day, the whole thing can start all over again. Marcus had experienced it all too often from a very young age. It was a beautiful, hard, but at the same time, simple existence. Nevertheless, the boy had his head regularly in the clouds, something that didn't seem to escape his father. Bertus, too, was a man of few words. He also understood that his son wanted to experience something different from time to time, something different than the daily goings on around their farm. And so it came that the man once, somewhere in high summer, approached his son...

The scythe had gone through the tall mature grass in the past few days, and the seeds from the ears now stood open and exposed to be absorbed by the soil again. The heaps of dried grass had been laid out in neat rows. They were put on the hay wagon by Marcus, Bertus, and a number of helpers, with the use of pitchforks so that the animals, on which the Pritchard family had become so dependent, had some dry food available to be able to get through the heavier seasons. Bertus walked up to Marcus.

'Marcus!' he shouted, walking towards his son with a smile. His tanned skin gleamed in the afternoon sun, and on his forehead, beads of sweat fell from his face with every step. 'Your mother and I had a conversation earlier, and...,' he rattled on for a while.

Marcus was already preparing a reply in his mind. *Yes, I know, Father,* was what he was thinking in his head. *You guys always go to the small side room when important matters need to be discussed, and you have probably been talking about me this time...*

'And,' Bertus continued, 'your mother and I have talked mostly about you this time.'

Marcus nodded.

'You have been part of our family business for quite some years now, and even though that is not more than logical, since you are our son, we believe that you have been doing very well so far and for a long time by now. You hardly ever whine, you do your jobs with the right commitment and diligence, and that is why both your mother and I want to reward you this year; reward you for your hard work and contribution.

'You will be entering education in about two months, and that is also your last big step towards full citizenship, towards a full-fledged adulthood, and that's why...,' Bertus did a little wooden dance to reinforce his enthusiasm. 'I want to take you to the annual market soon! And, of course, I don't mean the paltry fair of Glancebury by that, which is not even worthy of the name. No! I mean a real fair! The one in Light Town!'

'Wowww!' Marcus excitedly exclaimed. His pupils dilated like saucers, and he embraced his father, who stepped back a little uncomfortably.

'Haha,' laughed Bertus out loud. 'I knew this would appeal to you! We leave on early Monday morning. Be ready!'

Mentally, Marcus was already prepared for this, strangely enough. That night, all he could think about was this gesture that his parents had so coincidentally, but at the same time not so, placed in his lap. Peculiar was what Marcus had to think. Miraculous was the second word that came to his mind. *Was that perhaps how the world worked? If one could imagine things, visualise something, and actually believe in it, then could it eventually come true?* After all, it was not long ago, sitting in front of the windowsill, peering through the large window of his parents' farmhouse, that Marcus dreamed of distant travels, visiting cities that could enrich his little world of experience. And now, all of a sudden, such an opportunity indeed presented itself. Very special was what Marcus thought for the last time, and with a contrived image of Light Town in mind, he dozed off in an exciting but also tense sleep...

'Look!' said Bertus to Marcus on that very early Monday morning, around four o'clock. 'After all, education is the greatest asset that we know. Broaden your horizons while gaining knowledge so that you can enter full-fledged adulthood with the right intellectual tools, skills, and equipment. That is also one of the reasons why I am taking you to the annual market in Light Town, Marcus. Not only because you have earned this through your hard work but also because you will be going into education soon. Before long, on that upcoming moment when you will become ten years old, you will walk the path that we all have had to walk. It won't always be fun, son. Sometimes, you might hate it, but in the end, you will come out smarter and wiser. It will make you realise that education is an essential part of our existence and that it will strengthen your development.'

Yeah, yeah, was what Marcus thought somewhat lazily.

And as if fate itself was playing with the matter, Bertus mounted the farmer's cart with their only horse harnessed to it in order to visit a place that could well exceed Marcus' wildest expectations. The two took their seats on the trestle of the cart and now drove along a long, narrow, and almost straight road towards a place where it all seemed to be happening.

The journey was boring, long-winded, almost monotonous, surrounded by nothing more than farmlands and the natural beauty that the province of Lancastershire was so rich in. The ride was dull, alas, but the tension that began to settle in Marcus' constitution because of it seemed to temper the monotony a bit.

Passing farmlands, meadows, fields, and many a tree, they finally approached the city walls of Light Town. Bertus stationed his cart at a special spot just outside the city walls. He gave the supervisor some pence, and so the two could now, without too many worries, make this stronghold their own.

'Look,' said Bertus again, just as they set foot inside the bastion while the hubbub of the many festivities came closer and closer. 'You probably already knew this, but this isn't the first time that I've come here to take a look. Almost every year, your old man travels to these grounds to see whether certain developments have been made within my line of work. On these grounds, I have met many fellow farmers. We have exchanged our experiences and knowledge, and sometimes even exchanged or sold our cattle to each other by means of the so-called hand-clap. The animal market, the farmer's market, the horse market, and the weighing house are names indeed, but they are also places that are named after our trade and where we farmers can still be found when it comes to our merchandise.

'Now, I'm not going to bore you with that, Marcus. Someday, probably one day in the future, I will show you the way of this cattle trade, but for now, for this day, we're going to walk around in this big city called Light Town. We are going to try to take in as many impressions as we can, and we are going to try to make this day as fun as possible.'

Marcus smiled at his father, nodded in agreement, and then immediately began to work on the playful assignment his father had instructed him; taking in impressions and also experiencing what it is like to walk around in a city that he only dared to dream of a while ago…

The sun glided slowly over Light Town like a warm blanket that lit up its tall buildings and warmed the visitors as well as the inhabitants of this grand city with the sunlight that reflected through the high windows and the shop fronts. *Maybe that was where Light Town got its name from. A bit similar to Glancebury, which in turn got its name from its surrounding rolling and also shiny hills, partly thanks to the sun that, from time to time, so eagerly played with that scene.*

Marcus looked up at the luminous peaks of the city. He looked at the towers, facades, and battlements, all of which seemed to be ablaze and which, from his first impression of this place, already gave an almost archetypal image of what an imaginary dream city should look like. He looked upward, almost bulging his eyes out. His feet blindly took their steps, maneuvering through a crowd of people who all had come to join the festivities, as if he had been here many times before as if he could sense everything around him intuitively and thus create a path for himself, without bothering anyone, without disturbing anyone, and even without bumping into anyone in the crowd.

Marcus took in all the impressions and smells and, despite the large crowd and the therefore limited room for movement, still felt like a free man. He looked at the many market stalls that had been set up and admired their wares: the exotic nuts on display, the variety of spices, the artisanal cuts of meat and sausages, and the many other stalls with their nice jewelry, toys, postcards, and other keepsakes that he actually wanted to surprise his mother with.

He looked questioningly at his father, who stood a little further away and had become involved in what seemed to be an animated conversation. Maybe with someone he already knew, or maybe with a new contact, but Marcus' tacit plea under his breath was, of course, not heard.

He looked at all the rings and the glitter, at the bracelets and the chains, and also at the many cut-out and hand-painted figurines, and then thought for a moment. His father had given him five pence, a reasonable amount that he could probably buy something nice with. He had no clue what he was going to buy exactly, but buying something for his mother might be a bit unwise at this moment. Not that he didn't want to give her anything, but more because it was so unique that he was walking around in this place, and he just wanted to have a personal souvenir of this experience to bring home with him. He had no idea what this memorabilia was supposed to be, but he went voluntarily on the wind of this day and let himself be carried away by its relaxing current.

Bertus put a big hand on his shoulder, and pushed him a bit further along, which said to Marcus that the man was in somewhat of a hurry. They stopped from time to time for a viewing or an event. Sometimes, at a play performed by street performers who comically portrayed the former tyranny of King Henry the Sixth. Another time at a ring joust. Two armored horsemen were facing each other and had to knock each other off their horse by means of a thick wooden lance. A sound of splintered wood could be heard from time to time with the tin sound of a suit of armor slamming hard against the ground and deafening applause because of the spectacle, but also because of the courage of these two pseudo warriors, who were risking their lives for a bit of money and fame.

According to Bertus, these kinds of games were a remnant of feudal times, perhaps even from a time before that, from a certain class society. He promised that he would tell Marcus all about it on another day. Marcus nodded enthusiastically; he couldn't wait to hear more about it. Bertus ordered him to continue walking again. They had already stopped by this event long enough and their precious time was slowly running out. Plus, Marcus had to hurry up to get a souvenir. He quickly searched around while the clock ticked relentlessly. Before long, Bertus would force him to go home again, and he knew that this would be without concessions.

Marcus looked at the variety of stalls again, with all their paraphernalia and their gadgets, with all their toys, their jewelry, and other keepsakes. It was almost too much to choose from. The image of his mother haunted his mind again, and so did the smile that he could put on her face, although something in him held that back. He had to make the right choice; the well-known icing on the creamy cake. The hidden pearl in the, at first glance, simple and somewhat average oyster seemed the perfect choice to end this marvelous experience.

Marcus looked up for a moment at the skies high above

him. *Help me!* He almost implored, turning to the gods or whoever might hear him. *Help me to end this wonderful day in a sublime way.* And as if fate itself was playing with it; fate with its endless calculation of possibilities that, strangely enough, always knew how to influence the universe in a way and even seemed to be in cahoots with it, he heard, not far from him, a merchant shout. 'Get your books here! Come and get your bundled manuscripts here! Bound or stitched! With or without cover! There is something for everyone here! Books in a higher price range! And also books for the lower incomes! For young and old! For anyone who wants to add to their book collection and who dares to stimulate their mind and at the same time enrich their vocabulary!'

Marcus' heart seemed to skip a beat. That's what he was looking for! The beginning of something that could well become his personal refuge. The beginning of the end of this magisterial day, which could undisputedly be called mind-blowing and, in this case, could even have an educational outcome. He greeted the market vendor in a somewhat timid manner and tried not to show his enthusiasm too much because the man might then charge him a higher price for his merchandise. He eagerly, but in a controlled manner, began to rummage through his wares.

The merchant's books were neatly laid out in rows, also neatly stacked, and apparently sorted by subject. Many of the books were old, half-worn, and almost falling apart from misery, with many loose pages that the closed books held together due to their volume and, of course, due to gravity.

'This section is chiefly about the history of our country,' said the merchant to Marcus. His young and potential buyer looked like he could use some help in his search. 'This pile goes mainly about the animal kingdom and the many creatures that walk our globe. And this pile here...,' the man pressed a finger on the top book as if all these books were extra special, and as if he didn't want to sell them at all 'is about strange, and also foreign people; people who live on the other side of the ocean, for example, or who no longer exist at all.'

Marcus was amazed. His heart almost raced out of his chest, and his body experienced a sensation that could almost be labeled as a gold rush, only then in terms of knowledge-gathering. He felt book-hungry, and if he had the money, he would have bought them all, but unfortunately, he hadn't. He had only five pence in his pocket, and if he was lucky enough, he might be able to get one book for that amount.

A bookcase.... How neat would it be to own one? Marcus thought. His mind started to play tricks on him. He had to choose as Bertus was getting impatient to go home. *Good!* Marcus thought decisively and looked at the books about indigenous people with a certain eye of knowledge that he apparently carried within him. After all, he couldn't read yet, but the book he chose simply caught his eye...

'Good choice!' said the market vendor suddenly. 'Excellent choice, in fact! A book about the ancient Indians! And this one is even illustrated! You'll probably have a great time with this book, young man. That's six pence, please.'

Marcus looked at the five meagre coins that lay in the palm of his hand, looked at the market vendor somewhat bewildered, and then raised his hand.

'Hmm,' said the merchant doubtfully. 'We'll just have to make do with that, don't we?' He handed Marcus the book and wished him a good day.

'Look, Dad!' Marcus enthusiastically cried out as he walked up to Bertus. 'Bought from that man over there.' He pointed towards the book stall where a bunch of new customers were now standing.

'That's nice, Marcus,' said Bertus, somewhat unfazed. 'But what have you exactly paid for that?'

Marcus mentioned the amount he had handed over. Bertus quickly leafed through the yellowed book, with a number of pages whirling to the ground and with the cover of the book half detached from the spine.

'Five pence?!' shouted Bertus in dismay. 'Five whole valuable pence?! For this garbage?! Ridiculous! You've been tricked, Marcus! I won't let this happen!'

'But?!' cried Marcus, trying to explain that the merchant had already accommodated him by taking a whole penny off the price, but it was to no avail...

Bertus had already walked towards the stall with brisk steps and was now scolding the market vendor. Doing so, Bertus seemed to chase away the bookseller's potential customers because they understandably didn't feel for a riot.

Meanwhile, Marcus had also moved to stand next to his father, while the market vendor looked somewhat annoyed at his young buyer. 'You must understand, sir,' said the merchant calmly. 'That I have made a verbal agreement with this young gentleman here and not with you. The transfer of the product was done in full agreement, and on top of that, I also lowered the price for him...'

'Ha!' shouted Bertus in turn. 'This book isn't even worth three pence! Two at most! You should be ashamed for taking advantage of an ignorant youngster like this one! Of a young customer like my son!'

The trader had to grin for a moment and his somewhat brownish teeth bared as he said: 'Well, sir, those are the tricks of our trade. Supply and demand. To give what the fool wants....' He looked obliquely towards Marcus.

'I'm not going to take this!' yelled Bertus in an even angrier tone. 'Either you give my son his money back, or you make an agreement that we can work together as civilised citizens.'

'And what are you exactly thinking about?' asked the merchant somewhat laconically, turning towards some of his new customers, thus trying to disguise and soften this little debacle.

'You make it two books for this price,' Bertus demanded, 'or halve the price, simple as that! Or, in extreme cases, book back, money back, but I'll leave that choice up to you...'

'Hmm,' said the merchant pensively. 'Well, come on then, choose another book...'

Marcus immediately stood on his hind legs. *Another book,* he thought. *What a day!* And what a hero his father was for standing up for him like that. He eagerly again, and this time less controlled, rummaged through the stacks of books. He laid one book on top of another, making a mess of the sorted and categorised subjects, to the seller's dismay. He felt brave all of a sudden, mighty almost, because his old man stood behind him, and he did not want to let this opportunity pass him by.

Should I go for the animal kingdom? For the fauna of the new world, perhaps? Or maybe that of the old one? Should I choose another book about indigenous people? People who undoubtedly and regularly came into contact with these four-legged animals? With all kinds of winged creatures and whatnot? Or should I opt for a stitched collection about the rich history of Ingland? With its former princes and regents, undoubtedly dry fare but educational at the same time, that could give me a possible head start within the form of education that I would soon enter...

'Hurry up, Marcus!' snapped his father.

The market vendor could do nothing but tacitly agree. Marcus turned the pile of history books upside down and judged the books by their covers, but he still wasn't satisfied. He had to find a subject that had the potential to overwhelm him. Something he could learn from, something educational, but also with a wink, and preferably entertaining.

He was almost at the bottom of the pile when his gaze caught a book with some red cloth folded around it. He quickly picked up the book, to the now even greater horror of the owner, stripped it of its textile prison, and looked carefully at the front cover. 'I want this one!' said Marcus. 'I think this one would be fun!' Simply because he liked the cover.

'That one is not for sale,' said the merchant with a grey face and with a sour undertone.

'But why is it on the shelf then?' asked Marcus. 'Among all the other books?'

'This one belongs to my personal collection,' said the salesman. 'I have no idea what the book is doing there…'

Marcus looked questioningly at his father. 'Okay, okay,' said the man hurriedly because he understood very well what Marcus was trying to achieve here. 'I'll be honest with you. 'This book comes from my personal collection. It is indeed for sale right now, but this book alone is worth more than the five pence you have spent so far...'

'You had said two books,' Bertus retorted firmly. 'Two books for the price of one. I heard it coming out of your mouth just now, you were there yourself when you spoke those words.'

'Damn it!' shouted the man angrily. 'Are you trying to trick me or something?! Unbelievable, I have never experienced such stubborn customers as the likes of you. Fine! Actually, I want a shilling for it, forty farthing is also good, but I'll round it up for you. Come on, you two, both books for the paltry sum of ten pence, take it or leave it.'

'Ten pence?!' exclaimed Bertus indignantly even when it wasn't that much money, and the miser could do perfectly without it. 'Fine! I guess it won't be books then, and return our money, of course!'

'But, Dad?!' pleaded Marcus. 'I want the book about the Indians, but I also want this one. I want them both! Give me this opportunity, please. I don't just want to tell Mom something about Light Town when we are back home; I also want to show her something tangible...'

Marcus could see that his father was contemplating this. 'I don't know, Marcus,' Bertus said. 'We had a very pleasant day today, and what's wrong with taking home some good memories? Moreover, ten pence is household money, which we can live on for the next three days. You have to think about that sort of thing too, Marcus.'

Although Bertus had his doubts, the last thing that he wanted was a sulking Marcus next to him on the trestle of their farm wagon on their way back home. He also wanted to end this day as fun and as pleasant as possible.

'Besides!' said Marcus with conviction in his voice, trying to persuade his father some more, somewhat taking advantage of the wavering gap between a yes and a no, which his father was now visibly struggling with. 'I can't do much without a single book. But with two books, I could learn to read much faster, maybe even master it after a while.' He showed his father a charismatic grin.

'Well, come on,' said Bertus, pressing five more coins into the merchant's hand.

'An excellent buy!' said the merchant in a rousing voice, reverting to his role as a slick salesman. 'A nice book! A beautiful book even! Mysterious! Eye-opening! A book that is undoubtedly made for you!' The man smiled at Marcus for a moment, although the gesture seemed a bit crooked. 'I'm not going to tell you what it is about because you'll find it out for yourself, but the information within it had entertained me greatly, at least.

'Now, you'll have to promise me something, little man,' said the salesman and also looked at Bertus. 'Promise me that you'll never set foot in my stall again!'

He gracefully turned away from the two villagers and welcomed his next customer or potential victim, depending on how you look at it, with open arms.

'Hmpf, what a blowhard,' Bertus told his son as they walked towards the city walls again, towards one of the exits where their faithful steed, harnessed to the cart, was eagerly waiting on them. 'I still think that we've been fooled, Marcus,' he said, laughing at the matter; a possible nice anecdote to tell at home and also a confirmation that city dwellers were not to be trusted when it came to clinking coins.

'I don't think so, Father,' Marcus replied. 'I don't think we've been fooled at all. It might even be that I have two golden treasures in my possession right here...'

Marcus had not yet fully uttered these words when Bertus seemed to choke for a moment, although Marcus didn't really understand why.

'I hope so for your sake, Marcus,' Bertus coughed. 'I hope so for your sake...'

He tightened the reins, ordering the horse to walk, and the ride back home began...

Beginning of Education

Marcus had now two books in his possession: a book on the ancient Indians, of which the merchant had told him about, and another book, whose subject remained unknown but seemed exciting. He was proud of them. He regularly took them to hand, and looked at them for a while, although he couldn't do much with them for the time being.

The book about the old Indians already spoke to Marcus somewhat, partly thanks to its black-and-white illustrations. In broad strokes, he glided past the many drawings, absorbed them, and thus began to get an idea of what the book was all about. He could spend hours on it, looking at the drawings that adorned the book of those ancient people while also studying the cover of his mysterious second book. It spoke volumes, for there was something dark about it, something ominous, and Marcus couldn't wait to read it. Soon, perhaps, at least maybe in six months, when he had been in school for a while and hopefully had been able to master the basics of the alphabet.

Marcus could spend hours like this; all alone in his little room, often at the end of the afternoon, often until dusk, and sometimes even with a lighted candle by his side when the sun had already faded, and when the moon let its light glide over the surrounding fields, and over the rolling hills from which

Glancebury owed its name. But sometimes, he had enough of this: locking himself up in his sovereign chamber, the days that began to resemble one another, and the few souls he encountered by constantly doing so. There were days in between, however, when he did come out of this room, realising that it was also good to wander through his birthplace from time to time, and to talk to the souls who lived there. Moreover, Marcus realised all too well that he'd better spread his concentration and not let it burn out completely because he could put it to good use within the educational form that he was about to enter.

He always used to play with his younger sister in the yard of their farm, although that occurred less in recent times, and he didn't really know why that was. She seemed to reject him more often, seemed more and more 'absent,' which was partly because she always had something to do: helping mother in the household, collecting flowers to make bouquets, and making straw dolls to sell them in her small self-set up stall on the side of the road, which no one actually came to visit, but which she was nevertheless very passionate about, and in which she was stimulated by mother and father.

And so it was, after the umpteenth rejection from his younger sister, that Marcus decided to pay a visit to his friend, or rather, to his good acquaintance that he called the chicken farmer. He was a nice fellow, easy-going, a man well over forty, and always on his own, which seemed odd to most of the residents of Glancebury. Marcus didn't find this strange at all, and he could understand this phenomenon very well. After all, he also liked to be on his own. It simply seemed a method in which a person could think well and clearly and not be so easily distracted by the many quarrels and inflections that took place so often.

Perhaps his good acquaintance, the chicken farmer, felt the same. Perhaps the good man had figured this mechanism already out in life and was that why he lived the way he did: in total peace and quiet, not caring that much about those around him, who thought he was just a weirdo anyway, of course, never said this straight to his face, but sometimes let him know through their weird little mannerisms. It was something Marcus had thought about before, and perhaps today was the perfect day to confront the man with this question to reconfirm these thoughts…

The man was a very small-scale farmer. He lived a little off his crops, lived a little off his chickens and their egg production, and had odd jobs here and there when needed and when people could use his services. He was a jack of all trades, and seemed to be able to support himself just fine, although it wasn't exactly noticeable by looking at his house.

He lived in a small ramshackle farmhouse, had a small piece of land that was poorly maintained here and was also withered in certain spots. Behind his house was a large chicken coop, whose clucking sounds could be heard from a great distance and which, at first glance, seemed to be falling apart a bit. Marcus had been to this place many times before. He had noticed the poor dwelling of the chicken farmer, although he had never said a word about it. The man seemed to live here very well, and perhaps this whole house stood synonymous with the way in which he lived his life: somewhat chaotic, not exactly admirable seen from the outside, although it seemed with a strong foundation and remained upright like a real house.

It just wasn't Marcus' place, rebuking this man for his

standard of living as that of a clochard, although Marcus also knew all too well that if his parents knew that he was a regular hangout with this person, he probably wouldn't be allowed to go there anymore...

The man walked up to Marcus with a smile and gave him a friendly pat on the shoulder.

'So, are you here again, friendly giant? To what do I owe your visit? Will you come and help me with the chickens again?'

Marcus stoically shrugged his shoulders, told the man about the fair in Light Town, about the books he had bought there and had been looking at so many times lately, and that he was actually visiting the man out of boredom.

'Ha!' the man shouted. 'Well, that's fine, right? The bow can't always be tense. There has to be room for some pure time killing now and then; a putting of the mind to zero, and a realisation that life isn't about obligations all the time.'

Marcus thought that was a nice way to put it, especially coming from a, at first sight, simple soul like the chicken farmer. However, he also knew that almost everyone had a certain amount of depth if you looked long enough, and that was certainly the case with this man.

He decided to ask his good acquaintance something straight to the point. A question that he had been carrying with him for a long time now, something that he had wanted to ask the man much sooner but hadn't had the chance.

'Hmm,' said the man thoughtfully. 'So you want to know why I live my life as I do? All alone, and without a wife and children to enrich my life, and to secure my offspring with? Can I conclude from this that you came here not only out of boredom but also out of curiosity?'

And Marcus nodded.

'Well, I don't know, Marcus. I think it's quite a personal question. What if I suddenly told you things that could really offend you? That could put me in a different perspective. And so that you might not want to see me at all afterwards? Or would you like to hang out with me again? And all this out of a form of candour?'

A small grimace appeared on Marcus' face. 'And is that also the case with you?' he said very directly but at the same time also somewhat concealed.

'Well,' said the man. 'If that were the case, I probably wouldn't even tell you, for fear of becoming a pariah, for a fear that my honesty would be used against me. But you know, I don't think this is the case for me at all. Actually, you may know everything about me, although I do know that, simply because of the way how I'm living, some people look at me in a certain way. Because there is apparently a shadowy area between us, something which they cannot enter, something which they cannot place, or which they easily have access to. If I could describe the answer to your question simplistically, it would be that I just really like to be on my own, that I find pleasure in this way of living, and that I can do exactly what I want without being hindered by others. And the fact that I don't have a wife or children? Well, I think that stems from the fact that I feel like I don't have enough to offer, although that might be a bit painful to say about yourself. I'd rather not have a family than a family that I couldn't take care of….'

Marcus swallowed a wad of grief for a moment, and the pain was palpable in the air, although it didn't seem to bother the chicken farmer that much.

'Ah, loners, hermits, clochards, whatever you want to call them. They've always been there. New rounds, new opportunities, is what I always optimistically say.' The man looked at Marcus with a smile but also with a certain glint in his eyes. 'But,' exclaimed the man excitedly, 'there are more like me around, as I've heard. Did you know, for example, that we have a new resident in our illustrious village recently? A real cloth weaver. He, too, always seems on his own. He, too, is the subject of gossip and buzz, although that doesn't seem to bother him either since he is originally not from this town. Maybe you could pay him a visit one day? Perhaps you could ask him the same question? Even I am a little curious now….' And the man laughed loudly again.

'See if you can get something out of him, and then you can tell me all about it on your next visit here. Not that I need to know of certain things, but then we have some material for comparison!' And the man walked away with a chuckle, raising his hand in the air to wave goodbye to Marcus.

Marcus thought about this for a moment. A real cloth weaver? He didn't even know what that was, although it sounded interesting, somewhat decadent even. *That man is also a lot on his own…? Well…. Comparison material…? Maybe… maybe I'll make new discoveries this way. Maybe I'll even come to a new insight.*

An insight into why people want to live in such ways, although, at the same time, Marcus also got a bad taste in his mouth from all his. *Digging into other people's lives wasn't exactly decent behaviour, and what did you actually get out of it?* Perhaps he could ask the same question to this man, who apparently called himself a cloth weaver, as he had to the chicken farmer? Maybe… although Marcus also knew that, when it came to the research of social motivations, he probably wouldn't go through with this. He might ask the man this question, and perhaps it was a good opening to get to know the man somewhat better. Marcus was more hoping that he, if all went well, would gain a new acquaintance, whom he might learn something from, just like he could from the chicken farmer from time to time…

'A wooden school bag is ready for each of you students, containing a reading board, a slate with a pencil, a jar of ink, and a quill. Be careful with them! You can decide for yourself whether you take these things home or leave them here at school. The next two years will be dedicated to learning how to read and write, a little general knowledge, and some basic skills such as calculation.

'Cherish the inkpot and the writing quill well. Don't let any ink go to waste, and always close the jar tightly. If your inkpot unfortunately falls over, you have to knock on your parents' door for compensation for the loss. You can come to me for pointing the quill and for buying new ink. The same goes for sheets of paper. In the coming period, however, we will practice with the slate and the pencil. Do not press too hard with the pencil on the slate, as this will cause permanent scratches that cannot be wiped away. I wish you all the best in this very first school year. May our lessons be fruitful, and may God assist you all on this path towards full citizenship. Grab your slate so we can start right away.'

Marcus looked at the handful of students around him and decided to follow their example. He placed the wooden school bag on his lap, took out the slate, and then placed the slate on the wooden bag so that it could function as a surface for writing. Small markings were already scratched on the dark slate. These markings stood in rows below each other, and they almost depicted a magic formula. Marcus had seen letters, words, and sentences before, but they often seemed like a jumble of writings. They often looked interesting, but he had never been able to decipher them.

It would now take two years. Maybe two very long years. Maybe two very difficult years. Perhaps he would never be able to master this reading and writing completely. But he would nevertheless do everything in his power to at least be able to master its basics. He vowed to himself, and he just had the idea that he might be able to keep it.

'Weird, aren't they? Those peculiar signs on your writing board?' said Miss Tilly, the apparently friendly, perhaps somewhat stern teacher, who had to guide this small and young group of Glanceburies for the next two years in what she herself called 'formation.'

'Signs, sketches, markings, illegible, and also incomprehensible to you all,' continued Miss Tilly. 'Incomprehensible because this here, what is now in front of you, is a work of writing of the highest level. It's not that I want to throw you children in the deep end of the lake, but it's more that one day you might also be able to reach such a level. Not after these two years, of course. But maybe at some later point in your lives, when the urge for knowledge increases, and one realises that enriching one's mind is a great asset.

'I have written this piece of text also on your writing

boards. To welcome you, in my own way, to this first school lesson that we share together. It's one of my favourite poems. It is a piece of text recorded by the poet Mattheus van Heyningen Bosch. It has a core that applies to us all. The poem will also come up more often during this school year, so try to remember it at some point. I'm going to read it aloud to you now for the very first time:

> *Be diligent, my dear!*
>
> *Then thou shalt grow great,*
>
> *and then you have certainly*
>
> *always your bread.*
>
> *The sloth has to beg*
>
> *despised by each one,*
>
> *a carefree life*
>
> *gives labour alone—'*

One day, Marcus' mother sent him to the chicken farmer to get some eggs. The neat chicken farmer, that is. The one who has the largest coop in the village, with its hundreds of chickens, and where almost all the inhabitants of this town got their eggs from, and the abattoir its chickens.

But not Marcus. Unbeknownst to his parents, he got the eggs from his good friend, the smaller chicken farmer. *Eggs are eggs,* thought Marcus. *And chicken farmers are generally just chicken farmers, so I'm not really doing anything wrong.* He supported his good acquaintance with some money; the eggs were exactly the same price, sometimes even a little cheaper, and if his mother ever found out about this endeavour, he would just say that he didn't know that he had to go to a 'specific' chicken farmer. A chicken farmer, well, in

Marcus' eyes, was just a chicken farmer. His father probably wouldn't give a damn where the eggs came from, but his mother might be difficult about it…

'Haven't seen you in a while!' called the man as he walked up to Marcus in a laughing manner. 'How long has it been since our last conversation? Four, maybe five months already? Time flies! By now, you must have been at school for a few months. Do you like it?'

Marcus waved his questions nonchalantly away. School was okay; he learned a lot from it, that was for certain, but it was also very dry, and he didn't really feel like talking about it right now. Another time, perhaps, but not now. Marcus wanted to voice his grievances, this time his cries from the heart even, and with this man he was usually at the right place for that. He wanted to ask the man a pressing question, and of course, he wanted some eggs from him. If the man could only give him eggs, with some superficial talking on the side, Marcus might as well have gone to the big chicken farmer, with its hundreds of chickens and thousands of eggs.

Marcus still dreamed of Light Town, the city where the annual fair had taken place, and lately, this craving had increased more and more. He didn't know why that was exactly, but a certain force seemed to drive him towards that direction. As if deep down, he had a realisation that he was meant to do greater work. That he had a lot more to offer than the average person, and that he had to respond to that calling, or else this dream might slip between his fingers.

He had no idea what he would do there exactly, but that he wanted to be in that place, that was for certain.

'Chicken farmer?'

'Yes, good Marcus?'

'May I ask you an important question?'

'Another one?' the man replied. 'Well, go ahead, but if this is a line that is extended from now on and into the future, maybe even into eternity, then I will have to ask some money for it eventually! I could make a small fortune with all those questions of yours!'

Marcus chuckled.

'Well, it's like this,' said Marcus, seriously. 'Since I've visited the fair, my longing for the big city, you know, Light Town, has only grown more. I've always dreamed of Light Town, ever since my younger years, but now that I've actually taken steps in that bulwark, I'm completely sold. I want to live in that big city, too, absorb the many sounds, taste all the smells, and let them sink into my clothes. So that when I'm back home, and I press my pants or cardigan against my nose, I can smell this city of my dreams, and I know that I've truly lived! I want to gain knowledge, knowledge that I have accumulated from books, and I want to display that knowledge there. I want something like that in my life, living life on a large and also intellectual scale!'

'Well, well, well,' said the chicken farmer, somewhat surprised. 'Those are poetic words for someone who is only ten years old and with only four months of schooling behind him. Maybe that city is indeed where you need to be. Maybe you were indeed born for it. I have never heard a Glanceburie speak so animatedly about that city like you do. But I would like to advise you to take a step back. You are still young, very young, perhaps even too young to venture into such an immense city on your own. I advise you to wait a few more years, at least until you are fourteen, and if your dream is still valid, then I would pack my bags if I were you and just go for it! Because I agree with you on one thing: it is not always wise to live on a dream, but to have never chased a dream at all is also not a way of living.'

'Exactly!' exclaimed Marcus delightedly. 'That what you've just said is exactly what I mean! Do you have that too sometimes, maybe? A certain craving for knowledge? Maybe even for the big city?'

Marcus knew the moment he spoke that this was a somewhat stupid question. The chicken farmer was probably not like that at all, and maybe even the opposite. And the way Marcus asked him was almost as if he was trying to project his own dream onto this man in order to derive some form of confirmation from him…

'No,' said the man firmly. 'I never had that, actually, and certainly not in my younger years. So the fact that this is the case with you says a lot in my experience. But again, keep thinking about it, keep playing with the thought, but please wait a few more years on it; you'll thank me later for it….'

'Okay,' said Marcus in a somewhat minor key, nevertheless grateful for the wise advice he had just been given.

'Hey!' said the chicken farmer cheerfully. 'I may have never been to Light Town myself, but I happen to know someone who, at least from hearsay, seems to be from there. I have told you about him, haven't I? The cloth weaver? Apparently, you haven't visited him yet. I've told you about him before. He supposedly comes from there and even seems to have held a fairly high position there, although he is a villain, according to many. But go to him, hear him out, and then you can always decide if Light Town is the place for you....'

Marcus decided to do as he was told. He had little to lose, had little to do on this day, so he might as well pay this man, the cloth weaver, a small visit.

After Marcus had delivered the fresh eggs to his mother, he walked back into the village square of Glancebury with rapid strides to surprise the cloth weaver with his presence. The chicken farmer had passed on the cloth weaver's address, which was actually quite easy to find.

Marcus was welcomed in the cloth weaver's house, provided he was not touching anything. The good man, who indeed came from Light Town, held a high office, as he himself called it, and he made that very clear to the young boy. Marcus had quite a few questions. He wanted to ask this man all kinds of things: about Light Town, what he had done there, how long he had lived there, and how he actually ended up in Glancebury.

But it was almost as if Marcus had met his match. The cloth weaver, in turn, asked Marcus all of his own questions. But more than that, he too was quick with his words, and that he immediately wanted to show Marcus the ropes of the trade in which he earned his living. There was no arguing with it, at least not for the questions that Marcus would have liked to ask here now on the threshold of this dark cave. And it almost seemed like a test, as if the man was trying to gauge whether Marcus had the sharpness to understand this craft of cloth weaving and whether he cherished a certain fascination for it. But a test or not, Marcus actually found it interesting. And he could always ask his pressing questions later on, provided this man started to like him a bit and provided Marcus could visit here more often…

The man lived in a standard terraced house right in the center of Glancebury. From the outside, it looked sober, not that badly maintained, but dirty. The curtains of the house were always closed, and it seemed, if one looked at the house from the outside, as if no one lived there.

Inside the house, however, a completely different world emerged. There was a lot of activity, and all done by just one man, in a dark, somewhat musty cave, which was partly due to the fact that the curtains were always closed and that there was little ventilation going on. There were large tubs with water and also scaffolding on which large rugs hung, and there was a certain smell in the room that Marcus could not quite identify.

It was clear that a certain fabric, or rather textiles, were being used, but the how or what remained completely unclear to Marcus. Nevertheless, the man would tell him, in the way that Marcus was standing here so, in this muffled, somewhat musty room of the man, all about it in his own characteristic way, of course…

'Look,' said the cloth weaver in a calm tone. 'Actually, it's not that complicated at all what I'm doing here. Yarn is turned from fibers, or better said, spun, and then textiles are made from them. Textiles then can be used to make clothing or other artifacts. Have you ever heard of the word artifact, Marcus?'

Marcus shook his head because that was a word he hadn't

heard before, let alone known.

'Well,' said the man, 'actually, an artifact is a somewhat expensive and fancy word for an object made by human hands. It is simply a term that is used within our line of work, although I wouldn't break your head over it. Now, you shouldn't be thinking that I make this yarn myself because they are sometimes delivered to me or I pick them up myself at the so-called spinning houses. You know, from households that have the privilege of owning a spinning wheel and who can live partly off it. Here in Glancebury, you also have a few of those spinning houses, which is mainly women's work, of course, but you probably have seen them before…'

Marcus scratched the back of his head for a moment and couldn't really confirm this, although he decided to keep his mouth shut and not show his ignorance too much.

'Cloth…,' continued the man in his calm tone, 'is very popular among large parts of the population. The material is robust, wear-resistant, water and dirt-repellent, it lasts a very long time, and it also requires little maintenance. It's beautiful stuff! And I am honoured to be able to make it.'

The man looked beamingly at a wooden scaffolding with a large piece of cloth draped over it. Marcus followed his gaze and understood the story for the most part, although some things were still unclear to him. 'Oh,' said Marcus, somewhat surprised. 'And all this time, I thought that you were making pieces of fabric that people could use to sleep under, or they could drape a dining table with…'

'Yes,' the man said with a little laugh. 'That is indeed a view that is not correct. I, and many people with me, are engaged in the making of cloth fabrics, fabrics that are made out of wool.'

'Oh,' said Marcus for a second time. 'Learned something new today.' And even though he found the story of the cloth weaver somewhat interesting, and he actually learned from it, it was also very dry. He was wondering how long the monologue of this man would last…

'I use the so-called flat weave,' the man continued, without noticing that his story was starting to bore Marcus a bit. 'Also called the plain weave. The threads, the warp and weft, lie alternately above and below, below and above, and above and below again. A kind of mirror image construction, so to speak. In this way, the fabric gets a regular appearance and the cloth is very stable. Moreover, I myself find it the easiest method. After all, it does its job, so why do otherwise?' He smirked.

'The fabric is then felted by so-called foot fullers in those large wooden tubs you see over there. By the way, it's not that surprising, Marcus, that you've never come into contact with this type of cloth before because it's quite a luxury product. This is partly due to the complicated production process because of the many sub-operations that this product undergoes. And very high-quality cloth, which I do not make myself anymore, is even worn by nobles, even by the king of Ingland himself! Of course, ordinary citizens don't have the money for this product, and they mainly wear clothing made from home-woven fabrics. I get my own yarn from Light Town and not from a hamlet where we are now. In Light Town are where the real ones, the specialised craftsmen reside, those who still pay the necessary attention to their subproducts and who have the right knowledge of the many dyes with which they colour their fibers. But to come back to the foot fullers.

'And I must say, Marcus, be glad that you are the son of a farmer because this profession, this fulling of wool, is perhaps one of the worst professions there is. But anyway, the wool… the cloth has to be felted, the so-called fulling of the wool, and that happens in those large wooden tubs over there. We pour in a lot of hot water, piss in the tub a number of times, add some lumps of earth to the mixture, which absorbs the dirt from the fibers, and then the party can begin! By the way, don't tell other people that I said that; the worst profession there is… because I can really use my helpers in this work.

'But gosh, if anything is monotonous, heavy, and nasty, it is this fulling of wool. Anyway, when the tub has been given the right ingredients, the cloth is submerged in the water piece by piece, and it is tamped down with the feet for hours. That is why it is called 'fulling,' Marcus. Because this way of treatment creates a sturdy, waterproof fabric, that is less susceptible to shrinkage. It is a nasty job indeed, but necessary for the process, and the result is definitely worth it.

'Oh well, I treat my helpers in kind. They get paid according to the standard, and I haven't heard them complain for the time being, so for now, I'm good.'

School life was not as carefree as Miss Tilly made it out to be. And her character was not at all as nice as in those first few weeks. There seemed to be an increasing pattern in which corporal punishment was an issue almost daily, and strangely enough, these were almost always carried out on young Marcus. He didn't really know why that was the case because, in his own opinion, he didn't do that much wrong at all.

Perhaps it was because of his big mouth or rather said,

because of his wit, which Miss Tilly didn't seem to be tolerating. More and more often, she took out the rod and often when Marcus had made a certain remark. A remark that, preferably, a silenced student should not have made at all.

Perhaps Marcus' wit was seen as a form of insubordination, a form of rebellion, of a form of brutality even.

Perhaps Marcus' remarks were offensive to Miss Tilly because a child shouldn't respond to an adult at all.

Or that it was out of the question that a child, in certain areas that is, might be sharper of mind than an adult at times. But be that as it may, the rod—a set of branches tied firmly together—was often eagerly brought out by Miss Tilly when she felt hurt in her honour again, and she then hit it with quite some precision on the bare backs and buttocks of her defenseless students.

Today, Marcus had to bend over again, his shirt pulled up, and he once again endured his punishment passively.

'Ouch!' he sometimes shouted. 'Ouch!' in an even more pathetic tone. But actually, he didn't feel that much of it and often just pretended so that Miss Tilly wouldn't hit harder or go even more crazy with her sadistic procedures.

It wasn't for the blows, and it wasn't for the strange pleasure that Miss Tilly managed to get out of this. No, it was this shameful and also submissive posture in which Marcus had to maneuver himself again. Marcus was too good for this! This primitive behaviour infringed on his mental capacities! Oh, how he had come to dislike Miss Tilly in such a short time. And oh, how he began to denounce the grown-up world by now!

'Yes, take a good look, children,' was what Tilly said to the class while she took care of poor Marcus. 'I really don't do this without a good purpose, but this here is to teach you children some manners! Ways that you will desperately need to keep you standing in the big, bad outside world. No one has ever worsened from a good beating on his or her buttocks or from some coordinated corporal punishment here and there. And if you do not believe me, then you little sinners will only have to take a good look at the Great Book. For it is even written in the Bible, and I quote Proverbs thirteen, verse twenty-four: "He who withholds his rod hates her son, but he who loves him seeks him early with chastisement…"'

In Battle With Tilly

Now that Marcus had leafed through his book about the ancient Indians a number of times, and now that he was getting the hang of reading, he began to realise that the book contained quite the information. Information about people who apparently, somewhere on this globe, had set their footsteps, and perhaps still did. And even though it was a book that consisted mainly of illustrations and was apparently aimed at a somewhat childlike audience, Marcus decided to go through it completely this time. At least, to start it and then see how far he would get.

Marcus soon found out that Indians have different tribes, many different tribes in fact, although his book only discussed the four largest ones. He read about the Sioux, the Hopi, the Iroquois, and the Cherokees. How they originally came from Asia, how they crossed the Pacific Ocean, and how they first populated North Imerica tens of thousands of years ago. He could well imagine their journey, and with the words he read, short fragments of this great undertaking and its people were created in his mind.

Marcus saw how these first Imericans had spread over the north of this continent. How some of them lived in the woods, others in the cold north, some in the southeast where it was always warm, and some of them even in the hot desert of the southwest. He understood that since the environment was different everywhere, these groups of people had also developed different ways of looking for food, how they built their shelters, wore different types of clothing, and even had their own way of thanking the spirits. And over the course of thousands of years, these people formed hundreds of different Indian tribes, each of which had its own culture...

Marcus was now getting the hang of it, began to like the book more and more, and he eagerly read on.

The next chapter he read was about Indian knowledge, striving for knowledge that he also seemed to pursue in a certain way, and which was also one of the reasons why he now, up to this point, had his nose so deeply in these pages. The book told him that these first inhabitants had no written language at all. The only thing they could do was listen to stories and try to remember them as best as they could. And since the Indian children did not go to school, they learned everything by imitating the adults.

Marcus thought about this for a moment, and something seemed to dawn on him. He read the last sentence of this piece and, strangely enough, was able to link a certain comparison to it. A comparison that related to his own little world—a very small world within a very large nation called Ingland—which was traced back to the small hamlet that was allowed to bear the name Glancebury. Marcus put his finger on the last sentence and then read it aloud in his head: 'Children learned about their origins and listened to the legends they were told, and of course each tribe had its own stories...'

Legends, sagas, folktales...

Glancebury also had its own folktale that had been circulating within the village for generations and that should supposedly frighten the youngest in the community, probably to keep them in line. It was the story of the white death. A curse, or rather, a disease that seemed to affect mainly young children. People did not know where it came from or how it exactly reared its head. All they knew was that this disease actually existed. Almost everyone knew an acquaintance or a family member who had succumbed to it. If children had been acting naughty, this disease was raved about because, according to the story, it would mainly affect rebellious young souls.

Marcus could not help but to make this comparison. Was the story of the white death also nothing more than just a folk tale? The people, especially the older inhabitants, claimed that was not the case, even though Marcus himself had never known a victim close by, and no one had been affected by it for years. True or not, it was certainly a folk tale, a strange and mysterious story, which sent chills down Marcus' spine.

The warriors of the prairies wore feather headdresses, each feather representing a brave deed. And the tribes of the north coast... Marcus understood that this meant another area, other types of Indians, and other cultures... *depicted their stories on totem poles.* He looked at the drawing of a totem pole attentively and was so absorbed in it that he was startled when his mother called him for dinner.

Marcus closed the book, took a good look at the cover— at the person with the large feather headdress on his head, and then put the book away with some sorrow. He didn't feel like eating at all and also didn't feel for a joint silence at the diner table. He felt like being in the book, like an Indian on the back of a horse, spear in hand, looking for a mighty bison to cut it down and eat the animal's flesh at a time when it suited him, not when he was told to. He woke up with difficulty from this daydreaming, reluctantly descended the creaking, worn wooden stairs, and then unwillingly joined the rest of his family...

One day, Marcus overheard a conversation that took place in the small side room. The small room where his parents always retreated when major adult problems had to be discussed, thus safely shielded from the vulnerable children's ears who probably could not bear the suffering. Today, however, the door was ajar, and Marcus could hear his mother crying and how she poured out her heart to her husband.

'I don't get it either, Bertus,' he heard his mother say. 'I also don't understand why they act that way to us. Our family trees have resided here since time immemorial. We have just as much right to live here as they do!'

Marcus couldn't make more out of the conversation because the door was quickly closed again. However, their voices kept sounding for a while, and although he could not understand more of it because the walls wouldn't allow it, that something serious was going on was certain...

So there was a real cloth weaver in Glancebury, a high craft, which made it extra strange that the good man had settled in Glancebury. Some claimed that this fueled his arrogance. He enjoyed being looked up to because otherwise, you wouldn't live in a small hamlet like Glancebury, would you? Perhaps the man just liked his peace. Be that as it may, Marcus visited him from time to time, and so he did today since he was one of the few villagers who still allowed the cloth weaver a fraction of light in his eyes...

Marcus was walking across the village square to go to his

now good acquaintance, the cloth weaver, when a man suddenly bumped into him. His shoulder, somewhat vicious against Marcus, almost caused the boy to lose his balance and, at the same time, sending a small shock wave of terror through his body. When Marcus took a closer look at the man, it soon became clear to him that he had been drinking heavily, with movements like that of a heaving ship, complete with a double tongue and an unkempt appearance.

Yet this situation, in which Marcus had now suddenly found himself, did not seem to be a case of balancing problems. No, it looked like the man had deliberately bumped into him. The man had Marcus probably in his sight from a distance, and now that he had come closer, he fired his verbal bullets at the boy.

'Ha!' the man shouted closely at Marcus, speaking with some consumption, which was even somewhat felt in Marcus' face. 'Just walk on!' the man said intimidating. 'Just walk on to that friend of yours, that cloth weaver! That's also such a swindler!'

The man menacingly pointed out his index finger to Marcus, standing so close that he almost touched Marcus' nose and so that the boy could clearly see the black nail on the finger that was now rebuking him. 'Don't think you're better than us, you educated farmer's son! We have made this village great as it is! We have!'

The man spat on the ground in a disrespectful manner, after which he fortunately walked on, or at least, staggered on further.

When Marcus arrived at the cloth weaver, he immediately

discussed this incident and, at the same time, also expressed some of his own grievances. The cloth weaver listened to Marcus' story, although he didn't think it was all that special. 'Peasant life is a noble aspiration, Marcus.' The man laughed at the same time. 'No, you shouldn't take this too seriously. You shouldn't care so much about the gossip that goes on in this village. And let me tell you a little secret right away….' The cloth weaver moved cautiously towards Marcus while holding his hand to his mouth. 'The majority of the residents in this village are even crazier than a cuckoo's egg! But don't tell anyone….'

But Marcus was not satisfied with this answer, referring to the conversation he had overheard earlier from the small side room of his own home. His parents also seemed to suffer from this to a certain degree and there clearly was more going on than people actually wanted to tell. 'Why are they acting like this to our family?' Marcus asked the man. 'And why are they acting like that to my father? He is a good man. He works hard every day. He takes good care of us. And with his works he also ensures that other people have food on their table…'

The cloth weaver nodded. He understood very well what Marcus meant and explained to Marcus that Glancebury was originally a mining town. The miners were the real men, and the farmers weren't afraid to get their hands dirty either, but according to these people, they were afraid enough to risk their lives for their descendants...

'What nonsense!' exclaimed Marcus angrily. 'Everyone in this village needs one another, right? Everyone eats from one another, right!?'

'That's right,' the cloth weaver said. 'But try to tell that to these people…'

'Do we all have to chew on lumps of coal then!?' Marcus shouted sharply.

'You're absolutely right, Marcus,' the man said, 'but that's just the way people are. Seemingly, they like to think in terms of ranks and positions. Even a miner thinks that way apparently, with the dust of the mine still visible on his teeth...'

Marcus just couldn't understand this. He just couldn't comprehend the short-sightedness of this story. He decided to go to the church, a building where he hardly ever came, but today he did, simply to ask the priest who worked there for clarification.

The school lesson started piously, although it would probably result in a form of quarrel and conflict. Be that as it may, the students obediently took their reading boards out of their wooden school bags—the luxurious ABC board, which was covered with a layer of horn—turned it over as there was a text on the back, and the meagre class then read in unison:

'Our Father who art in heaven,

hallowed be Thy name,

Thy kingdom come,

Thy will be done,

as in heaven, so also on earth.

Give us this day our daily bread,

and forgive us our trespasses, as we forgive our debtors,

and lead us not into temptation, but deliver us from the evil one.

For Yours is the Kingdom,

and the power and the glory forever.

'You just keep making a mess of things, Marcus! Learn how to act normal!'

'But I can't help it, Miss!' Marcus exclaimed in despair. 'I keep sliding with my hand over my own writing, I really can't do anything about this! I'm left-handed!'

'That's really your own fault, Marcus,' Tilly said unreasonably. 'It's a punishment. Left-handed people are simply sinful and bad, that's in their nature. Take your fate as it is, and accept it...'

'What nonsense,' muttered Marcus to himself while at the same time feeling a certain anger igniting. Firstly, because Miss Tilly was once again not open for debate, and secondly because of this unreasonable statement.

'Bad...?' Marcus muttered again. 'Bad...?!' he suddenly shouted a lot more clearly, for every classmate who wanted to hear it. 'The only thing that's bad here are these annoying writing pens! Why can't I get a goose quill for right-handers? With the tip slightly bent to the left? It might look a little weird, but it will definitely help. I dare to assure you that the side of my hand will turn out less black, and there will also be a lot less stains on the paper...'

Marcus started to smile a little, looking with his head slightly bent at the sheet of paper that lay on his wooden school bag, a sheet of paper full of black smudges and stains. After all, it was a good argument; soon, his sheets of paper would undoubtedly look cleaner.

Marcus looked up, tried to find out if Miss Tilly felt the same way about this, but then suddenly felt a painful blow under his right cheekbone. He felt startled with his hand above his cheek, then looked at the floor next to him where the object had fallen with a thud, and saw the "unlucky bird" lying there; the sand-filled object, that was made of textile, and which could only mean one thing: punishment, a small calamity, and that usually in the form of a beating!

'But?' said Marcus aloud. 'And?' in an incredulous tone while he reluctantly brought the unlucky bird back to the desk where Miss Tilly was already waiting for him with some pleasure in her eyes.

Chastisement in the form of spanking was something Marcus was bound to get, so he decided to take it up a notch. Five extra blows might not be so bad. A few extra blows might be worth it to get to the truth, to get the truth above the lectern behind which Tilly had managed to entrench herself with piercing eyes.

Why did he receive this reprimand in the first place? Marcus just had to know! 'This is not fair!' he exclaimed. 'Why are you chastising me? I've done nothing wrong at all! I only came up with a good alternative to solve this problem!'

'Shut up!' Miss Tilly snapped. 'I have no intention to argue with a brat like you! And certainly not with a left-hander!'

'But?!' Marcus replied in despair.

'Hold out your hands! Now!' Tilly shouted.

'None of it!' Marcus shouted in return. 'Tell me the truth! And then I will undergo my fate!'

'Damn it!' Tilly shouted this time. 'Disobedient and rude youngster that you are! The shame board for you today!'

'Fine!' yelled Marcus again. 'Hang the sign around my neck, but tell me the truth!'

Miss Tilly turned fiery red. She did not feel like lowering herself to the level of one of her students, although at the same time, this seemed to get out of hand, and this could even cause her a certain degree of loss of face with the rest of her students. She could even permanently suspend Marcus from school, although that would eventually affect the meagre wages she was earning already.

In the end, she decided to only partially meet Marcus' clearly stated demand, although, of course, she did not show it. 'I'm not going to argue with any of my students! Know your place, disobedient child!' was what she said once more, and at the same time thinking of a proper form of concession. 'I threw you the unlucky bird because you clearly don't know your role within these four school walls! I'm the teacher here! I call the shots here, and I also make the decisions! And you just have to listen and obey!'

Marcus decided not to say one more word, bent over a little, and then got the heavy wooden shame board hung around his neck. He knew the procedure, and he walked out of the school doors without wanting to hear another word from Tilly. *Take a good look, bystanders!* was what he thought when he stood outside the school, for every spectator to see what a rude and uncouth disciple he was. *Take a good look at the victim! Rejoice in his suffering! Talk about it for miles around! For anyone who wants to hear it! One day, I will no longer be a victim, but I will also not be a perpetrator! One day, I will be free! Free from these erected facades and this unreasonableness! One day, I will be free! Free of mind and also of body and limb! So that I can put anyone in his or her place who tries to slow me down with his or her own shortsightedness!*

Marcus' grandfather had often told him about earlier times. And even though he didn't understand a word of it at the time, more had stuck with him than he had initially thought. Not so much the details of the conversations but more the moments. Marcus, therefore, approached his father to ask him about this knowledge and to get a certain clarification about the conversations he once had with his grandfather in earlier times.

'I really want to tell you about them, Marcus,' Bertus said to him. 'But before I do that, I would like to discuss something else with you. You know, I'm almost starting to feel regret for the fact that I gave you those books,' Bertus said with a friendly smile on his face. 'And I understand that you want to practice reading, and apparently, you are starting to develop a certain fondness for it, but I also need you here on the land, Marcus…

'Stand by your old father, try to divide your attention between your school work and that of the farm, and take up your daily chores with the diligence you have shown us all those years before, before our visit to the fair in Light Town.'

'Okay,' said Marcus somewhat hesitantly, as if what Bertus had just said hadn't quite gotten through to him. 'Can you tell me about earlier times? About the times in which grandpa had grown up?'

Bertus nodded and then started to tell. 'Your grandfather's grandfather worked for a feudal lord. The man had no land, the man had no possessions, the man only had both his hands, and a tool to work the soil with. Every day he had to toil in the fields, sometimes for twenty hours on end, in order to be able to yield sufficient harvest every year, together with many others. Reap what was to be ceded in part to the kingdom. And if this harvest was scanty, people like your great-great-grandfather for example, felt the consequences. The king, also known as the liege lord, was given priority. So, no matter how hard the serfs had worked that year, they still had to bite the bullet at the end of the ride…

'It was not an easy time, Marcus. And even though people like your grandfather's grandfather were assured of a certain legal certainty, safety, and also social security, these were still very harsh and uncertain times.

'And even if a war broke out, these so-called serfs were obliged to fight in battle, fighting for their liege lord, with probably nothing more than scythes, rakes, pitchforks, and flails to defend themselves with. No, those were indeed difficult times. They had no possessions, little or nothing to say, and they had nowhere to go. Because providing for themselves was damn difficult to do in those days, so they were, literally and figuratively, bound to the clod…'

'But how did we, the Pritchard family, get our land then?' Marcus asked his father.

'Yes, that's a very good question, son. I don't quite remember how it went exactly, but times change. My grandfather regularly spoke about a class society, and what he exactly meant by that escaped me a bit, but it looks like we don't live in such a society anymore. At least one of his sons, that of my father's father, was able to come into possession of this piece of land, partly thanks to the hard work and the good name of your great-grandfather, and so this piece of land here had become family property...'

'So these fields have only been in our possession for three generations? That's not that much either!'

'Ha!' exclaimed Bertus in return. 'The Pritchard family have been walking with their heels in this clay soil since the Middle Ages. For even though this piece of land may not be called our property for that long, we had already earned it back amply and much sooner.'

Marcus swallowed for a moment and even started to feel a bit dizzy. He even seemed to feel a kind of despair, even though he didn't let his father know. The story was much clearer now, and it even implied that this baton, that this stick, was already partly placed in Marcus' hand and, therefore, only had to be handed over to him. But was he actually ready for this?

Did he actually want this? It gave him a lump in his throat. He already had done so much work with his ten years of living, and so much work still lay ahead of him. He even had to take care of offspring in the future, and raise them in a proper way. Could he actually do this? Were his back and shoulders big, broad, and also strong enough to manage all this? Did he actually have it in him to be a real Pritchard…?

Marcus got more often the idea that Miss Tilly was not just after him. She picked him out of the group of students more and more. He had to come to her desk more often than usual. And when that happened, he got a tap on his fingers with the pointing stick, with the rod, or had to stand in the corner as punishment while facing the wall, which he sometimes didn't find that annoying at all because then he didn't have to look at her face. Most of the time, he felt like he had done nothing wrong at all, but he still ended up in these kinds of situations more often than the average student, and this started to gnaw at him. Today, it was such a day again, simply because Miss Tilly claimed that she was in possession of high-quality woven cloth at home, and according to Marcus, this could not have been the case because this high-quality product was only intended for the rich and the noble among the population. A fact that he had learned from his good acquaintance, the cloth weaver, and that he definitely believed this man, who practised this high craft, over a simple primary school teacher, who wasn't even a qualified school teacher at all, but a sexton of the local church, and did this teaching on the side for some extra money in her pocket.

Miss Tilly almost jumped out of her skin at this. Marcus was just a simple farmer's son! He shouldn't think that he was an intellectual or that he was well-read like a churchgoer! But Marcus had had enough of Tilly's subcutaneous sneers, and he decided to tell her the truth...

'Well-read like a churchgoer?!' Marcus shouted loudly. 'You are just talking in your own lane! You only say that because, in addition to this meagre job, you are a sacristan within the church! It is noble of you to be teaching us, but you cannot support yourself at all with the little teaching that you do, and therefore you are dependent on the church for money and the work that you do there! I don't think you like being a sexton at all, and you seem to take this out on the class because that is clearly reflected in your way of teaching!'

Having this said felt like a liberation for Marcus; nevertheless, he also swallowed a wad of despair because he had now clearly gone beyond his remit. He had now trampled on Tilly's soul, had hit her somewhere far below the belt, and that was actually far from courteous on his behalf. He had never wanted to say these words. They had always been assumptions that he had managed to keep to himself. But the frustration that had been bubbling up, and also the accumulation of subcutaneous remarks on Tilly's side, had now evoked this outburst in him.

Marcus simply could not stand injustice, and today, this came to him in the form of a cold, perhaps even unreasonable, truth. But he was a little ashamed now, even felt himself becoming somewhat smaller, and even though it was at the same time a weight off his heart, it also testified to a certain bravado that he apparently carried within him, and in the end, he was glad that he had said what he had. After all, it was no longer possible to reverse the situation, and now it was only a matter of waiting for a verdict that would soon unfold in all its intensity; a verdict like he had never known before…

Miss Tilly could now seize anything to her benefit. She could pull out all the stops to torment young Marcus. Several unlucky birds would fly around his ears. All his fingers, and perhaps all his toes, would be covered in sore spots of the pointing stick. The rod would be called in to flog his bare back and buttocks without mercy. He would forever have to wear the donkey sign around his neck in the classroom, and he would have to take the big heavy shame board home with him to carry this heavy object, both indoors and outdoors, with him for many years to come. To show everyone what a shameful, improper, and rude child and pupil he was. Miss Tilly could have imposed all that on him, but instead, she did nothing.

All she did was look at Marcus very tightly, more penetrating than she had ever done before, while an almost ominous grin adorned her mouth. 'You don't know anything about me, Marcus,' was what she suddenly said in a calm tone. 'And I'd like to keep it that way. You are just a simple farmer's son, in the line of other simple farmer's sons, who are trying to take over our beautiful Glancebury. In addition to my work here, I am indeed a sexton, and I am very proud of that.

'Working in and around the church gives me joy, and also a satisfaction, that you don't know anything about at all. It is working with brats like you that often bothers me instead. Working with children who cannot muster respect and who do not know their place around grown folks. Children who do not appreciate education and the knowledge that is taught to them by us.

'Besides!' Marcus was startled for a moment at these words. 'I come from a miner's family. From a line of hardworking people who made this community so great with their own blood, sweat, and tears; who made it to what it is today. And that! Haughty young Marcus! You will never be able to take away from us! Remember that very well in that rebellious thick skull of yours. Because that is the only and the real truth…

'You are still welcome in my class, and fortunately for you, as well as for me, your full term of education is almost over. But if we ever meet each other on the street after this teaching time, which will undoubtedly happen in this small community, don't expect a greeting from me, and certainly don't expect a chat because I—just like I do with others whom I despise—will walk around you with a very big bow.

'Take it from me, Marcus…' And the woman pointed with a long, thin finger at a young boy who was now staring at his wooden school bag with his head somewhat bowed, hoping that this discussion would finally come to an end. 'People like you will undoubtedly meet themselves in life. Take it from me. And I even dare to swear by that. You are typically someone who will amount to nothing, doomed to a life as a clochard, like a wandering soul, always looking for solace for which he himself seems to make no effort at all.'

Marcus had been in school from his tenth to his twelfth birthday. And even though the other village children had always hated it, he had never found school life that particularly bad. Okay, it was always somewhat stuffy in the classroom. Miss Tilly had always been quite strict, and he could still feel the wooden pointing stick or the ruler on his fingers, but how stern and dutiful Miss Tilly may always have been to her pupils, it apparently had helped.

The young frolicking Glanceburies had now mastered reading and writing, and so also, of course, young Marcus. And while the other boys lingered in activities that they had always done before this school period—running after girls, stealing fruit, annoying the older residents, and bullying young animals—Marcus often walked right past them, while sometimes not even noticing his peers, because he was once again lost in his thoughts. Almost every day, Marcus couldn't wait to go to his good friend, the cloth weaver; a friend indeed, but on top of that one with an additional plus. A privilege that was not for every Glanceburie but for the cloth weaver because he was a well-read man. How that came about and why the man had chosen a craft for which he only had to use his hands, Marcus didn't quite understand. But for now, Marcus had quietly crawled away in a corner of his buddy's cramped room. He had opened the pages of the newspaper in front of him and let the words come to him, which then became sentences and images.

One day, however, the cloth weaver looked up from his loom and spoke directly to Marcus: 'I'm getting the feeling that you only come here for that newspaper, Marcus. Because when the newspaper is here, you're just sitting in the corner and you're just being quiet. But if the newspaper is not here, you just stick your head past the doorpost, say hello, and you're off in no time. I'm almost starting to think that I'm not interesting enough.'

The cloth weaver laughed for a moment, but, of course, he also meant what he said. Marcus blushed for a moment and then decided to vent his heart.

Reading the newspaper was simply an outlet in addition to working on the land. The information from the newspaper almost had a healing effect on him, and he wanted to know as much as possible about the world around him.

'I think you're very nice,' said Marcus sincerely. 'And I am very grateful that I can visit here and read the newspaper for free. But what can you teach me that I can't find in the newspaper already? I mean…I know that you are a well-read man and probably a lot more mentally developed than most in this village, but you still work with your hands and not with your head. Yet you live and work in a hamlet like Glancebury, while the other inhabitants seem to look down on you, while calling you a swindler. I just can't wrap my head around it. You should put them in their place with the knowledge you possess instead of entrenching yourself in a dark hole while you're manufacturing cloth for people who don't even seem to appreciate it in the first place.'

The cloth weaver was silent for a moment, although he decided to express his own inner grievances at that point; his soul stirrings to this excellent young man called Marcus, who the cloth weaver was happy to call a friend and also a young man who regularly managed to hit the proverbial nail on the head. 'I am indeed a swindler, so that side of the story is mainly true,' said the man, somewhat sad.

He told Marcus in broad strokes about his former life. That he had lived in Light Town for quite some years, that he was a member of a real guild at the time, and that he made the highest quality cloth available for miles around, together with his partners. How he had tampered with cloth seals, and that he, partly because of that, had lost his credibility, or rather said his integrity, as a specialised craftsman, as an artisan. He had indeed made an intensely stupid mistake, a life-changing choice, although it wasn't necessarily done with bad intent. The pressure was simply too high at the time. The cloth quality had to improve, and at the same time, the production process was to increase. The inspectors who had to check the quality of the fabric became stricter and stricter, and so more and more pats were applied to the leaden seals. At a certain point, the cloth weaver had to tamper with the product simply to cope with the workload.

'It's not good what I did…' the man said. 'But I have always been a craftsman, an honest one at that, and I stand guaranteed for that. The fact that people don't see me like that anymore is their own problem because I just happen to know the real facts. That's actually the main reason why I'm here right now in this small town, to continue to pursue my passion, in some small hamlet called Glancebury, with a little friend by my side, who always comes here to read the newspaper.'

'But why weren't more people appointed to compensate for the increase in production?' Marcus asked, cutting immediately trying to find a solution to the dilemma that this man found himself in back then.

The cloth weaver looked annoyingly at his loom. 'Well, Marcus, in the end, that was all talked about afterwards. Of course, in the end, it was all about money, or rather said, skimping on it.'

And it immediately became clear to Marcus that his friend didn't want to talk about it any further. However, the man told Marcus that there was much more to this work than meets the eye and that his own outlet was simply working with his hands and that of Marcus, apparently with his head. Moreover, Marcus had to be careful with having his judgment ready so easily because one day, he may become arrogant. Ultimately, the cloth weaver was rather an alleged swindler than a self-righteous and inflated blowhard.

'But maybe you should start working with your head, Marcus,' was what the man said to him. 'Maybe farm life just isn't for you at all.'

Marcus thought about this for a second, even though this saying only made him even more gloomy. It just wasn't that simple.

Because of Marcus' bubbling yearning for knowledge and because of his frequent visits to the cloth weaver, a man who came from Light Town, had once made this city his own, and had held full citizenship there, Marcus began to dream of a life as a bon vivant again; of a flamboyant person who would bring Light Town even more colour than this city already had of its own. Throughout the school period, he had fantasised about Light Town and how he experienced the most diverse adventures there. It was actually always, but especially after the trip with his father, a funny game that he had managed to make for himself. During the day, he thought about this city as much as possible so that he might actually be able to walk around there again at night in his dreams.

However, because of this, his work around the farm began to suffer visibly. Since this persistent daydreaming occurred, he carried out his jobs and chores on the land a lot less attentively. In a dreamy way, he often walked around the yard, picking up less and less out of his own accord. Sometimes, he moved so slowly that it almost hurt the eyes, even the farm animals looked surprisingly up at his way of movement.

One day, Bertus had had enough. 'Son!' he said in a somewhat loud voice. 'You have to understand that we are farmers. Be proud of us kin. We are simply not highborn. I am almost beginning to feel regret that I've given you those books.' Even though he still said it with a smile. 'I understand that you want to keep practising reading and apparently have developed a certain fondness for it, but I also need you on the land, Marcus. Please stand by your old father also. Try to divide your attention between your books and the farm work, and pick up your chores again with the diligence that you have always been showing us all those years prior to our visit to the county fair.'

But Marcus didn't seem to care that much about his father's words. Okay, he had understood them, and maybe he should indeed put a little more effort into the jobs around their farm, but he only had a limited amount of energy and motivation. He had just finished the school period, which had not exactly been a bed of roses. He had his books that he wanted to read in and learn something from. He had some social contacts, such as the small chicken farmer and the downturned cloth weaver, which also took time and a certain enthusiasm. And he also had a deeply cherished wish that he might want to do more with in the future.

Marcus was the type of person who wanted to focus his

motivation, energy, and also his enthusiasm on one thing specifically. This seemed to give him a certain peace of mind, a certain overview that he could work with and through which he could accomplish things. The words of his father may have been well-intentioned, but they also put a certain pressure on his shoulders. More and more balls were being thrown in the air, balls that Marcus was less and less able to catch, let alone that he could juggle skillfully.

His father had increased the pressure on Marcus' life with his words. A pressure that he couldn't handle very well because he was losing a certain overview, and thus began to feel more and more nervousness that was still foreign to him in his younger years, or at least had been spared to him back then. It was a certain imposed pressure that Bertus did not seem to realise, probably because he spent too much time focusing on his own working patterns and wanted so badly that Marcus would also conform himself to them.

A Thorough Reading of the Indian Book

The Iroquois lived together in a so-called longhouse, an elongated wooden structure in which ten, sometimes even more, families of a clan lived. These clans were often named after a certain animal, for example, a bear, a turtle, or a beaver.

These people, the Iroquois, grew a lot of corn, beans, and also pumpkins, and these crops all grew together.

But as peace-loving as these Indians might have appeared, these clans had fought a lot with each other. Their struggle was so fierce, and it raged so on, that about eight hundred years ago, five Iroquois tribes formed a special group, the so-called Iroquois Confederation.

These gathered clans were so tired of fighting that they established a group peace so that they could once again live peacefully side by side within their common territory...

Wow! thought Marcus. *So that's how it can be done! And actually a fairly simple solution to a major problem.* The young farmer's son mused further about what the world would look like if he was in charge; a global and overarching confederation, having people with their differences, but also with a common vision and a clear line of thought...

Marcus read on; he could not stop reading this book about the ancient Indians. He noticed beautiful openings that, when he had just got a hold of it, might have considered as somewhat insignificant.

Marcus started the chapter about the inhabitants of the southeast of this ancient world: the Cherokees.

A tribe that grew its crops in the fertile soil that this area had to offer. They built small villages in the vicinity of rivers, and they often owned two houses: a rectangular summer house and a conical winter house that was covered with clay or woven mats...

Well, well, well, thought Marcus for a moment, *let's be expensive... Two houses? That's not bad at all. It could even be labeled as somewhat decadent.* However, he understood that they needed those covered shelters to defy the annual weather elements.

What these Cherokees mainly grew was corn, beans, pumpkins and tobacco. And corn was so important to them that it could only be eaten after a certain ceremony that was held every year and after all the crops were sufficiently ripe...

Remarkable! thought Marcus this time. *So, corn was so important to these people that it was almost declared sacred?* Curious... was also a word that haunted his head for a while. *Dairy is very important in our own community, and that certainly applies to our family,* even though he had never seen anyone put a cow on a pedestal before, at least not in this country. In any case, he would never do that. He actually thought that cows were stupid animals. And he was even a little afraid of them. Not because of the fact that they could hit so hard with their hind legs but more because they were such clumsy, almost silly, animals. The day had yet to come that someone died because of one. Not because of a kick or swipe from those crazy animals, but mainly because of their constant slipping, their falls, the sudden danger of being crushed under their weight...

But his father, on the other hand? Yes, his father could undoubtedly one day label those reckless and clumsy wretches as saints. Gosh, his father was actually just an Indian! Marcus chuckled. No, his old man was actually far from that. His father was more of a cowboy...

Marcus decided to read some more, although it was almost enough for today. He read that during their autumn ceremonies, the Cherokees danced and shook their rattles made of gourds in order to thank the spirits for the good harvest they had given them...

Funny... Marcus had to think. *We also have an annual harvest festival here in Glancebury. Festivities, ceremonies, they were actually a bit alike. Maybe we are not so different from this people after all? Perhaps these kinds of customs are used all over the world? However, in a slightly different form?*

He thought this was a nice thought to put the book away with, to thank the spirits somewhat playfully for this beautiful book that had come his way, and maybe to go out on the field to ask if his father could use some more help. Nevertheless, the book continued to beckon him... With the concepts that he would never have encountered otherwise, but which he nevertheless began to understand more and more. The ceremonies, being in contact with a higher spiritual world, and smoking tobacco in order to come to oneself. Even nature, on which people were so terribly dependent, and which was placed on such a high pedestal that it almost blurred the line between hunter and prey.

Marcus hungered so much for knowledge about these people that he decided to read on for a while. He quickly turned the page and then read the next heading:

The Sioux, the bison hunters of the prairies...

The prairies of America were a sea of grass on which many animals grazed, and the bison was one of them. For the Sioux, the bison was the most revered animal on the plains.

Naturally! thought Marcus. *That does not surprise me at all!*

Every year, large herds of bison roamed these plains, and the Sioux used their meat for food and their skins for making both clothing and teepees.

If the bison moved to another territory, the Sioux followed. The horses of this Indian tribe ran faster than the bison, and they taught their faithful companions to run alongside the bison so that the hunter could skillfully and purposefully stick an arrow, or spear, in the neck of the beast to kill it swiftly...

Wow! thought Marcus for the umpteenth time. And even though he thought he had already read this fact in a previous chapter, he was very impressed by the efficiency and also by the animal friendliness of this action. In his imagination he saw how such an immensely powerful animal would fall to the ground as a result. How it would feel little pain. And how it would take its last breath with a second targeted stab in a vital part of its immensely muscular body.

It would not even surprise him if these Indians would honour this animal on the spot where it lay, hold some type of ceremony at that moment, and thus calmly guide the soul of the animal towards the eternal hunting grounds. Of course he didn't know this for sure, but if these people were capable of anything, it was definitely such a big and honourable thing.

Marcus started to feel dizzy again. He wanted to stay in this book and not close it to wake up again in a gray environment where everything went slowly, where most of the people were sullen, who seemed to think about only a few things and were only concerned with survival, only with making it through another day. But as efficiently as the Indians could kill a bison, the knowledge could only be used if one could fully concentrate on it. He closed the book again, indeed woke up in a pale and somewhat gray environment, and tried to, with some Indian enthusiasm that is, add some colour to it...

In the days that followed, Marcus could not stop thinking about the pieces of text that he had read earlier in his room. The pieces of text about the ancient Indians, and their respectful working methods when it came to animals or nature as a whole. After all, they didn't just see these animals as hunks of meat on several legs. But they actually saw them as full-fledged beings, sprouted from the womb of Mother Earth, with a soul, an emotional life, and a way of living within their natural habitat that instilled both respect and awe within these Indians. He had come to respect these views and supported them. Simply because they felt right and, at the same time, were also very logical. It was a way of thinking that seemed to be completely out of touch with the gray reality in which he found himself in, as soon as he had closed this book again.

Okay, most Glanceburies had a certain bond with their cattle, and they took good care of their animals, certainly, his father could not be blamed when it came to taking care of his cows, but there was still something that gnawed at the young Marcus. It was not because of the life that these beasts led that caused him to arouse wrath. It was more because of their certain death, which was anything but acceptable to him. From one day to the next, crammed, piled up, and loaded on a cart that was far too small for them, a bustle, a panic, and a mooing of the cows, as if they already knew what unfortunate fate awaited them. And the actual death blow? How was that actually carried out? Marcus had really no idea. The boy had never set a single footstep in the slaughterhouse, in the so-called abattoir, but it would probably not be pleasant at all.

The abattoir... was what Marcus had to think with derision. With its beautiful and also chic name for slaughterhouse. A place where intelligent life forms were killed in rows in a way that was probably anything but animal-friendly, let alone respectful.

Actually, we should eat meat only sporadically... was also a thought that slumbered through his mind. *And maybe we should practice ritual slaughter as well, just like the ancient Indians did... Because a ceremony was what these animals seemed to get anything but; rather a bloodbath, with a razor-sharp meat hook as the ultimate reward, although fortunately the damage had already been done...*

Marcus began to get more angry and upset with these inner images, which danced before his mind's eye. It was, therefore, not because of the fact that these animals were butchered down—after all, meat would always be eaten to a certain extent—it was more because of the unreasonable and animal-unfriendly method of the final job, not wanting to make it more animal-friendly, let alone thinking about it or considering this issue.

No, Marcus was a bit fed up with the infantile thinking of the Glanceburies. The people within this village, and probably also the ones outside of it, seemed to lose connection with their food more and more. He just had enough of this way of thinking, a certain awareness had to be cultivated, something had to be done!

One day, Marcus stood in front of the abattoir, clutching a number of targeted statements in his hand. He had carefully written them down on a sheet of paper at home, with some writing material that he still had in his possession from school, and so he was now standing in front of the large wooden gate of this meat processing company. He looked around to make sure no one saw him. Fortunately, dusk was already setting in. He took out the hammer and nail, which he had borrowed from his father without asking, and then riveted his personal manifesto to the thick wooden gate. He looked around cautiously for a moment, carefully put the hammer back in his pocket, and then quickly left.

The wind eagerly played with the note for a moment, although it seemed to be firmly enough attached, while Marcus was already complacent on his way home, and while the wind let its invisible hand glide over the following words that, probably in the very early morning, would be read by several people:

People seem to have lost touch with their food!

There was something going on in the village, and if it wasn't for that unknown disease that was called the white death, then it was for the residents who didn't allow each other the light in their own eyes. Marcus started to plunge even more into his own world. He read his book about the ancient Indians and sometimes, for a brief moment, glanced at the other book that he owned. He dreamed more and more about visits to the big city, partly thanks to the stories of the cloth weaver, and he began to feel more and more inclined to make his long-cherished boyhood dream come true.

His only two friends were actually the chicken farmer and the cloth weaver, two people who had also followed their own paths or at least had chosen a certain way of life. And even though they had been roads full of bumps and barriers, they were also roads that seemed to be the right ones for them, that seemed to have been specially mapped out for them. Marcus also wanted to be such a person. He also thought that he had found such a suitable destination, that he had found his own mapping. For now, there was only one important thing to do. He had to present it to his parents...

His mother put a hand over her mouth when Marcus expressed his deeply cherished wish. Bertus looked a bit exasperated at his dinner plate, sometimes looking at Marcus with scorn and then again questioningly at his own wife.

'So, you would like to be a reporter?' was what his mother asked Marcus somewhat surprised, and she also looked questioningly at her husband.

'Yes, mother, that's right,' was what Marcus said in a serious tone, but also with some doubt in his voice.

'I really want to be a reporter. I want to work at the newspaper. I want to display the things that I know, entertain people with the knowledge I have gained so far in my life, and also touch people with all the situations that take place in the big cities, in the whole of Ingland, and perhaps even of those beyond its borders...'

His mother now stared into nothingness with wide eyes while his father once again snorted his nose, even though the man decided not to say anything for now.

'This just doesn't come out of the blue,' was what Marcus added. 'I have thought about this thoroughly. I've read a lot of newspapers by now, gained a lot of knowledge myself, I apparently have a certain wisdom that has to come from somewhere, and I think I could just make it in that world...'

'But...?' his mother said in a surprised tone. 'You decided all this for yourself after reading just one book? If you have read it at all in its totality...? After just finishing primary education? Do you have any idea what it takes to pursue such a goal? You're still so young... Aren't you getting too carried away in a certain boyhood dream?'

Marcus felt a certain hint of despair come over him by

these words. Simply because his mother's words touched a certain core that, of course, did not leave him untouched, and that Marcus himself had often been worrying about. 'No!' he said very resolutely. 'I may be a bit young, but I could definitely roll into it, right? I know I've been a bit quiet lately, maybe even a bit aloof, but that was partly because I've been pondering about this for a while. I just know that I have it in me!

'I somehow have the intellect and a kind of innate wisdom that has to come from somewhere. I can oversee situations quite well, actually see a story in everything, and I can work hard if I really want to. I am eager to learn, I am good with words, and I also have a certain imagination that allows me to give a certain spice to stories. What more can one expect from me? These are all skills that a somewhat skilled reporter, or journalist even, should have...'

Marcus beamed with satisfaction.

'Journalist even...,' Bertus remarked somewhat laughingly. 'Do you actually realise what kind of education you need to have for such a profession? I don't think your boyhood dream, how well-intentioned it may be, is completely correct. You are walking past yourself, son. Your sketched picture may be nice for a story, but I don't think it is particularly realistic...'

Bertus looked at his wife with laughter, after which Marcus stared somewhat ashamed at his dinner plate.

His mother, on the other hand, now looked somewhat sternly at her husband and then turned to her son: 'I think what your father is trying to say... And I actually kind of agree... Your vision of the future doesn't look very promising. You simply need a certain knowledge of things, Marcus, not only a large vocabulary but also a deeper knowledge of language and how to put it on paper in the right way. You at least need a certain prior education, one that we cannot afford at all. You have to radiate a certain self-confidence and also come from a very good family, perhaps even from a prosperous family... I don't think this is a profession meant for a simple Glanceburie Marcus...'

His own mother looked somewhat disappointedly at her still untouched plate of food, an evening meal prepared with love, which was healthy and nutritious but was also somewhat simple and made with products that mainly came from their own land... She nevertheless still seemed somewhat hopeful, even seemed to be a bit behind Marcus, even though she did not show it at all. She simply sided with her husband, which was what a good and benevolent woman ought to do, even though she also seemed to feel some remorse for the words she had spoken earlier. She perhaps even felt a certain nurturing for the courage that Marcus had previously shown by expressing his inner desire and because of a certain ambition that he tried to pursue.

Nevertheless, she also stuck to her point of view, simply because Bertus expected this from her, while he did not hesitate to express his unvarnished opinion after everything that had already been said.

'I've told you this before, Marcus...' Bertus looked intensely and seriously at his son, while Marcus even detected a certain anger in him, one that his father wasn't planning on showing too much. 'I've told you this before... You are a farmer's son and probably always will be. You were born that way. We are all pulled out of the clay, and you will have to find a certain peace in that... You shouldn't think that you can control the whole of life, Marcus. You shouldn't think that you're untouchable because that's how you seem to behave lately. Wait and see...' Again, his father looked at him intensely, with a certain inflexibility that the young Marcus just could not understand, let alone appreciate...

'Be very careful, Marcus!' the man said again in a paternalistic way. 'Because one day the white death might come and get you too...' Bertus looked at his son somewhat ominously, with a certain childishness at the same time, which Marcus thought he had long since transcended.

Yes, Father... was what Marcus had to think in his mind. *Keep on dreaming...*

Marcus knew this story, this folktale, by now, and it was not that he wanted to fob it off as a fabrication because the consequences of this pandemonium were very clearly felt throughout the community, but he decided to stick to his own truth. He had passed his twelfth year of birth many months ago. And if this ghost, if this disease that was called the white death, had wanted to pursue him, it surely would have done by now.

Marcus looked at his mother for a moment, looked at his father, was reminded of the stories of the white death, and then thought the following: *maybe it's better if I keep my guard up for now...*

Marcus went to the cloth weaver the next day. He had become somewhat confused by the words of his parents, and especially those of his father. He had a dream that welled up inside him, a vision of the future that he felt was so real that he could almost touch it. He had to speak to someone who could support him. A person who could appreciate ideals, did not diminish them as childish impulses, and also a person who understood his conflict, a conflict between his parents and his ambition as a future reporter. A conflict that ignited a certain fire in him and also a gnawing doubt that extinguished that same flame...

The cloth weaver had the following to say about this matter: 'As you already know, Marcus, is that I'm a newspaper reader. I can rightly tell you that the eighteenth century, the century that you just had to miss because of your date of birth, was quite prosperous for Ingland. And these glory days only seem to increase on top of that... What I am trying to say here, Marcus, is that that old man of yours never really knew very hard times himself, at least not as his own father knew them, and actually, he was basically a Sunday's child himself. It seems, now that I have heard of your dilemma in this way, that your grandfather had transferred his dissatisfaction to your father, and your own father seems to do the same to you again... I call this the dejected tradition, Marcus. It actually occurs in all generations, and I wouldn't worry too much about it because maybe you'll do this to your own offspring too one day...'

The cloth weaver had made a clear point, and Marcus was glad he had said it, even though the good man still hadn't given him an unequivocal answer about Marcus' deeply cherished dream. But hey... What could he expect in this matter from a man who seemed to go where the wind took him? The cloth weaver did not seem to lead an easy life either, although he just did what he liked the most: exercising his passion, regardless of what one thought of him and regardless of the environment in which he exercised it.

Actually, the cloth weaver was the perfect role model, a man whose example to follow. Nevertheless, he did not seem to feel the ropes of his supporters pulling so vigorously on him. He seemed to be able to go wherever he wanted, and this seemed to be anything but true for Marcus. Marcus decided to keep this question, this dilemma actually, to himself for the time being. Maybe he could put it in someone else's hands soon. Perhaps there was someone in Glancebury who understood this question of his, and who might be able to steer him in the right direction...

There was a knock on the door of the Pritchard family's farm at a time when, in a hamlet like Glancebury, one would not expect. Marcus, sitting at the top of the stairs, entrenched himself behind a wooden stair bar because he might already know what they owed this unexpected visit to. He kept quiet, pricked up his ears, and then heard his father speak to this uninvited audience:

'No,' he said. 'Marcus has already gone to bed, why?'

'Well, it's like this,' said an unknown male voice, trying to explain a few things to Bertus. 'Do you recognise this handwriting?'

'Yes,' said Bertus modestly, 'but I just can't imagine that he would do this kind of thing...'

'We prefer to talk to him ourselves,' was what another male voice said. 'Nevertheless, we also realise that he is still young and that he can use his good night's rest. Keep an eye on your son a little, Bertus,' was what the man added somewhat ominously. 'You are a good man, and also a hard worker, and also a great asset to our village, but please don't let your son grow up for the gallows and the wheel...'

'No, no, I understand,' said Bertus quickly, while at the same time Marcus let out a deep sigh that reached almost all the way to the bottom of the stairs. 'I simply cannot understand that my own son did this kind of thing; so terribly ill-considered, and also an action which brings me into a certain disrepute, since I am also a cattle farmer, and since I also have a good business relationship with the abattoir to maintain... I am, therefore, deeply ashamed, gentlemen. I am sorry for this foolish act of my son, and I would like to apologise sincerely for the fact that my son had tried to discredit both you and your company.

'This will by no means happen again. I will put him through his paces tomorrow at the crack of dawn, and there probably will be a beating involved as well. But tell me one thing, gentlemen... How did you know that this note, that this letter, with those strange writings on it, came from him?'

And these two men, with their confident voices and their clear undertones, told Bertus that they had summoned Miss Tilly in their investigation. She quickly caught the culprit, simply because she didn't know anyone else in the village who had such strange handwriting...

'Great,' responded Bertus sarcastically. 'That's all very nice. So he is not only an offender but now also has strange handwriting. And that poor guy even has a career as a writer in mind... I just don't know where that boy has been with his head lately...'

Marcus, well hidden above the sound of these voices and clinging to the stair bar, could just feel how his father shook his head sadly because of his childish boyhood dream. He was also very disappointed in the action that he himself, and only a few days ago, had considered so very noble...

Marcus had heard enough by now. He was quite horrified and, with a desperate lump in his throat, dove back into his now cooled-off bed. The front door was closed again with a loud bang. Bertus' heavy footsteps were still audible and could be followed into the living room, after which the silence in the house suddenly returned...

Will it still be so quiet tomorrow at the crack of dawn, Marcus thoughtfully wondered. *Or would his father tell him the truth? And show him how much he had disappointed him?*

A certain mutual understanding that Marcus had been experiencing more and more lately? Marcus would find out eventually, but he was actually hoping for certain words from his father. The silence had already been so present in this house lately. It was a saying of nothing that could make Marcus only guess; a guessing he had never been very good at. These were things that may not even have been an issue but which he seemed to relate to himself within his head. It was this increasing of guessing that confused him more and more...

Marcus looked up at the lowered wooden ceiling of his bedroom and thought for a moment. *So Miss Tilly was called in to see if she could identify the handwriting.* That had turned out to be a bull's eye. Of course, she recognised Marcus' handwriting. He simply wrote his letters in a strange way and had often received comments about it. He liked them; his letters had something graceful, and he didn't really understand the whole commotion. Nevertheless, his writing style was the first thing that exposed him. His earlier action had not been smart; it even could be called ill-considered, but perhaps he had secretly wanted to be caught. Anyway, for now, it didn't matter that much. He simply stood behind his statements, and everyone was allowed to know it...

The next day, there seemed to be little, if anything, going on in the Pritchard residence. No angry father to drag Marcus out of bed early in the morning to give him a beating. No heated discussion between his mother and father in the small side room where the problems of this family were always discussed. Not even bullying or unreasonableness, where Marcus had to get the feeling that he had done something wrong without it being openly said. None of that...

Bertus had just gone back into the field early, as he did every morning. His sister might have been to a friend's house, sitting in her own room, working in her stall on the side of the road again, or making straw dolls in the field nearby. And his mother was either out for some errands or she was just serenely doing some housework. They had even left Marcus in bed. He had even been able to sleep in a bit, which almost never happened.

This was rightfully weird and different, but he was actually fine with it. It gave him a feeling that they didn't have that much to say about him, that he could decide for himself how he organised his life, and they themselves had to take that into account. It was a certain sense of power that pleased Marcus. And even though this was unique and probably not so consciously planned at all, it was also a state of affairs that he could get used to…

Marcus decided to take out his Indian book again. It had almost come to an end, and he thought today was the perfect day to go through it again, finish it, and then bury it somewhere deep in his memory, where no one could reach it with their grasping fingers or could take this knowledge away from him... *Okay, where was I,* was what Marcus thought when he found the crease and opened the page. *Oh yes! The*

Sioux! What a magnificent book you are! He gave the Indian warrior, who was looking determinedly into the distance on the cover of the book, a big kiss on his forehead.

Marcus' finger slid over the words and sentences again so that he soon found himself in the landscape that he, with pain in his heart, had to turn his back on a few days ago. He saw in his mind's eye how the Sioux lived in conical tents, which they called teepees. They were movable houses, which were very useful to these nomads because when the herds of bison moved, and they did this at a rapid pace, the Sioux always had to be ready to follow. They, therefore, made a travois, a kind of sled, by tying the poles of the teepee behind a horse so that they could quickly transport their belongings...

Clever! thought Marcus. *And handy, too! The poles of their shelters were multifunctional... Those Indians were certainly not dumb folk!* Maybe one day, he could tell this fun fact to someone who owned a horse and cart. He could even tell this to his father, although the man would probably not be open to it or debunk it with a clincher... No, one day, Marcus would tell this fun fact to someone if he ever had the luxury of riding with someone who owned such transportation...

Inhabitants of the Mesas

Marcus had now arrived at the last Indian tribe that the book revealed. He still had a few pages to go and felt some despair running through his soul. In the not-too-distant future, he would have to say goodbye to his dear Indian friends. It already hurt him, but at the same time also filled him with a kind of pride. A pride that he had this special collection of information on his bookshelf, and also an additional feeling of hope because he could always, and at any time, return to the savannah and plains if he wanted to; there where the dust rose high above trampling and shining hooves, and where he could calmly smoke his peace pipe in the vicinity of his cone-shaped home...

The Hopi tribe lived in the hot desert of the southwest for thousands of years. Their houses, which were built on top of the mountain hills, were called mesas.

In ancient times, these mesas formed a natural protection against an attack by the enemy. Their houses were made of sandstone and adobe, a sun-dried clay. Moreover, these Hopi houses were built on top of each other. The roof of one house thus formed the terrace of the house above, and people climbed from one house to the other via ladders...

Fun! Marcus mused for the umpteenth time while he had stuck his nose so deep in the book that he could smell the musty fragrance of the pages.

Teepees? Teepees?! He didn't want to own such a biodegradable tent anymore, such a raised tarpaulin with sticks, in which the wind sometimes eagerly managed to find a passage and wherein people had little knowledge of what was going on outside. He now wanted to live high up against a mountain cliff, in a beautiful, somewhat rectangular, and brown sandstone house. With many noises around him, blowing in from all sides, and with a purple sun in the distance that sometimes managed to raise the mountainside to a work of art and that cast a shadow over these piled-up houses when this celestial body passed over the mountains again at the end of noon.

Marcus wanted to live in such a setting, mighty beautiful

and wonderful in all its simplicity, peering over the desert grounds, looking for potential intruders, who first had to look for a ladder if they wanted to reach his beloved tribe anyway... But he clearly digressed again and then read on about the customs that these Hopi had made their own. On the page was an illustration of a petroglyph that had once been painted there by a Hopi. The drawing represented TAWA, the sun god, but the spider woman was also depicted there.

For when the earth first existed, they sang a magical song so that the animals, the birds, and also the insects came into existence. Only then did they make man...

And, of course, Marcus had no choice but to muse about this as well. *Funny, wasn't it,* was what he had to think; the way in which people were able to attribute greater meaning to the things they experienced in daily life, and which they encountered in their immediate environment... *And, of course, I know that I better not say that to the pious people in our own community, but it is still a funny and also extremely interesting phenomenon...*

Another illustration showed Kokopelli, a mythical flute player with a humpback, dancing for the people and whistling at them when they were feeling sad... *Nice,* Marcus thought again. *All very nice...*

Corn has been very important to these people for thousands of years because it grows very well in the desert climate.

In addition, they also grew beans and pumpkins. But in order for the crops to really grow, it had to rain, of course, and the rain spirits helped with that. Hopi artists even made wooden dolls that were supposed to represent the rain spirits, and the Hopi girls received them during their rain ceremonies...

Again funny, thought Marcus, *and again recognisable.* His own younger sister also made such dolls, only she did not make them out of wood, but from dry straw. And not to thank something or anyone. No, she actually made them purely for profit. Marcus had to chuckle about it for a moment. *Oh well, she didn't really hurt anyone with it. Moreover, they were quite beautiful creations.* Maybe he should tell her that someday...

Marcus had now reached the last few sentences of the book. And he had to swallow a few times while he was already silently starting to say goodbye to his distant bosom friends.

The young Hopi women wore their hair in two buns until they got married...

You can't mean that... thought Marcus. The last sentence of the book was about hair buns? *Huh yuck! Because if there was one thing this young Glanceburie didn't like, it was hair buns. Womanly? Womanly?! Women's hair had to be wavy, curved, long, at least up to the shoulders. They would never get a man this way, now would they? But maybe real love was hidden in the bun. Perhaps that was the true reward for a man who could see past such a hair nest.* Marcus finally closed the book and rested his hands on it for a while. *What a magisterial information! And what a beauty of a book you are! What exceptional adventures I have had in it! And what a pity that it had to end this way! Hair buns...*

Conversations With the Priest

Marcus was a rebellious young boy. At least that was the idea he got from his parents and also from some villagers. Marcus had made a mess of his schooldays. He had gone through the curriculum well. Only the relationship between him and Miss Tilly had been far from amicable.

Marcus had been squandering his duties in and on the farm for quite some time now, and he had also discredited his own father by nailing his impulsive statements—which Marcus still supported himself—to the gate of the abattoir. His mother had already expressed her concern for her son several times, his father Bertus, his disappointment many times more, and how did Marcus anticipate all this?

By having read the Indian book even more thoroughly, and even by having looked at his second book, actions that his father Bertus began to vilify more and more because these stories seemed to make Marcus' head spin. He seemed to undergo his tasks around the yard with a certain lethargy, a certain laziness that Marcus had never shown to such an extent before reading these books. Marcus was fine with it, though. He was anything but happy about this widening gap between him and his parents, between his deep-seated ambition and a future life as a dairy farmer —which had apparently already been mapped out for him. But nevertheless, he had made his future dream known to them. The truth had finally been put on the table, and strangely enough, this made Marcus less confused because both parties now had something that could be worked on.

Nevertheless, Marcus was not yet completely satisfied, and he hoped to find answers in the church life. A place where he had knocked on before but where the door remained closed at the time, simply because no one was there. This time, however, that was not the case.

Marcus soon became friends with the priest and told him about his books, at least about the beautiful Indian book he had read inside out. He told the good man also that he had another book in his possession. Had already skimmed through it a number of times, but he didn't really say much more about it.

He liked to keep that book, that subject, to himself for now. Actually, Marcus didn't understand that much about this book currently. He didn't quite understand the underlying meaning of it yet, although he just had the idea that this second book of his contained a certain message that was not quite suitable for everyone.

This second book also did not seem to fit quite well within the little world where Marcus came from. Moreover, the subject also seemed to be inconsistent with the teachings of the church, and Marcus had to be careful about revealing its message too much. It was Marcus' own little secret, a secret that he might share with the priest one day, but not for now. Even though this man was probably to be trusted because he was a man of faith, Marcus also knew quite well that the expression of unconventional ideas could eventually turn against him, that it could arouse certain suspicion, and that, in the worst case, he could even be called a heretic, with all the consequences that entailed. Perhaps he could share this book with someone someday, perhaps even sooner than expected, but in any case not before he himself understood the main message of it somewhat better.

Not before he had read it—just like his Indian book—from front to back, and he could conclude with an inner certainty that this book—now almost forbidden—could bear the light of day, and he could tell the people around him about it with verve...

However, the priest knew nothing about these kinds of subjects and had never even heard of them, and this surprised Marcus, to say the least. Marcus thought about this for a while and soon came to the conclusion that he apparently knew more about certain things than, for example, this man, who was so highly regarded within the community, also as far as intellect was concerned. It made Marcus shudder a bit. Shudder, because there was still so much knowledge in the world that Marcus knew nothing of and that he would like to master someday, which also would take a lot of work, perhaps not even achievable within a lifetime.

It also made him shudder that there apparently were people in high positions and high functions who actually did not even possess half the knowledge and skills that they should have for such professions. This made Marcus shudder. Yes, it indeed did, but it also gave him a sense of hope, pride and enthusiasm. Hope, because such a high-ranking position might be feasible after all, even for a lowborn individual like himself. A position that he one day might be able to obtain by just studying very hard and demanding of himself to have the necessary knowledge for it, knowledge and skills that were simply needed for such a post.

He also felt a certain pride. A pride—because he had already learned so much in such a short period of time that he began to realize that he had a certain wisdom that he could fall back on and that he also possessed a form of intellect to get where he eventually wanted to be.

And finally enthusiasm; the enthusiasm to find out even more about things, to be able to give them a place for himself, but also a place in the world around him. And perhaps even to be able to teach people about them, perhaps even people who were higher on the social ladder; an exchange of intellectual knowledge that gave Marcus the feeling of belonging, of being somewhat special as well. A certain reciprocity, but also a certain equality, which the young Marcus apparently craved so much...

Marcus trotted on again, and that didn't seem to escape this priest either.

'No,' said the priest. 'I really don't know anything about this people you call the Indians, but I find it very interesting to hear about them. Moreover, I think it is admirable that you already have a certain knowledge of things, especially at your age. Maybe you could tell me more about these topics? About the books that apparently occupy your mind so much?

I think that would be very nice and also a reason for you to show your nose more often around this church...'

And that was exactly what Marcus did during those days. He could place many of his questions with the priest. Their mutual bond seemed to become more and more flexible and also more defined, and so a form of openness arose that Marcus could appreciate, and that he had been looking for in the first place. The priest and Marcus had become good acquaintances by now, perhaps even friends, and they talked about a variety of subjects.

The priest had already familiarized Marcus with the doctrine of the church he practised, a doctrine that he tried to propagate as much as possible because that was his calling, and also his work. Marcus asked the man about the Roman Catholic Church, an institution he had heard of before.

He also wondered why there were so many movements within this belief since it was so prevalent in Ingland alone. The priest found this a good question, and he answered it with a certain open-mindedness that Marcus initially had not sought behind the man, and certainly not within the seemingly strict beliefs that always seemed to go hand in hand with church life...

'Ah, Marcus,' said the priest.

'People just do certain things, don't they? Our movement, my movement, calls itself Anglican, but in the end, we are also just a hotchpotch of Roman practices and Protestant ideologies. At least I'm still from the Low Church, but please don't let me spew my bile about the High Church because this movement has paved its own street completely for itself. Even celibacy is no longer a virtue! Oh, well, I'm actually not that better...'

'How do you mean?' asked Marcus with interest.

'Are you also guilty of lusting after a woman?' But the priest looked fixedly at the boy.

'This has nothing to do with guilt, Marcus. I've made a conscious choice about this. Sexuality is simply one of the strongest drives of man. And in my view, perhaps an animalistic instinct, nevertheless an inner urge that is almost insurmountable. Let me not antagonize our Good Lord, but if I may name one sin that is difficult to control, that is intertwined with the urge to procreate, with the latent excesses of our subconscious, and also our tendency to dominate, it is the human sexuality...'

Marcus paused for a moment to reflect on these words.

'But if sexuality is so insurmountable, as you so beautifully call it, how does one escape it?'

'Well,' the priest said thoughtfully. 'That requires discipline and perseverance, little friend. And even though I'm doing well so far, I have a struggle with it almost every day...'

'But isn't it actually unnatural what you are doing?' was what Marcus asked while the priest had to laugh at the sharpness of the question.

'Another good question, Marcus! But I don't see it all that way. As I told you earlier, I see sexuality as an animalistic urge, something natural, of course, but nevertheless also something that can keep you grounded. If you merge more with the higher divine, then that drive also disappears more and more into the background. Then you realize that we are truly one and that, in the end, that drive is also somewhat inferior. Then, there seems to be no more lust. Only love...'

'Phew...,' sighed Marcus. 'It's all so confusing... I would love to have a girlfriend, but I'm starting to believe more and more that this jar doesn't fit a lid at all...'

Of course, the priest had to laugh about this. 'You are a beautiful human being, Marcus,' was what the man said. 'And if women don't see that, then that's their loss. Besides, even if you are a twisted pot, then there's really only one thing for you to do...'

'And what's that priest?' asked Marcus again interestingly. 'That's looking for a twisted lid yourself, Marcus...'

'I don't know, priest, he said. I just don't know...'

'Dear little Marcus, stop worrying so much. Your time will eventually come. Moreover, you can always join the church if you can't figure it out in the long run. But let me give you some advice if that is the case with you...'

'And that is...?'

'And that is...?! The priest repeated, in a slightly different tone of voice this time.

'Listen to your heart. And whether that applies to women or men in your case. Our Good Lord simply does not discriminate—you should take the following consideration very carefully into account in your subsequent choice:

'It is still better to lust after a woman or man than to burn with a deep-seated desire...'

Marcus, of course, paused for a moment to reflect on those words. And even though they were very nice words, they were at the same time also very difficult...

'I thought this was a nice conversation Marcus, very enlightening. You've told me something about your interests, about your books, among other things. And I have told you a bit more about the church movement in which I find myself and about the faith that I profess. You can always knock on my door if you want to know more about this church, Marcus. The door will always be open for you...'

And that was exactly what Marcus did. The next day, he stood again, very early in the morning, at the door of the church. He wanted to know everything about Anglicanism. Because it was fascinating stuff, interesting to hear about, and it was also a large chunk of free knowledge with which he could fill his frame of reference, knowledge that he might one day be able to tap into, that he could teach people about—just as the priest had done with him the last time that they've spoken and that he might even write an article about one day…

'Look,' said the priest delightedly, glad that his little disciple stood again on his threshold and at the same time delighted that his stories were still interesting enough and that he himself, at his age, was still worth listening to for the youth.

'Look,' he said again to reinforce his story some more.

'Even though Roman merchants and soldiers who were connected to the church of Rome brought Catholicism to Ingland, this ecclesiastical movement that we now know in its current form arose from a marital dispute.

Long before your time, there was a monarch in power, the revered and noble King Henry. The first Anglican bishop we have ever known and I will not mention his name because that may be a little too much information at this point—brought about an annulment between the marriage of the king and his first wife and declared his second marriage as valid.

Now, all of a sudden, dear Marcus, a new princess was born in that year. The supreme leader of the world church of Rome, the pope, was somehow not happy with this situation and therefore relieved the archbishop of his ecclesiastical function and excommunicated him to use a fancy word.

King Henry again did not agree with the decision of the pope, and with his interference on Ingland's soil, and therefore entered into a conclave with his own people. The king, therefore, submitted a bill to his parliament: the so-called *Act of Supremacy*. This was, of course, accepted, and so King Henry immediately became the most powerful person on earth. He stood directly under God, and with this law, he was also the head of the church of Ingland. The separation of the Roman church and its papal authority had thus become a fact.

Ingland now took care of its own ecclesiastical structure, with its own liturgy, even though many Roman influences still remained in force. Anglicanism was thus born, with its two branches: the High Church and the Low Church, which I, and many with me, are a part of. But now you are to guess, Marcus, what did the king carry out as a first measure and as the head of this new church?' But Marcus shrugged his shoulders. 'I've no idea,' he said. 'Maybe implement more freedom within certain areas?'

'Indeed!' shouted the priest. 'Very good, Marcus!' The first thing he implemented was a more liberal marriage law. Isn't it beautiful?! That which had previously worked against him so much, and that had caused him such a burden, was now the first thing he did to disempower with his newly acquired power...'

'Well, it's just what you consider as beautiful,' said Marcus dryly. 'In my experience, it sounds a lot like a form of opportunism...'

'Indeed,' the priest added thoughtfully. 'But that's just in what kind of world we live in Marcus. People will always try to bend the rules, especially if they can work them to their own benefit.'

Marcus thought about this for a second, wanted to tell the priest the truth, and then also wanted to tell him that the good man might be giving away his life or was handing it over to some kind of puppet show. Nevertheless, the priest thought that he could already silently detect this opening. It was something that he had undoubtedly thought about before, but it was something that he had resigned himself to because he had found a certain truth within it, and it was also something in which he could find a certain peace.

'I know what you're thinking, Marcus,' was what the man said.

'That this church movement is actually not all that much, and that it originated from a certain human gain, but I see it differently...

Power games are always a part of it. Because from the early Middle Ages, and from the beginning of the class society, the nobility, but above all the church, have always been in charge. Even though these two classes work together and are in close contact with each other, they also keep a very close eye on each other. Perhaps that was the main reason why King Henry, under the guise of a personal dispute, had regained some of the power.

Of course, I don't know this for a fact, Marcus. I simply wasn't there when all this occurred, although I try to get as little involved as possible in power politics, and I've never been a strategist at all, either...

I have simply found peace within this church movement. I like to hold a certain position in it, and faith in it is simply the highest good for me.

In addition... And to finish my story... Catholicism, and later Protestantism, all already existed. And especially within the church that I adhere to, the Low Church, these two movements have come together somewhat. I can therefore, agree with both of them, with their joining of hands. And even though we are somewhat cut off from the worldly church, we still belong to it a bit, I have so the idea...

That evening, Marcus had a hard time falling asleep. The more he talked to the inhabitants of Glancebury, the more a map began to emerge in his head of their interests, their ideas and views, and the way in which they lived their lives. Marcus found this an interesting fact, and visibly enjoyed it, and it also created a healthy tension within his body that made it difficult for him to fall asleep that night.

In the late morning, after working in the fields and yard for a few hours, Marcus stood on the threshold of the church again to ask his good friend, the priest, all of his questions.

'Priest?' was what he asked to get straight to the point. 'Can you tell me some more about the church, and especially about Anglicanism?'

'You want to know everything, don't you?' the man replied with a smile. 'I like that! In my opinion, it testifies to a certain interest in our fellow human beings. A curiosity about life even... But beware, Marcus! One day, you will understand that a person has to resign himself to something, to feel a certain peace about something, even have a particular goal in mind; otherwise, you may be searching forever...

But enough of this seriousness, what more can I tell you about? We have already largely talked about the origin of the Inglish Church. Maybe I could tell you some more about my church? About the Low Church?'

Marcus nodded enthusiastically, of course, and that afternoon the priest told in detail about his own church and about *The Book of Common Prayer*, a book that formed the backbone for the Anglican Church and for its decoration. It was a book that contained not only the prayers but also the texts of the various liturgical actions and models for the organization of the church services.

The priest told Marcus about the sacraments that they considered important and which they honoured. He talked about the different degrees of ordination that a person had to go through if one wanted to grow in function within this church movement, from deacon to presbyter—as the man himself was—to maybe even a bishop if you tried and worked really hard.

And he told Marcus how the entire Anglican Church was divided into dioceses. And how these dioceses were united again in a church province. That within such a province, there was only one archdiocese—where the archbishop resided— and that this archbishop was at the same time also the metropolitan—in other words the head—of this province. The influence of the church was great, and the power of the supreme archbishop was far sufficient.

For this person was not only the head of the church in Ingland, but he was also the head of all ecclesiastical provinces, stood—when it came to religious matters—even above the king himself, and this person even sat in parliament, on a seat that was not intended for an ordinary minister...

Marcus began to enjoy the conversations with the priest. It was something different for a change from the lighthearted conversations he had with the small chicken farmer or the more earthly chatter with the cloth weaver.

Marcus had been thinking about a subject at home that he could discuss with the priest, and he thought he had already found two. Two questions had already popped up in his mind while he was still sitting in Miss Tilly's somewhat dim and stuffy classroom, with the heavy wooden school bag resting on his lap and the writing quill in his left hand.

Marcus told the priest about the corporal punishment that Miss Tilly had always used and that she always seemed to choose him for it in particular. He just couldn't understand this. How could fear, intimidation, and also physical chastisement, make a child a better student? Let alone a better person?

Marcus could still remember Miss Tilly's words, for she could not chant them often enough when she took out the wooden slab or the sharp pointing stick and then called one of her disciples to her. She got her justification from the Bible, and Marcus had remembered the words in all their details: proverbs thirteen, verse twenty-four, and this time it was Marcus, and not Miss Tilly, who quoted:

'He that withholds his rod hates her son, but he who loves him seeks him early with chastisement...'

Simply hitting children seemed to be seen as a responsible

method within education. Marcus did not agree with this at all, had literally experienced this firsthand, and could, therefore, be called an expert by experience.

In any case, it had not taught him anything. Only a hatred for his teacher, walking on tiptoes that had always managed to give him a certain inner tension, a despise of the old-fashioned form of education they were in, and even a certain suspicion of adults in positions of power in particular, and perhaps even a growing suspicion of all humanity in general.

Marcus just couldn't understand this because his inner feelings seemed to be the right one. He, therefore, placed this issue with the priest, and the priest, again, seemed to have a wise judgment at hand. The priest understood Marcus' point of view, although corporal punishment was at the same time, and on the other hand, just a method that is used in this day and age. Either Marcus was very sensitive, too sensitive perhaps for a teenager of his age, or Miss Tilly had indeed gone too far and had indeed picked up the rod too often; picked it up too often to be able to channel her own frustrations.

'Anyway,' the priest said. And with this, I quote one of my brothers in faith: 'Chastisement is a bitter pill, one that should be gilded in wisdom and given in love.'

Marcus understood what the priest meant by this, and the way the man had spoken these words also seemed correct.

But gilding corporal punishment in wisdom? And giving it in love? Ha! Thought Marcus. That was anything but what Tilly had done! She seemed to enjoy it! Seemed to want to apply this as often as possible!

'I actually have another issue that bothers me,' said Marcus, in a very mature and also very wise tone.

'Well, let me hear it then!' shouted the priest, delighted. A man who clearly took pleasure in hearing all these questions from Marcus while at the same time pondering about them. Marcus was a sensitive boy, that was quite clear by now, and maybe even too sensitive.

A certain sensitivity that should be cherished by the world that could give the living environment a certain helping hand and that could give the world a bit more colour, perhaps, by means of its details that would have quickly eluded a somewhat blunt or duller person.

It was the character and nature of a painter, of a poet, a writer, or an interior designer who knew how to arrange the various fabrics, the colours on the walls, and the furniture in the house in such a way that the atmosphere within the house seemed to elevate itself, and whereas the person within could make himself feel benevolent like a king or queen.

Marcus also seemed to have this kind of magic in stock. He, too, saw the details, tried to point them out to people, and thus created a world in which he, too could feel peaceful and at home. But this was quite difficult to achieve somehow...

The outside world was often harsh, unreasonable, and also ignorant in many areas. It was often just a matter of carrying on, putting shoulders to the wheel, while people often just did things without any thought behind them, or were often not even satisfied with the lives they were leading.

And that was exactly where the point of contention lay. There, on that plane, and at that moment in time, one could appeal to that delicacy, to that magic, which some seemed to possess—some a bit more than others—although it was often not noticed at all. The magic soon faded, the tenderness was quickly crushed down by callousness, and the delicate souls among us were soon weighed down by guilt, stress, and a whole lot of other tensions. It seemed more and more the way of the world. However, more of a dead end. A certain path that Marcus also seemed to take more and more because this was somehow expected of him. Even though he fought against it with all his might while he clung to every wooden sign that he encountered along the way, and while an invisible force field pulled him towards a despondent and also hopeless abyss in which so many had already been swallowed...

'Well, let me hear about it then,' was what the priest said for a second time, and to be able to get Marcus out of his daydreaming.

'Whenever I was in the classroom, trying to get words and sentences on paper, I always got the wind from the front. My writing technique was never good enough; my papers were always stained, and according to Miss Tilly, that was my punishment because of my left-handedness. She made left-handedness appear as a bad thing. As if I had been born with an evil disposition, couldn't do anything about it for the rest, and I just had to accept my fate in this...'

However, the priest had to laugh aloud about this. 'You are laughing now,' said Marcus in a serious tone. 'But I'm actually quite serious. What do you think about this matter? And what does the Bible actually say about this? Should I really be concerned?' The smile on the priest's face soon faded.

The man was more in the mood for humour today, not for all that seriousness, even though he thought it was another beauty of a question from young Marcus, and he weighed his answer carefully.

'You know, Marcus, as far as I know, I have never come across anything in the Bible about this issue, about that alleged evil origin of left-handedness of which you speak. I can't give you an unequivocal answer about this. The only thing I can give you is my vision. My view on this particular phenomenon sprouted from the bosom of reason, reasonableness, and also logic. The way I see it, left-handedness is also simply laid down by nature. And shall I tell you something else? The master painter Michelangelo also seemed to have been left-handed! At least, he had the creation of Adam, a part of the mural that can be admired on the ceiling of the Sistine Chapel in Vatican City, placed with his left hand.

A man who was typified as a man of God. A man who was said to possess certain gifts, to be able to see beyond dimensions, and in all probability, who possessed the Holy Spirit. Not bad, hey! For a lefty!' And the priest gave Marcus a pat on the shoulder and also a playful wink to reassure him somewhat, and thus hopefully suppress his somewhat foolish thoughts with some hard facts, or at least to be able to contain them a bit...

In the days that followed, Marcus often walked the streets aimlessly. The rolling hills that flanked the fields and arable land in the distance, which could be seen from time to time, from which Glancebury owed its name, and which shone due to the dew and raindrops which the sun seemed to shine eagerly on even today, laid there peacefully. Even on the only paved path in the village, the dewdrops sparkled in the full light of the morning sun and sometimes blinded Marcus with their sharpness.

Marcus had visited the chicken farmer, but he didn't seem to be at home or was still in his bed, perhaps sleeping off his intoxication from the night before. Marcus had also passed by the terraced house of the cloth weaver, with its tightly sealed door, where no one seemed to live, and with the heavy curtains that always hung in front of the window.

Marcus had walked past it quickly, had thought about knocking on the door, but eventually had decided not to. He knew that the cloth weaver was at home and could even hear the foot-fulling, or maybe it was some other activity, through the walls of the building, but he didn't feel like paying a visit today. Today, Marcus didn't feel like sitting in a musty and dark cave where a man was constantly working, without sometimes speaking for an hour on end.

With a newspaper opened in front of him that was interesting but also difficult to read because of the ever-dimmed light in the room. And also a room where it smelled so heavily of chemicals that Marcus felt like he could faint at any particular moment. No, Marcus didn't feel anything about that today.

After all, the weather was beautiful today. The air felt clean and crisp, and Marcus sniffed his nose a few times, took a few deep breaths of the cold, clean air, and then, almost unconsciously, walked towards a place where he had spent more often lately. Towards the threshold of the church and towards its supervisor, a man whose house stood always open for everyone, and of course also for the young Marcus, for whom the man even seemed to have a surprise in store today…

'Look at this, Marcus!' said the man, elated. 'I have a law book here. And after our enlightening conversation about chastisement in education recently, I looked it up and gazed through it. I have, therefore, come across a number of clear guidelines. And even though, in theory, and as a rule, it is often written more beautifully than it is applied in practice, these are still the guidelines that one must adhere to and that one can be pointed out to if one wants to flout the law.

Here, I'll read them out loud to you.

Initially, there is little opposition to corporal punishment, but there are all kinds of rules and conditions that are to be taken in account.

And here are some of the guidelines, Marcus, so pay close attention:

- The child must experience the punishment as justified.

- It must understand the sense of the punishment.

- The punishment must be adapted to the age and person of the child.

- Every punishment must have a clear beginning and ending.

- The child may not be reminded of a given punishment all the time.

- And when one has undergone the punishment, everything is forgiven and forgotten.'

'Chastisement is a bitter pill, one that should be gilded in wisdom and given in love.

I've said this before, Marcus. If teachers would adhere to these guidelines in a better and more constructive way, then corporal punishment should continue to be permissible as far as I am concerned, as long as they are applied in all reasonableness.

Especially the last guideline appeals to me: "When one has undergone the punishment, everything is forgiven and forgotten." I get the idea, Marcus, after listening to your stories, that Miss Tilly did not apply this last guideline at all?'

'No, indeed...,' said Marcus somewhat angrily. 'She always knew how to rekindle old suffering. She just couldn't get enough of reminding the students of their mistakes, even if the punishment had long since been served, and one should, literally and figuratively, have to start with a clean slate.

No, Miss Tilly didn't know anything about those guidelines, and I am therefore glad that you have been able to clarify that through this book of law...'

'Look, Marcus,' and the priest let out a bubbling fart to reinforce his statement.

'If the universe wasn't good, then eh, well, yes, well, then eating would be like a turd, and then pooping would really hurt. It rhymes even! Okay, I may have put it a bit simplistically, but that's basically how it is, isn't it?

And I want to add something else to it, Marcus. Something that actually has nothing to do with what we have just discussed but which I would like to express to you in a personal way.

If you can't figure out certain life questions, just try to keep things as simple as possible. Do not dwell on them for too long. Keep things as superficial as possible, and try to accept them for what they are. Life is simply incredibly straightforward, but intensely complex at the same time. Try not to wander into that complexity, Marcus, if you aren't yet ready for it...

Well! the man suddenly exclaimed. Has this story become profound after all, huh?! After that lighthearted and airy opening of mine...'

And the priest gave Marcus another playful pat on his shoulder. 'You think too much, Marcus. Leave that complexity to others...' And the man looked cautiously at the sky above him.

'...for there are plenty of entities who deal with issues that would make both your and my head spin like wooden spinning tops...'

Marcus had by now looked often at the two books which he had in his possession. He had read the book about the ancient Indians from front to back, and he had also opened the other book; the book full of mystery and ominous creatures, from time to time.

Partly because of this, and also because of the newspapers he had regularly read at the residence of the cloth weaver, everyday farm life began to bore him more and more, and his dream of working as a reporter in the big city of Light Town began to impose itself on him even more frequently than before.

Marcus therefore, and once again, presented his deeply cherished dream to his parents.

A while ago, he had already made his ambition known to them, with an indignant and sometimes mocking father on one side of the table, and a worried, somewhat suspicious mother on the other end. Marcus had expressed his grievances at the time but had received no solace, although it had nevertheless become clear to his parents that Marcus was dead serious about this matter, that this was not some sort of whim, and that he had thought about this very carefully, and also very thoroughly.

His parents seemed to be getting a bit tired of Marcus, 'Marcus-tired', as he had thought to himself with a chuckle.

It was; therefore, a strategy, a last resort, and the little plan seemed to work out; to irritate the people around him for as long as possible, and to confront them with his wish as often as he could, so that they got sick and tired of it, and eventually went along with it, in order to get rid of it.

Marcus had now presented his dream to his parents for the second time, and this time, it seemed that he had managed to push it through. His father's dislike continued to take a clear form, and his mother's anxiety did not exactly diminish, even though she continued to support her son for the most part and seemed to do this tacitly. Because even though we draw the beginning of the nineteenth century; a century with many changes on the horizon, certain changes also had to wait a bit longer.

And even though male-female relationships were not exactly fair up till now; the wife, for example, had to submit to her husband, and her only right seemed to be the kitchen sink, often, and in practice, this wasn't applied at all in reality.

Okay, also, in the nineteenth century, it was a man's world. And yes, to the outside world, men liked to show some macho behaviour now and then; with a silenced hen next to their side to reinforce their masculinity somewhat more. But when push came to shove, the roles were really reversed sometimes. And the man at times realised very well that he would never make it without his wife, and he sometimes even resigned himself— even though he would never admit it out loud himself—to a somewhat more submissive position.

That's how it also seemed to go in the Pritchard residence from time to time. This time, the wife decided to stand behind her son, awarded him his chance at success, and if all didn't work out eventually, he could always return home and resume his everyday farm life.

Bertus didn't agree with this at all, was anything but happy about this, but had to give in because his wife expected it of him. Bertus also, and finally, complied to Marcus' great surprise, but also to his great happiness. Yes, Bertus had also changed his mind at that point, but only on one condition: If Marcus' dream were to fall apart in one way or another, he had to abandon his ambitions for good, resign himself to his fate, pick up farm life again, embrace it, and never, but then never, look back.

Marcus nodded with a lump in his throat, hugged his mother tightly, and shook his father's hand exuberant, even though the man didn't even look at him in that process. In a few days, Marcus would make the big crossing. Not by boat and over water, but by a bridging of rural life to a more urban one. A crossing from boyishness towards a more mature posture. And hopefully one of still reasonable superficiality, to that of a more general self-development.

His father, Bertus, didn't like this one bit. In his eyes all this was just a waste of money, time, and also that of precious energy. Marcus would soon come home from a rude awakening.

His son would once again learn his lessons through the hard way of life, stubborn as he was, while his wife just let it all be. Bertus didn't like dreamers, and he didn't like impulsiveness. But deep down inside, even though he probably didn't even realize it consciously, he didn't like idealists or creative people. Perhaps because they got so little done, amounted to so little, or could be seen as lazy people. But perhaps also because they had the courage to grab life by the horns and were not afraid to express their feelings, an aspect that Bertus always seemed to close himself off from.

Either way, and whether Marcus was a dreamer, a lazy soul, or a creative idealist with a perspective in his future, Bertus deep down hoped for the former. He had always known his son as a dreamer, and Bertus always enjoyed seeing him wandering across the lands and with his head in the clouds while still neatly completing his tasks and chores.

Marcus hurt his father with this splurge, and this just didn't seem to get through to his thick skull.

Bertus looked somewhat melancholic over the fields and lands and then thought the following: soon, everything will be back to normal. Soon, my son will join me again, and we will once again dig up the land together and offer the cows and also the pigs their daily care. And all of this will be nothing more than a bad daydream, a nasty gust of wind over the fields and lands of the Pritchard family, pieces of land that have been cultivated by us for centuries and that hopefully may remain in our possession for many years to come…

John McAllister

Marcus had regularly stood on the threshold of the priest's house.

He sometimes had difficult but enlightening conversations with several residents of Glancebury.

He had chatted with the chicken farmer on a regular basis and become acquainted with the seemingly easy interpretation of his life's path. Marcus had spoken frequently with the cloth weaver, an alleged bon vivant who had to turn his back on the big city due to personal and business circumstances. An urban environment in which Marcus, in turn, tried to find a certain solace.

Marcus knew the hard work and the toil in the fields. Adults who didn't seem to give him a single hand's breadth. The immense quarrel between him and his parents. And his brief foray towards a certain recalcitrance at the time of nailing his idealistic views to the gate of the abattoir, with all its consequences.

And now young Marcus stood once again on a threshold. Not that of the church this time but that of a new phase in life. However, Marcus turned out not to be the only dreamer within the small hamlet called Glancebury, seated within the diocese of Lancastershire, which in turn was situated in the powerful nation that many other world powers called Ingland, and which was feared by many because of its influence, power and global reach.

Marcus had gathered some of his belongings. He had come up with a plan of action. And now he waved goodbye to his parents, who watched from behind the large windowpane as their eldest and also only son tried to break free from their parental grip.

Marcus walked down the village path in a controlled manner. He had a few sandwiches in his suitcase, some sheets of paper, the pencil, and the inkwell that he still owned from his school days.

A certain fear took hold of him, of course, but also a form of healthy enthusiasm and a belief in his own abilities that was, for the most part, the reason for this, hopefully, professional escapade. A belief in his own abilities that he had carried within him from an early age on, for as long as he could remember, and that no one had been able to take away from him, no matter how hard they had tried.

Marcus walked further down the village path. The paved road soon became unpaved, and at the beginning of what was to be a new chapter in life, a companion, a partner in crime, already stood waiting for him. He was a cheerful man, friendly, and with a certain hopeful expectation of life in his eyes.

Marcus knew the man only by name, had seen him before of course—since almost everyone in Glancebury knew each other by name or had seen each other pass by in their steps—but Marcus had never actually spoken with him. The man had been patiently waiting for a customer and today, on this very early morning, that customer was the young Marcus. The man, whose name was John McAllister, was already standing by the side of his trusty steed, with a cart stretched behind the horse to take Marcus to his new destination, a destination most likely full of hills, potholes, and barricades, but hopefully also one of new opportunities, maybe even fortune, and a place under the common sun where Marcus could finally and truly spread his wings.

Marcus jumped on the trestle of the farmer's cart and handed John the meagre but precious pennies that his mother had put in his hand—a sign that gave Marcus a certain hope and showed that at least one member of the family stood behind him for as long as his dream flight lasted—Mr McAllister then let go of the reins, after which the horse started to walk, and the cart started to move.

Marcus had never spoken to John before and did not know him that well yet, although he could already conclude that John was cut from a different kind of cloth than the average Glanceburie.

John was spry, frank, and almost flamboyant, character traits that were not often found in these generally stiff residents.

It almost made Marcus doubt, doubting whether he was doing the right thing about this subterfuge, as it was often labeled by his parents. And a doubt that he was trying to look for something in the big city, something that might also be found in Glancebury: Frankness, a certain depth, a form of living outside the established rules, but at the same time still being able to secure a place within this whole. It made Marcus hesitate for a moment when he looked at John, who himself kept his view on the road in front of him and had to wait and see what this young passenger had to tell him.

Marcus indeed felt a doubt for a moment, but not for long. The other pennies were still ringing in his pocket, given to him by his dear mother who, despite her often passivity, had always shown him unconditional love, and that also seemed to give him a certain courage to continue on with this.

The farmer's cart had been on its way for a while now. The path was somewhat linear but also admirable because of all its surrounding natural beauty.

Before long, Marcus and John would get to know each other somewhat better.

For today? For today the first cornerstone for this starting relationship would be laid... It had been quiet between the two for a while now; a silence as the very long path ran down before them, and while the natural beauty around them changed with every rotation of the wooden wheels of the farmer's cart and with every step the horse took. It wasn't an annoying silence, but Marcus was still in the mood for some chatter, and he just thought that John wouldn't mind either. A topic of conversation was therefore not far away. In Marcus' little world of existence, there were always plenty of topics to talk about, and Marcus decided to ask the man about the most common thing. He asked the man about his profession: about commuting between Glancebury and the big city of Light Town, about transporting passengers on his farmer's cart, and how much money the man actually earned with it.

He asked about his seemingly simple job, how John had come up with the idea of doing it, and if he didn't find it a bit monotonous.

John explained to Marcus that there was a bit more to this work as it seemed at first glance. He didn't like it when people had their opinions ready so quickly, although he could appreciate Marcus' directness. It was, in any case, better than people who had a firm opinion, who did not express it, and thus keeping people in their immediate environment in the dark with their beliefs.

No, this was anything but an easy or simple job, maybe

Marcus would understand that one day. Simply nothing in life was easy, even if it looked so from the outside...

'How so?' asked Marcus boldly. And even though he didn't want to provoke the man at all, he stuck to his own point of view that this job seemed even simpler to him than, for example, herding chickens.

'Isn't it just about keeping the horse in line and following a dead straight road?' But the horseman, who still bore the name John McAllister, looked at his young passenger in amazement. 'Ho, ho, ho,' he said, even if it wasn't against the horse.

'There is really a bit more to this all. How about the maintenance of the cart? The care of the horse? Ha! Even harnessing the horse and harnessing it in front of the cart is quite the job. It all seems so simple, Marcus, because you are sitting here next to me on the trestle, and it all seems to go by itself, but it is really not as simple as it seems. Look, my joints might have become a bit worn out by working in the mines at a young age, but...'

'Wait!' Marcus exclaimed suddenly, and the man was about to tighten the reins to bring his trusty steed to a stop.

'No,' said Marcus, 'please ride on. I would like to talk to you about the mine. I have the feeling that something has happened there. Something that has made the people in Glancebury bitter. Or is this bitterness perhaps the result of losing a form of livelihood?'

But the man made it clear to Marcus that he did not want to talk about it.

However, he did say in a somewhat concealing way that if Marcus tried to find out a certain truth, he would just have to find it out for himself...

But Marcus thought that was a strange remark. Surely, the

man was sitting next to him on the trestle right now, wasn't he? He apparently knew a certain truth, didn't he? So why didn't he just say it out loud? Finding out the truth? Looking for it somewhere? Start some kind of search? A search for what?! He did not have to do these things at all if there was a certain truth to be found in the first place.

The man only had to tell him this truth. This was not a matter of searching at all. This was a matter of honesty, and Marcus had the feeling that he was sitting right next to it on the trestle. But this man was apparently also less candid than he initially pretended to be.

Yet, Marcus liked this man in a certain way. The man apparently wanted to keep things shallow, and Marcus had no choice but to go along with it. Marcus was simply a person who liked in-depth conversations. And even though he knew that about himself by now, it was also a character trait that he would never want to let go of. It was a trait which characterized him, and he would never want to give it up; not for any resident of Glancebury.

Nor for this man who, in the meantime, had changed the subject on his own accord and that was now talking about all the ins and outs of his, not so long ago, newly acquired profession:

'In any case,' the man continued. 'Because my joints are largely worn out by working in the mines, and I really had to look for a new profession, I specialised in something that I call passenger transport. Something that is actually very convenient, because it isn't really that hard work and besides, there was no transport service like this already between Light Town and Glancebury. Which I actually thought was quite resourceful of myself, and also a bit of great luck, because I don't know what else I would have done careerwise. Weaving perhaps?

Or maybe even spinning? Although I actually think those are more women's jobs, and my fingers are too thick for that anyway. Moreover, this work that I do can also be very sociable. Anyway, where was I...?

Oh yes! What I am trying to say is, is that this new profession of mine has forced me to delve into everything that is involved with this passenger transport. What kind of cart I would use? What type of horse is most suitable? How to apply the beam and shafts? And which strands are most suitable for this? By now, I know almost exactly how to do this. For example, how many hand widths there should be between the different parts? In such a way that it puts as little strain on the horse as possible and so that the horse does not get stretch marks or friction marks on its skin. Yes, haha! There is really more to it than you think. But if you want, I can tell you much more about it on another day. For now, however, the ride is over.

Because just look ahead and behold! We have finally reached our destination! Here it is! The great city of Light Town!

Marcus didn't have to search very long.

He could still remember the vast central square of Light Town quite vividly—ever since his trip with his father a few years back—and also how to get there on foot.

He had agreed with John that he would meet him in eight hours at their drop-off point, so Marcus had plenty of time to carry out his plan, and he also had a considerable margin of time because who knew what could happen? Maybe he would be appointed right away? Maybe he had to get to work immediately? It could all be the case, and Marcus had done well to take this into account. After all, it would not be appropriate to have to say on his first day of work that he could not actually start until the next working day. It might be possible, maybe his superiors wouldn't even mind it that much, but John's shuttle service wasn't exactly free, and Marcus' parents, who supported him financially with these rides, simply did not have a lot of money and every penny counted as one. In the big city, time was money, and a number of pence soon became a shilling, and a number of shillings quickly became a pound. And Marcus tried to keep this small debt to his parents, which he was already building up a bit today, as small as possible.

Marcus walked through the grey, somewhat dilapidated alleys and really only had to follow the noise that would lead him to the great central square. Marcus walked past a number of housewives who were hanging up the laundry or that were scrubbing with the strength they possessed in their forearms on a scrubbing board that lay half submerged in a tub full of cold water. Here and there, drunkards and paupers were wallowing in their self-pity, while Marcus also saw how a number of young children ran after an emaciated stray dog with a couple of tree branches that they must have collected somewhere outside the city walls.

Marcus thought that this scene, in which he suddenly found himself, was an interesting image. And quite frankly, it was a perfect reflection of the day-to-day goings-on in the back streets of a big city like Light Town. Marcus kind of liked it. He didn't feel intimidated by it. And in his somewhat scruffy and everyday clothing, he even fitted a bit in, even though this was a standard of living that he himself didn't have in mind at all for the future. A life as he envisioned it was a little bit further down this road, about ten footsteps away from where he stood now, and also a life as anyone had probably imagined it for themselves at some point, just before the ravages of time would intervene, fate would let its power resound, and thus throw everyone back to the place that seemed most suitable for him or her...

Marcus was amazed when he approached the end of the alley, and when he looked out over the large central square that led to it. The noise was almost deafening. Hundreds of people hurriedly walked past each other. Some bumped into each other and then quickly walked on again without even looking up—or back. A grand market had been set up, and all of its stalls were crowded. Horses and carts, many porters, and even a single carriage sometimes protruded above this mass, while the people within this hustle and bustle had to be careful not to be trampled underfoot by a horse, let alone by a fellow human being. It was a scene that would make many a farmer's son or another youngster who was not familiar with the harshness and anonymity of a big city like this one—turn around and never want to return as well.

It was indeed an immense bustle and at the same time, an explosion of impressions, stimuli and energies, which could make a light-hearted person crawl back into his or her shell and chase the person away towards the city walls so that he or she could rest a little bit from it, while throwing off his or her cloak of uneasiness, and while seeking refuge in a somewhat quieter environment.

Marcus was well aware of this, and he would no doubt have felt this uneasiness, too., if he hadn't been here before already. Marcus was basically still a child nonetheless, in the eyes of this zeitgeist, considered as a young adult, and he had come here with a mission. Marcus knew exactly where he had to be, everything else: the many impressions and the choices and possibilities that could lead him astray from his path, merely a side issue. Not exactly of great importance, and it was therefore incidental, and he needed to walk past it with blinders on, and pay as little attention to it as possible.

Marcus had now also joined in the tumult of the large central square, occasionally looked at another passer-by, a market stall, or sometimes swerved before a horse-drawn cart, and then walked towards a stately building of which he almost certainly thought he had to be there.

It was a building complex that had previously caught his eye during his first visit to Light Town with his father. A building that he had thus managed to engrave in his memory and which he now, after three long years, stood in front of on his own to hopefully be able to get a story out of it because even though at the time—during the annual fair visit with his father—and when he could not yet read the many words and sentences that surrounded him, this building had simply struck his keen eye because young people were constantly walking in and out of it with piles of bound newspapers stuck under their arms.

Marcus paused for a moment, took a very deep breath, walked up the wide staircase that led to the door, and then stepped into the building. The door then closed behind him with a ringing bell, together with a placard that adorned it on the front and which read the following:

Welcome to the Gulden Gazette!

A daily newspaper like no other!

Of course, it didn't work out the way Marcus had envisioned it in his most ideal experience. Marcus had come here on a mission, but his boyhood dream, which had been cherished for so long, was soon nipped in the bud. He had quickly found the editor-in-chief's office, had imposed himself with a nice story—since the man in question had not really counted on a spontaneous applicant at all—even if it was a story by Marcus that was by far a lie. That was laced with an eager ambition and perhaps with a form of enthusiasm that was not entirely to be called realistic. Nevertheless, the editor-in-chief was happy with Marcus' visit.

After all, they could always use more manpower, and Marcus was allowed to work at this illustrious newspaper provided he started at the very bottom of the ladder, and preferably even a step below of that. And who knew? The man stated. Maybe one day he would become a book printer? A bookbinder? Maybe even a real local reporter? Although they would probably be talking about five, maybe ten years further from now...

Marcus pretended not to have heard the latter. All he had heard were these four words: a real local reporter. His ears began to glow, his eyes grew larger and larger, and he could finally focus his enthusiasm on the purpose for which he had come to this great city of Light Town.

The good man had made the working methods of this newspaper globally clear to Marcus.

Of the guidelines and also of the rules of conduct that an employee of this newspaper had to adhere to, and the man had set up a small provisional contract with him. Marcus shook hands with the man with all his might, thanked him with good fortune in his eyes for this extraordinary opportunity, and said that he would give everything that he had, do his very best, and probably even more.

'We'll first see and then believe,' the man said. 'Do your very best, work very hard, start at the very bottom of the ladder, and then in time we'll see what more we can do for you...'

Marcus was happy to sign for those words, and he put his

scribble under the simple contract that lay in front of him. Marcus was now working for the newspaper, and his mission was accomplished! He was now almost a local reporter in the making, and in not too long, he might be able to rub this under the noses of his everlasting critics.

Marcus once again shook hands with his superior while the man looked at this new worker with some surprise. Marcus snatched his part of the contract from the table, folded it neatly double, and then put it in the front pocket of his vest in a controlled manner, after which the man showed Marcus his new workplace. Marcus was indeed working for the newspaper now, and he could hardly believe it. His mission had actually succeeded, and he would give everything that he had within him. Even if the skins of his hands would hang down on the sides and even if he would fall down from fatigue. This was what he had come for. This here would be his new life, because this here was his calling!

The Terrible Routine of the New Platen Press

Marcus had been working at the *Gulden Gazette* for almost a week now. And even though he didn't really liked the work at all—he actually had to start at the very bottom of the ladder because that was how it was agreed during his first introductory meeting. He tried to complain as little as possible and also not to show his annoyance too much.

The best moments of the day were actually the drive to work and the long drive back home. During the conversations he had with John McAllister, sitting in silence from fatigue next to the man on the trestle when dusk had already risen high, and when the moon let its light glide over the surrounding landscape. John was a jovial, easygoing, even very sweet man, although he was also a bit simple, or rather said, had a somewhat simple outlook on life.

Marcus always had plenty of topics for conversation; he had always carried this within him. Although John always wanted to talk about the profession he was now currently practicing: about driving the horse and about the maintenance of his wagon. These were subjects that Marcus knew by now and that he had to listen to almost every day. And even though they were quite fascinating, and Marcus even learned something from them in a substantive way, he often craved a good and also eye-opening conversation. Something he hadn't really experienced since he had turned his back on his good acquaintances in Glancebury because Marcus also had to choose a life's path for himself. Maybe he could have such an eye-opening and enlightening conversation again. Soon?

Maybe even with a newly acquired contact? Because he didn't seem to be able to find that in the workplace either...

In the meantime, Marcus was back on the stand, sitting next to John. His daily work lay ahead of him again at the end of this long, almost dead straight road, which nevertheless remained special and even entertaining, while he himself kept his mouth shut for a moment and left the talking to John.

According to John, he could read the proportions between the parts of the cart and those of the body of the horse almost exactly already. He called these hand widths, and he literally used the palm of his hand for these measurements. Marcus had heard this story before and he started to understand it a lot better now. It was actually very handy—no pun intended— and very logical, too. Marcus wondered if John had come up with this idea himself or if he had learned this from someone else...

'Well,' John said. 'This poor creature has had to endure a lot at the beginning of our joint venture, and so have I. By the way, you can still see the bald spots under her withers and around her armpits. Oh well, it was a learning process for Betsy—and he patted the animal kindly on her behind—as well for me. Fortunately, the friction spots have healed quite well, and she doesn't seem to be bothered by them at all anymore, although I think it's a shame because of the, here and there, still visible spots. It still gives the impression that I don't take good care of my horse, and I, of course, know better. But for the picture, for the overall presentation of my services, it would have been better, or nicer, if she still had a flawless skin...'

That's how it often went during those rides. Nice conversations—good conversations, but a bit linear in terms of topics. Marcus even started to find it admirable after a while. The man just endlessly kept talking about the tools he needed for his profession. And even though it was all a bit of the same, it was also true that the man had something new to say about it every time. It was indeed admirable but also a bit straightforward.

One day, Marcus was looking for another topic to talk about. However, he didn't have to look far. All he had to do was dig deep into his mind, although, in the end, he decided not to.

John seemed like a man who loved to talk about things that were tangible, which stood in reality, and that he could literally focus his gaze on. He didn't seem to like things out of the blue, that came from the top of the head, actually the exact opposite of Marcus' approach of subjects.

Marcus had to make do with this man. He was grateful for his service, liked him as a person, and wanted to accommodate him in his personal mannerisms. Marcus didn't have to look far for a new conversation. However he normally did this by looking inside, but this time, he looked for it on the outside. Because every time he drove to work with John he saw a castle in the very distance, around a quarter of their way. It was a castle that he regularly had nightmares about as a child simply because his parents and many villagers with them claimed that it housed an evil person. And every time they drove by there on their way to Marcus' destination, Marcus always fixed his gaze on that castle in the distance.

And sometimes, just sometimes, he thought he saw a small figure walking there.

A small stature indeed, although it could also be a tree that the wind eagerly managed to play with...

Marcus grabbed the bucket with ink in it for the umpteenth time, dipped the horsehair brush in the solution, smeared it on the base of the printing press, put the sheet of paper on it, pulled the lever, and then felt for the umpteenth time how the leaden letters imprinted themselves in the piece of paper. He placed paper by paper on this base plate, pulled the lever, and then saw how pages of newspaper were created.

The brush went back into the bucket, and after wiping the ink over the bottom plate again, the lever was pulled towards him again so that this short-term circle was completed for the trillionth time.

Day in, day out, week after week, and month after month, this cycle continued. And with a Marcus bending, toiling, and sweating to meet his daily quota.

It would perhaps take years before he could work his way up and before he could find an opening to the reporter position he aspired to so much, which now motivated him to pull this dragoon of a lever towards himself.

A routine that he underwent with pain in his heart and which he tried to endure as best as he could. *'Years?'* Marcus thought to himself. *'Years?! I have absolutely no intention of doing this for that long! I may be a newcomer to this profession and a layman within the form of journalism that is practiced here, but I just know that I have way more to offer than this!'*

Marcus looked at the dripping brush in his hand from which many drops flew, causing black stains on the floor which he was now standing on. He looked at the iron platen press that seemed to laugh at him and that challenged him to see if Marcus had any more muscle power within him than he already had shown so far.

Marcus looked around for a moment and saw how everyone was busy with their own work. Several platen presses were used, buckets of black ink were dragged in constantly, and piles of paper were constantly supplied, but no one saw how young Marcus was struggling with all this.

An inner urge that began to bubble up more and more inside of him and that wanted to kick over this entire bucket of ink and tear off the lever from this annoying iron device.

'Is this what I am destined for?!' was what Marcus had to think for a moment. A life filled with monotony and with already enough knowledge of things that could overthrow this entire establishment? As long as he got the chance to do so?

Marcus let go of the lever, took the sheet of paper from under the press, and put it on the designated pile for the umpteenth time, but left the now-dried bottom plate for what it was.

The brush rested comfortably against the inside of the bucket again while Marcus walked on high legs toward the editor-in-chief's office. With an order in mind that he now really had to make clear to the good man. A demand that would hopefully hit the mark, and that could make or break his further career and the coming long period ahead of him...

Marcus became more and more depressed, and his work of less and less quality, and that didn't seem to escape the editor-in-chief's attention. The man apologized for the fact that he had been stringing Marcus along for so long, although he basically had no other choice:

'You do your job generally properly,' said the man to him.

'And I understand all too well that the top link within a company cannot function without the bottom one, but... But you also have to understand that even the most inexperienced printer within our *Gazette* is more well-read than you are, let alone the freshly starting reporters. Moreover, almost everyone here comes from the big city or the cities that surround it, and they all have had some kind of writing education at one academy or another.

It simply wouldn't be fair to give you a chance of being a reporter, while some of them don't even make it through the preliminary procedure, even with their backgrounds...

I'm sorry, kid. You are a nice lad, but we just can't work with this. Moreover, you are the only employee from Glancebury, and we all know that that is not the place that entails the most intellect that our fine province has to offer. Maybe it would have been better if you had just stayed there? At least then, you could still become a farmer or something along those lines? Because here at least, and so it seems, you're not having the best time of your life...'

But Marcus loudly started to cry all of a sudden. He started sniffling and also began to stutter somewhat. And all the tension, frustration, the empty promises that had been presented to him by this man lately finally seemed to find an outlet through his tear ducts.

'But, but...,' Marcus sobbed and stammered. 'I may be just a simple farmer's son, and maybe I don't have that much knowledge yet or have read that much in my life up until now. I do have my qualities, on the other hand! I am curious, eager to learn, I can read and write, and I have largely taught myself grammar and punctuation and, and... And if you would give me just a chance? Just one minor chance? I promise you... I will go for it with everything that I have!'

And he quickly wiped away some snot and tears with the sleeve of his vest.

The editor-in-chief let out a long and also deep sigh and then said the following:

'You know what? I can tell that you really want it. And I can't help but agree that you've been doing a lot of chores for us lately. I will, therefore, make a certain arrangement with you, but you must promise that this will remain between us and that you will not talk to anyone else about it...'

And Marcus nodded exuberantly to this, of course.

The man continued:

'I want you to look for a story in your spare time, outside of your working hours and daily routine, which is so good that it could be on the front page of the *Gulden Gazette*, and on top of that, this story must come from your own hand...

If you succeed, you can apprentice as a local reporter... But beware! I'll only give you one chance! So don't keep coming up with useless and meaningless stories because one: I don't have time to read them. And two: you will lose your credibility that you have it in you to come up with a good story, let alone write one. So... keep this in mind, do your very best, and remember: you'll only get one chance...

Now, quickly get back to work because there is still a big pile of paperwork waiting for you at the platen press that needs to be printed...'

That particular evening, during dinner time, Marcus told his parents in a rousing tone and with many hand gestures that in the not-too-distant future, he might actually become a real local reporter.

His mother reacted with pride to this fact. 'You see, Bertus, it will all be fine,' although his father didn't seem to believe all of this yet.

'What do you want to write about then?' was what the man asked his son. 'Surely nothing ever happens here, does it? And those books that you are always reading, you know that they have been written by someone else, don't you...?

Well boy,' was what he finally said. 'Do your very best. But if all this comes down to nothing, please listen to what your old father has to say to you: get your head out of those clouds! And go back into the fields! After all, it isn't too late yet. In spite of this, my own age is increasing with time, my bones are becoming more brittle, and my muscles are becoming more stiff. And I really have to make a decision about the farm within a few years...'

The man suddenly got up from the table, looked at his son dejectedly for a moment, and then quietly walked away...

Marcus had imposed a certain discipline on himself: 'printing with a certain feeling' was what he called it.

In this way, he still gave a bit of himself once the customer had the end product in his hands and once the individual had opened it in front of his nose. But after a year or so, this feeling also started to fade away somewhat. Yet, it was not all doom and gloom that prevailed. After all, he had now gained certain access to information, so he read the newspaper more and more often for free these days, and people were sometimes surprised by the amount of knowledge that this—at first glance—unworldly boy seemed to carry with him.

In the meantime, he had even acquired a small local historical awareness; partly gained from the newspapers he had always read in the house of his good acquaintance, the cloth weaver.

He seemed to have transcended his parents on an

intellectual level by now, although it also seemed that they, at the same time, tried to keep him a bit small in his own opinion. An opinion that, of course, didn't just come out of the blue; an opinion that began to gnaw at him more and more often and also more by the day...

Marcus had had it all over again with the platen press to which he seemed to be bound for quite some time now. His dissatisfaction with this apparatus began to grow on him again, and this fact didn't seem to escape the attention of the head printer—his superior on the work floor.

He, therefore, took his youngest employee aside for a moment while at the same time telling him god's honest truth:

'Be happy, Marcus...,' the man said to him. 'Not so long ago, we had completely different kinds of platen presses standing here. A while back, the pressure still had to be applied by constantly tightening a spindle. Now, all you have to do is pull a lever towards you. The work is nearly as hard as it used to be a few years ago! You don't know how lucky you are with this development boy!'

And he looked at his youngest, but also his most dissatisfied worker, with a certain contempt in his eyes. 'Pfff...,' the man finally said, '...the youth of today...' While he walked away with an air of superiority...

Marcus had been working at the *Gulden Gazette* for three full years now. And after asking at least ten times to be apprenticed as a local news reporter he began to lose hope in his deep-seated dream bit by bit. And more and more often, when he made the long journey back home on the seat of the horsedrawn cart of John McAllister, and he could see the illustrious castle looming in the very distance, he began to notice feelings of liberation within himself for whomever or whatever might live in that castle. Because his parents, and especially his father Bertus, wanted Marcus—just like himself—to live in a large and comfortable house later on in life didn't he?

Well, this character, whomever or whatever it may be, exactly seemed to do that, although in that case, that didn't seem to be quite the right thing to do either. It was never good either way, it seemed...

Marcus had seen the castle in the distance many times by now at the beginning of his career. However, he had not noticed it that much, perhaps because he was too busy with himself or with John, with his endless monologues about his horse, about his farm cart, and about the pride he experienced to be the first shuttle service between Glancebury and the grand city of Light Town.

Nevertheless, Marcus began to notice the castle more and more often lately. There seemed to be a person living there, someone mysterious and somewhat elusive, and who was also reviled by those around him, just as Marcus felt sometimes.

The work on the platen press was monotonous, a prospect on a career switch seemed to be out of the question for the time being, and perhaps it would never come at all. And his urge for adventure began to increasingly impose itself on him. Marcus needed something to fuel his inner fire with. That could be a good book with an entertaining story in it in which he could doze off dreamily. Conversations with good acquaintances to confirm each other's suspicions about everyday life, to experience a form of cohesion, and preferably to learn something new.

Or simply by following a new passion in life. Something he could start his day off with, with some form of enthusiasm; working towards a certain end goal that could give him the proper satisfaction.

At least something! Something that could give him some purpose again. At the same time some fresh life energy to cope with everyday grind. Marcus had been looking for something like that for a while now. The bone-dry work on the platen press had almost gotten him down, but now he finally seemed to have found a new and also personal project. His fire had been rekindled, and the project lay there in the far distance, with its great looming towers and its tall shadows sweeping over the surrounding fields. The castle was his new challenge for now! A structure with a resident in it from which he might be able to learn something.

A resident who might appreciate Marcus' presence. A resident who would hopefully let him in. And above all: a place which, in all its splendor, could hopefully inspire Marcus...

Marcus' First Visit to the Chateau

Marcus didn't really know what to expect from this escapade. What was he actually doing here? Why was he here in the first place? Why did he peer along the high walls of this huge castle, trying to catch a glimpse of its high-pointed towers?

And why did the large, heavy wooden door before which he now stood seem to beckon him with its weathered appearance and with its mysterious door knocker?

Marcus had been standing at this gate for at least five minutes now, with a certain nervousness in his limbs and even with a slight fear in his constitution that had remained foreign to him until this day. But somewhere, deep down inside, he actually knew why he was visiting this erected fort at this particular midday hour. It would be something different, a breakthrough from the daily routine, which he began to dislike so frequently. Perhaps this visit would come to nothing, but it would result in a completely new experience, and he would not come to know this until he had made his own presence known...

Marcus reached for the heavy metal door knocker although he withdrew his hand at the very last moment. Because what if the inhabitant of this castle liked to be left alone? Who liked to isolate himself? And resided in a place like this just to avoid people? People like Marcus, for example?

Marcus thought deeply and carefully for a moment. He thought of a small ruse, although knowing himself, it probably wouldn't work out that well. Maybe it would even scare this dweller, and he would lose his chance to learn more about this place. Maybe Marcus should just go for honesty. Speaking truth had always worked out well for him up till now, and why would it be any different this time?

Marcus could tell this inhabitant that he came from Glancebury, that almost everyone in this area knew each other, and that he wanted to get acquainted. He could compliment the person on this beautiful accommodation, perhaps ask the question how he or she ended up here, and perhaps even better, tell the man or woman in question that he would like to break the monotony of everyday life with this unexpected visit, and whether the resident agreed on this and stood open to it...

Marcus started to feel a bit braver again and came back to himself a bit more through these reassuring thoughts. He took twenty steps back, looked at the building in almost all of its glory, and then thought the following:

A person who lives in such a magnificent stronghold is bound to be somewhat eccentric.

A person who walks the corridors of a place like this will undoubtedly be able to look past erected social conventions. Marcus could also put that argument forward in his defence; some type of flattery that the person in question could surely appreciate, and on top of that, might also approach a certain core.

Marcus took another twenty resolute steps forward. He wielded the door knocker for what it was intended, and the three blows on the woodwork ensured that he had made his presence known by now and that the door to his new adventure could be opened now at any minute...

The inhabitant of the castle was a friendly middle-aged man at first glance.

He had opened the large wooden door to his fortress in a controlled manner. Marcus had made his intentions known to him, and so the man had invited him to take a look in the immense fortress that he apparently could call his home.

The two had gone through a number of long corridors, crossed a large interior space, and finally climbed a narrow and stuffy spiral staircase, after which they had arrived in the man's personal quarters.

Marcus had sat down somewhat timidly and quietly on a wooden chair for the moment while at the same time admiring the decoration of the room with an almost open mouth.

Here and there stood large bookcases, all covered with a thick layer of dust, although Marcus had the opposite idea that these books were regularly inspected.

Stone busts, staring into nothingness. Large and small paintings on the walls clearly had lost colour already. And opposite to him, a beautiful, and strangely enough, shiny— teak wood desk, behind which his host sat. The man was friendly, quiet, and a lot more hospitable than Marcus had initially expected. He let his guest get used to the ambience in which he suddenly found himself, to the interior, which was anything but ordinary.

The desk that the man was sitting behind was littered with strange trinkets, objects that Marcus did not recognise at all but that somehow appealed to a certain imagination. Marcus' host was a controlled man; Marcus had already noticed that, and the good gentleman probably also possessed a certain tact.

Because even though Marcus had been sitting there in

silence for quite some time now; something that could have created a certain mutual tension between two strangers. This man seemed to influence Marcus' peace of mind with his inner calm, and it almost seemed as if the two had known each other for quite some time now and that they had already met earlier.

Marcus decided to shake off his little cloak of awkwardness. He complimented the man—with sincerity in his voice—on his beautiful dwelling, also complimented him on his great furnishing skills, and he wondered how the man had come up with the idea of dressing this space, but also the other rooms that the two had crossed before, in this way...

The man looked up from the pile of paperwork in front of him for a moment. He seemed to examine Marcus briefly and unobtrusively and then said the following:

'Well, first of all, bright young man, I would like for you to call me Count. Anyone who thinks they know me a little calls me that way, even the people in the neighbouring town of Glancebury, where you apparently come from; a community, I have the idea, where people gossip about me on a regular basis...'

And the man looked at Marcus with a certain glint in his eyes, but also with a crooked grin, where the boy for a moment felt the discomfort of the uncomfortable mantle that slowly tried to creep up again.

'Well...,' Marcus, however, said boldly, 'that could well be the case, but that is anything but the reason why I knocked on your front door. I...'

But the man raised a hand before Marcus could finish his sentence. 'It's all right,' the Count said. 'Let's not tire ourselves with trivialities and peripheral issues that can only lead us astray from our personal paths.'

Marcus could not help but agree with this, even though it

was actually the Count who had started talking about this on his own accord. And even though Marcus wanted to say this to him, in the end he decided not to, mainly because then he would indeed indulge himself in trivialities, and the Count would still be right on this.

Nevertheless, Marcus was already enjoying himself. Purely because of the fact that he was welcome in this new world of the Count, a world that Marcus had only been allowed to see from the outside—on the trestle next to the horse driver John McAllister—and of which Marcus had already created a bit of an image in his head that strangely enough, corresponded reasonably well with the reality in which he now suddenly found himself.

And even though Marcus was reasonably pleased and also very happy with this newly acquired contact, he had the impression that he had to be a little careful with his choice of words and take into account the seemingly fickle, strange, and perhaps even capricious and unpredictable character of his host. A suspicion that could only hint if Marcus would be allowed to visit here more often...

'But to come back to your previous question,' was what the Count said suddenly.

'You wanted to know how I got this accommodation? Or at least, how I came up with the idea of organising it in this way?' And Marcus nodded enthusiastically.

'Indeed, Count,' he said. 'I really think that you have a beautiful home. I can hardly name it or put it into words, but I really think that it has something special, almost something majestical...'

And the Count had to laugh aloud at these words. 'Well...' he said. 'This entire castle, and everything in it, has a so-called Gothic slant. Gothic...,' the man continued, and he looked proudly through his abode for a moment. 'I could tell you all about it. Paintings, sculptures, architecture... Actually, it's just art! Art in almost all of its facets!'

Hmm... thought Marcus, *so Gothic is what it is called...* And what exactly attracts you so to this art form? But frankly, the Count had already answered this question, so the young Marcus decided to take a different approach. 'What I really mean to ask is,' he continued, 'when did this period approximately begin? And how did you get so involved in it?'

'Well, that's a very good question', the Count said. 'And actually, a question to which I don't have an unequivocal answer so quickly...'

'But Count!' exclaimed Marcus suddenly as he jumped up from the wooden chair and planted his palms on the teak worktop of the desk he had been sitting opposite for some time now.

'I thought you knew everything?!' And even though it was a kind of rhetorical question, and Marcus didn't really know why he had stated it in the first place, it nevertheless was an assumption that seemed to fit this man.

'Well,' the Count said again. 'Art forms are often gradually adopted. Some of that is used, some of the other is copied, and so a new movement seems to emerge over time. Periods seem to merge into one another, overlap one another, so to speak; I don't really think that there is a suitable answer to this or a specific year or date to be mentioned. Moreover...true art—at least in my book—is simply not to be grasped...'

Marcus, in turn, thought about this, and he actually had to agree with this since he himself knew almost nothing about this subject.

Nevertheless, he found it almost admirable how the Count

was able to skillfully avoid certain questions that concerned his own persona, but that he still seemed to have an answer to almost everything...

Lately, people have had fewer remarks about Marcus simply because the young boy did not give them cause to do so. In a kind of daze, he did the small jobs and chores in and around the yard of his parent's farm. In a certain dreamlike state, he sat on the trestle next to the always good-humoured John McAllister. And at work, he printed his quota of newspaper pages while he was secretly looking forward and almost longed for the next visit to the Count's address.

Even the little subcutaneous sneers that his father occasionally passed on to him seemed to bother Marcus less, or the anxiety that his mother always showed him when she pressed a few pence into his hands in the very early morning, and Marcus could thus again take a seat next to John on the trestle of his wagon.

'Say, Count,' was what Marcus said to the man one day when he had once again taken a seat on the wooden chair that seemed to have been carved out for him.

'Let me hear it, little friend,' was what the man replied while running his hand over a shiny black stone that lay in front of him on his worktop.

'Well,' said Marcus. 'As you already know, I'm from Glancebury. And even though we are regularly looked down upon by the more educated people outside, so to speak, I occasionally have had quite a few profound conversations with some of its inhabitants.

I know a priest, for example, with whom I have talked about both love and lust, and I think he said something like that in the end: lust was something of an animalistic drive, and I think love was hard to find... No... I don't think that was what he said.' And Marcus gazed a bit silly in front of him for a moment.

'No, that was not what he had said... That if you are a twisted jar, it might be wise to also look for a twisted lid, something along those lines...'

Marcus scratched the back of his head for a moment. 'I'm sorry, Count, I don't remember it exactly. I only remember that it was quite profound and also a blockade difficult to overcome, something like that...'

'Well...,' the Count said. 'It seems very likely that you have been in conversation with a wise spirit, someone who knew very well what he was talking about. But what is your question exactly? What is the true meaning of this question that you have raised so suddenly?'

Marcus seemed to understand the context of this sudden counterquestion but strangely enough, didn't fully understand the content of it, perhaps exactly as it had happened during the conversation with the priest that the two had had at the time...

'Well...,' Marcus said again, hoping that he was somewhat right and also that his sensitivity and his empathetic antennae, would not let him down today.

'I just want to know what your thoughts are about these subjects: women, love, lust, and everything that comes with it...'

But the Count suddenly laughed out loud. 'Well, dear Marcus, I can actually be very short, concise, and also very clear about that. And I'll tell you exactly what it is that I'm looking for in a woman... I want to bite her in the neck, Marcus, not hard, but playful. All night I want us to be absorbed in each other and afterwards be able to have a good conversation; a conversation in which our souls get the chance to merge with one another. That's what I'm looking for,

Marcus! That's what I'm looking for in a woman!'

'Well!' Marcus exclaimed sarcastically. 'Good luck in finding that!' While he, at the same time, had to laugh scornfully. But the Count looked at him angrily and also provoked: 'It's possible, Marcus,' was what he dead seriously said. 'Believe me, it's possible...'

Marcus began to enjoy the visits to the Count's address. The two had only just met, but it was almost as if they had known each other for much longer. The meetings were casual, nevertheless very profound from time to time, and Marcus never felt that he had to justify his little person; had to answer to the infantile and also daily opinions, which seemed to circulate so firmly and persistently in the minds of the people outside this raised fortress.

Marcus seemed to be at home there, within an ambience for which he began to feel a predilection while being entangled by a higher intellectual movement that he had so eagerly been seeking and which indeed seemed to suit him so well.

He could, therefore, be found more and more often with the Count. The man seemed to be fine with it for the time being, and today Marcus was again in his presence while, without Marcus having uttered a word, the man not only managed to touch the essence of his being, but he even managed to pierce it with an accuracy that seemed almost out of this world.

Marcus deliberately allowed himself to be carried away by this current, looking up to a man who he began to feel more and more admiration for...

'I'm getting the idea that you don't like your fellow man that much, Marcus, is that right?

I'm getting the idea that you consider yourself superior to the souls who cross your path and who may, therefore, have the privilege of being in your presence...'

The Count had to laugh out loud about this because it was, of course, sarcasm that prevailed here, nevertheless, also a wafer-thin truth that Marcus now tried to debunk with all his might.

He looked with a blush at one of the table legs that supported the count's worktop, after which he looked in the direction of the Count again with some more decisiveness.

'That is anything but true, Count...' he exclaimed indignantly. 'Okay, I don't feel myself inferior to anyone else, and at least always equal regardless of position or rank, but it's just certain people who know how to get under my skin, and strangely enough, there are many of them. People who try to keep me small and who seem to want to shout me down with an ignorance that they themselves seem to be blind to. That tires me gruesomely Count, then I'd rather prefer to stay alone and with myself because that is a fight that simply cannot be won.

And even though I would really like to put them in their place, In the end, I decide not to—because firstly, I don't want to stoop to that level, secondly I do know my place, and thirdly I too am ignorant to a certain degree, just like all of us in the end...'

'Neat!' the Count shouted triumphantly. 'Neat, neat, neat! I partly agree with you, Marcus, and I'll tell you why.'

I, too, have thought about this regularly, and I am of the opinion that there are three types of people roaming this planet. Nevertheless, I would like to tell you about it another time when you walk with your head bowed down again, and I can cheer you a bit up with that. For now, however, I would like to talk to you about the fourth type, the somewhat more elusive type: a group of people who walk through life seemingly carelessly while whistling their carefree tunes but who can still be clearly identified if you know what to look for.

They are the people who seem to be able to forge the environment around them into their own perception, and I like to call this group the enlightened ones, Marcus.

The so-called alchemists. Those who know how to bend the pale, common, and somewhat devalued lead into the more precious, rarer, and also somewhat more shiny gold.

And that, of course, has a symbolic meaning, Marcus... Because it implies that with little to no resources, you could achieve something very big simply because you know how to tap into and use the power that lies slumbered deep within...'

Marcus didn't know what he was hearing. His ears chattered with these words. And his spine experienced a tingling sensation for a moment. That was the kind of person he wanted to be! Even though he lately felt like he was duping his environment with his inner dream, which he had been chasing so stubbornly for the past few years.

As if he indeed, as his father Bertus lately so often claimed, had been brought up with a valuable shiny silver, perhaps even golden spoon, and he managed to bend this instrument little by little, and bit by bit, into a piece of rusty cast iron that he—at some point—might not even be able to put in his mouth any more because then he might contract a certain form of metal poisoning...

Still, Marcus was pleased to hear all of this because, even though it all pointed out to the fact that he didn't have it in him to be such a person, it at the same time gave him some peace of mind that others apparently did succeed in this...

'So...,' the Count continued. 'And if you take a good look around you and see what wonderful things man has managed to create for himself over the many centuries; from the earliest history up to this point, you can probably imagine that there have been a lot of alchemists roaming this globe, and most likely plenty still do...'

'Masterful!' responded Marcus enthusiastically; the only expression, the only superlative, that seemed to fit this phenomenon.

'That's what I thought!' the Count responded back while at the same time giving Marcus something to think about...

'Look, Marcus,' was what the Count said to him one day. 'I do like it that you come by here now and then. And I can certainly appreciate your visits and presence from time to time.

But I don't really feel the need to act as a babysitter, Marcus. What I am actually trying to say is, is that I am looking for enrichment. For a walking on paths that are still partly uncharted; for a coming together of insights that we could largely uncover together and that we could discuss further. Can you do that, Marcus? Do you have that in you? Do you know about certain knowledge matters? Or at least have the potential to look beyond the ordinary pale world? And could you perhaps give me an example of that...?'

But Marcus had to swallow a lump for a moment because he had not expected this turn of events at all. Marcus had asked the Count indeed all kinds of questions since their very first meeting.

And this could indeed have given the Count the idea of being an endless source of information, of being some sort of teacher just like Miss Tilly had been only then a lot more mystical.

Marcus had to swallow another lump, felt a certain pressure imposed on him, because the Count could, any minute from now, show him the door at that point, simply because Marcus wouldn't be interesting enough.

Nevertheless, Marcus also felt a healthy tension coming up at the same time, a surge of enthusiasm because he knew very well that he carried these facets that the Count was now so suddenly asking for within him.

He thought about it for a while and then decided to broach a subject that, at this point in time, he knew the most about...

'For many Indians, the eagle is a symbol of strength and courage....,' was what suddenly rolled over his lips.

'Yes, that could very well be...,' replied the Count dryly.

'Have you ever heard of Indians?' was what Marcus asked the man, and the Count nodded while another characteristic grimace appeared on his face.

'Yes, I certainly have,' he said. 'And even though there certainly have been exceptions, I do have a fairly clear image of them in my head...'

'You do?' asked Marcus interestingly. 'How do you see them?' And the Count told him his vision of them:

'Yes, the Indians...,' he said thoughtfully. 'I could tell you all about them, but unfortunately, our time is not extensive enough for that. I know you are in a difficult position, Marcus, because I can almost always read that from your face, and I may also know why.

You have a certain sparkle in your eyes that tells me that you want to get more out of this life, but that you are hindered in this by people close to you. You don't have to tell me all about it personally, and I might be wrong, but I have the idea that these loved ones could be your parents.

Now let me tell you something about parents in general,

Marcus; the biological hatches that gave you life and how the ancient Indians saw them...

The ancient Indians, my soul brothers, and whom I have taken to heart, saw the earth—that little sphere floating in the infinite universe, and which your father countless times has torn open with his iron plough—as the true mother.

An immeasurable source of nature and life, which gives and takes, reproduces and does everything in its power to give us the building materials that we so desperately need every day.

In addition, however, they saw the creative power—the great elusiveness, the cosmos, so to speak, as the true Father.

A power that watched over its children and that worked together with Mother Earth in order to provide a protective cradle for their children so that they could raise their descendants in a rocking way, with the means that were given to them.

With this, I'm trying to say, Marcus, is that they honoured their biological parents and had a certain respect for their self-sacrifice, but that the Indians realised only too well that their parents were also but children after all; oscillating in the cradle of life in which we all find ourselves.

And since they realised this it also created a certain equality which everyone had to adhere to...

I am also trying to indicate with this, Marcus, that no matter how difficult your parents make it for you sometimes, and no matter how well-intentioned this may seem, they too are often blinded by their own fears, by their sometimes childish thoughts, but also because of a pursuit of dreams that they themselves may not have been able to realise, and that they would like to see realised through their own children.

So this actually means, in harsh terms, that they are trying to steer you in a certain direction in order to feed their own ego.

It is a difficult matter, Marcus, and parents remain creatures who must be treated with the utmost respect, but if there is no room for the realisation of your own dreams and ambitions, for your own growth through this life, then they have not really understood much of this concept, and they basically hinder you in a certain growth, which they themselves probably have not been able to achieve in some way...'

Wow! That was what Marcus had to think. *That's exactly what I'm up against!* And he again looked up at the Count with wide, almost astonishing eyes.

'You can look at me however you want, Marcus,' was what the man observingly said to him. 'With a certain look that puts me on a pedestal. But these are insights into life that go back many centuries, perhaps even millennia, and that this ancient people already understood; in all their so-called simplicity and in all their so-called primitive customs, looked down upon by a masses who was probably stone-blind to its own flaws...

Never forget this, Marcus: the earth is your true biological mother and the creative force as a father you never knew, but which you can always fall back on, wherever, in whatever state, and whatever place you might find yourself in...'

Lately, it seemed as if Marcus had only been sitting with the Count. Moments and fragments of his visits to the chateau had piled up more and more, and it was almost as if ordinary life; as if the ins and outs of the daily pressure and routine were completely faded away into the background, and even almost engraved from Marcus' memory.

The Count just seemed to have such an influence on the young Marcus. His castle just had such an effect on him when

Marcus once again had the privilege of being allowed to set foot in that place.

Marcus found the conversations with the Count wonderful, powerful, magical even, but lately, he also felt that he himself had to come up with something better if he didn't want the Count to lose interest in him.

Simply because he didn't come up with anything interesting, only standard clinchers that the average commoner could come up with, if they had the privilege of meeting a person with an allure that only the Count seemed to possess...

One day, Marcus stood in front of the gate of the castle again, although this time, something strange seemed to be going on. It was not the attraction of the chateau that had made Marcus appear here again—almost as if in a trance.

And it wasn't because of the infinite silence that always seemed to reign here, a fortress that had been erected and rested in its cutoff bubble of both geniality and a convulsiveness that Marcus just couldn't seem to place. And perhaps that was one of the reasons why this castle had such a hold on him; why it seemed to beckon him every time.

The castle was enigmatic, and Marcus simply just didn't hesitate to put on the detective's nose so once in a while.

No, the remarkable thing about today was that the door stood open. The large wooden gate was ajar for any unwanted visitor to enter the Count's domain and thus be able to snatch the priceless treasures he had entrenched in it and have them turn back into more devalued lead—wherever the alleged thief went with them...

Marcus banged the gate with the bronze door knocker hanging from it and called in a few times in a loud voice, but there was no answer... Marcus paused for a moment, thought deeply for a brief second, while his gaze had already passed the threshold of the fortress, meanwhile scanning the long, dimmed corridor of it for a sign of life, and in this way, actually already had entered the vestibule of the Count's residence.

Marcus had two options at this point. And even though he already had a bit of an idea of what choice he was going to make, he still wanted to play the moral knight for a while; let his inner ethics speak, so to say.

He could close the door at this moment, turn around, and come back another time when the Count, indeed, would be home. Or he could rummage through the rooms on his own accord in search of mind-blowing treasures and at the same time look for unwelcome intruders and thieves whom he had to prevent from taking his good friend's valuables—intruders of which he himself was one now either.

Marcus made the crack between the door a little bigger by exerting a lot of force on the gate. Slipped, no, almost slid inside the vestibule, and at that moment, he had actually committed some form of trespassing; something he didn't quite realise but also did at the same time...

Marcus walked through the grey corridor with its high vertical windows on both sides that still let some light through.

He entered the middle part of the chateau and then immediately decided to make a left turn. He walked up a narrow stone spiral staircase and ended up on a balcony that looked straight out onto the middle part of the castle, with a large shiny altarpiece in the distance that he kept as a gauge for now.

Again, high windows with colourful glass in them seemed to float above his head and, for a moment gave the young Marcus the idea of functioning in some type of work of art.

He walked a bit further, looked halfway through a transparent window this time, and saw how protrusions of the building disappeared into the depths again and how they partly seemed to support this enormous structure with the building blocks of which they consisted.

Arriving at the end of this passage—with the altarpiece diagonally below him, which reminded him of a performance as it was sometimes exhibited in the local mass of the priest's house—there was an old, weathered door that seemed to enchant Marcus with its deep grooves and dark wooden knots.

Marcus was able to climb another staircase but decided to descend one, and thus walked along a wall which the earlier altarpiece probably should have been behind, towards a place that would appeal to his imagination and where he could probably find what he was so desperately looking for: treasures, alleged intruders and thieves, but above all a place where the Count most likely harboured his deepest secrets.

Marcus again walked through a narrow corridor and now probably had to be somewhere in the back middle, maybe even at the bottom right of the castle.

How many rooms and quarters would actually still be above him? How much surface area had he already uncovered and discovered of this enormous structure? The tension in his constitution began to increase again. The urge to explore was increasingly fueled, even though he could not afford to lose sight of the entrance to this maze. Marcus knew very well how far he could go; to a point where he learned more about this castle without discrediting his good friend through these impulsive excesses.

The narrow and dusty corridor through which he strolled once again was completely illuminated by hanging candlesticks with burning candles in them, which gave him a glimpse of where he would probably find his ending point during this run.

So he walked to the end of this passage, looked at the bookcase that made him block his way, and then stopped for a moment because he couldn't go any further anyway.

Is this all there is? Was what he had to think for a moment. *Only one bookcase? In all the steps I've done so far? That can't be, can it?* Marcus looked at the dusty, cobweb-overgrown, but nevertheless handstitched books, and then read the titles that adorned their sides.

It was all paperwork, some were encyclopedias even, containing many different categorised topics. Books about amphibians, reptiles, and fish, books on religious subjects and some on art movements. Even books about the history of Ingland: about its monarchs and about its developments over the many centuries. Nevertheless, there was nothing among these books that made Marcus fall back steeply.

They were fascinating subjects, undisputed, and also reference works that Marcus would like to read with all pleasure—one day perhaps, if the ticking of the clock would allow it—but nevertheless, there was nothing among these works that made the Count for what he simply was: an enigmatic figure, with a knowledge of things that an unpurified individual would not, and probably never, come into contact with...

Marcus looked carefully at the space he was now in. A long, narrow corridor... An old, weathered bookcase that made him block the way... Why would anyone put such an obstacle there?

Why would such a long aisle lead to something that seemed of so little significance? Something wasn't right here. There seemed to be no addition to this space whatsoever.

It was just one endless big void that actually could have been used much better…

Marcus turned around, walked back a little, and then looked at the luminaires of lighting shining on the walls around him, the hanging objects that had so pontifically ignited their enthusiasm within him. It won't be, will it?

Marcus pulled at all the candlesticks he could find. He tried to move them both to the left and the right, but there was no swell in them to be made. No creaking noise, or even a mechanical sound, and no mysterious hidden passage that would suddenly open up to him and that could speed up his search for now.

It can't end here, was what Marcus thought. *There must be something to be found here...*

Marcus walked back to the bookcase and looked at it more carefully this time. Cover by cover was what he was looking at with the swiftness of a cheetah, and also with an observation technique that only a bird of prey carried.

His gaze, therefore, lingered on one book, a many pages long, densely bundled manuscript, which did not have the dusty characteristics of its other siblings. He was already standing on all of his toes, pulling on the still reasonably intact book, when...?

When it fell half opened at his feet, a key was what came rolling out.

Still, no mechanical sound to be heard, still no cogs that were set in motion and that might push this bookcase aside and thus give Marcus passage to a universe as only the Count knew so far.

Marcus looked at the clavis with only a small note hanging from it: *altarpiece number 1* was what was written on the small piece of paper. Now Marcus knew only one type of altar:

the large ornament and decoration that he had encountered and seen before during this stroll, and to which he now quickly walked to see if it could provide him with a little more openness of affairs.

Altarpiece number 1... Thought Marcus despondently. Discouraging...

There could be a dozen of such works of art in this stronghold; in places where Marcus had not yet set foot and that he might not ever see...

I'm still going to try! he nevertheless thought cheerfully. *Let's see if it works! And if that's not the case, then it will be enough for today and I will hand over the key to the Count the next time I see him, and also honestly confess how and where I got the object...*

Marcus was now standing in front of the large altarpiece and looked at it carefully.

His heart was pounding in his throat. The transpiration was clearly felt in one of the few underpants he owned, and he put the clavis in the only lock he could find. Ironically enough, in a miniscule treasure box, that a cute-looking little cherub was held in front of it as a gesture to the world.

A shifting sound was indeed what followed this time, and at the foot of this splendour of images, at the end of the nave of this chateau, a hole suddenly appeared in the floor where a group of bats flew out of to gauge who it was that had disturbed their resting place.

But better yet, to see if there were any insects left to pick from the sky in this room. Marcus looked at the inky black opening in the floor, and then decided to take his chance.

Shaking his head, he descended the wooden ladder realising that he might have gone a bridge too far by now. In the dark, and by touch, he felt around him and could notice some paperwork from the nerve endings of his fingertips. This is wrong Marcus was what he only could think. This is an actual infringement of personal belongings and also that of a trust that a good friend has placed in me.

I don't need to know everything was what his conscience told him. *Only one aspect that could arouse my curiosity.*

Marcus grabbed an object by touch, quickly climbed up the ladder, let his eyes get used to the light again, and then saw how he held a scroll in his hand.

Out of a sense of guilt, he read the scroll cursorily, let the header get through to him, and then quickly threw the rolled-up paperwork back into the dark hole. He swiftly put the key back into the lock of the little treasure chest, turned it over, saw how the floor part slid back into its place, and then rushed through the opening hall and out of the gate again. The gate slammed against the thick doorpost a few more times, after which it still remained slightly ajar; exactly as Marcus had encountered it at the beginning of this escapade.

With a feeling of guilt, a blush of shame, and a deep regret, he walked again along the lands and fields that were to lead him to his home; with a dark red colour in the sky, black clouds that probably predicted rain, and a blood moon above his head that knew exactly what Marcus had been up to this evening.

Could the Count ever forgive him? Would Marcus still be welcome in his abode? And would he still consider him as a friend? He would soon find out. Provided the Count would let him back in and Marcus would dare to confront him with what he had done prior. In the meantime, Marcus had become afraid, and in a frightened state of being, he entered his parents' farmhouse in order to quickly walk up the stairs and leave his parents in the dark of his presence.

He quickly crawled into his bed, to hopefully soon forget what exactly had transpired that day.

He lay restlessly on his side, eyes now closed, and not fully realising that the stinging sensation that he felt in his groin, and which he tried to ignore as good as possible as he turned with his body, was still the skeleton key that he carried around with him in his pocket...

A Crash Course in Gothic

Marcus had ended up at the Count's address again. This time, however, a visit gave him mixed feelings.

Of course, he wanted to speak to his good friend, the Count, again. And he liked to take a seat on the wooden chair opposite to the worktop, which the man was always working behind. But at the same time Marcus was tense, nervous rather, and there was an obvious reason for that.

Nevertheless, he decided to play the fool, pretended that his nose was bleeding, and let the Count do the talking, while he himself was mainly worrying about how he should confess his last misstep and whether he should tell it at all...

The Count was speaking again, seemed to pluck the interesting insights and topics of conversation effortlessly out of the air, and Marcus offered the man a sympathetic ear.

'Look,' the man suddenly said, and for no particular reason.

'I was born under the constellation of the big buck. I, too, like to look at society from a certain height. I also like to be on my own for the most part. And like my totem animal, so to speak...' Marcus wanted to jump out of his seat instantly since he immediately had to think of the old Indians. He decided to hold back because—in all fairness—what could the Count learn from someone like him, for God's sake? '...I also make crazy buck jumps often.'

The Count continued, 'In addition, I am also gifted with a nervous character...' And the man suddenly took out one of his many jars, took out some brown powder with a silver spoon, threw it in a glass of water, and then started stirring furiously...

The man then took a few sips of the brew and then shrugged his shoulders somewhat indifferently.

'This stuff just calms me down. It's called valerian, and it just works for me.'

The Count suddenly seemed to be pondering over the situation.

'Valerian...,' he said thoughtfully. 'Was that what it was called? Damn it, I'm starting to get forgetful. Or did they call this stuff catnip, on the other hand?'

The Count seemed to dig deep into his mind for a moment and then began to murmur to himself: 'Don't be so foolish, Count, because you know damn well that the infusion of this root has several uses. You know that it has an immense appeal to cats, and you also know that it has a lot of other names, in whatever language you can think of...'

The Count looked through his quarter for a moment and then began to mumble further as if Marcus wasn't even there. Almost shameless, even though the little reporter in the making found it fairly interesting.

'Multiple names for sure...,' the Count continued. 'Yet, I dare to swear that in old Germanic, it was called the goat weed... My writings! My apocryphal scrolls and papers! Where have I laid them?!'

'Don't weaken now, Count,' was what he also said to himself. 'Knowledge is simply the only thing that you...' But before the sentence had completed itself, and while Marcus tried to pierce his field of vision through the walls of the castle because he might have had an idea where they could be found, the Count had already fixed his gaze—and without Marcus noticing it initially—on his still young unsullied face; with a smile that is.

'Yeah, take a good look around you, Marcus. Take a good look together with me. Because I know all too well that you have been wandering around in my quarters...'

But strangely enough, Marcus didn't seem to be frightened by this, and in order to not lose any more face he decided to meet the Count halfway instead of spluttering against him.

Of course, Marcus could tell him that the gate stood open on that day and that he wanted to make sure that there were no intruders to be found in the castle at that time.

And even though he let his inner ethics speak at this point and he sincerely meant what he was feeling, it was at the same time also a lie. Marcus' curiosity had once again prevailed on that day, and he could keep using 'keeping out intruders' as an excuse or as a way out, but actually, if he really let his conscience speak, this would come down to lying.

Marcus sighed deeply for a moment, looked at the Count in a serious way, and then decided to go for honesty...

'Astrology, herbs, the phases of the moon, and their perfect attunement and thus also the most beneficial interaction with the human body... That is the scroll Count. That is the scroll you are looking for. And with all due respect, and of course, you know this by now, obviously, I took a quick look at it the other day. My curiosity had once again won over reason sir; I'm deeply sorry. I should have asked you nicely before I tried to expose your personal belongings...'

'Expose even!' the Count exclaimed. 'Ha! And that's why your nose is so big, Marcus. I already thought... How on earth does a little guy like you get such a big snout in the first place? But now I understand! The pieces of this puzzle finally seem to be falling into place!'

But the Count laughed just as loudly. 'No, without all craziness. Bring me this scroll, bright young man, and I will be forever in your debt. Or at least, for how long I have left, that is...'

And Marcus did as he was told and brought the man his personal property.

The Count spread the scroll over his worktop, weighted down the points with some objects and trinkets that were nearby, and then rummaged through the text.

'Darn,' he said. 'I just can't seem to find what I'm looking for. And I used to be so adept in these things...' The man then looked at the inscription of the scroll again.

'This has to be the right text. It can't be otherwise…

I was born under the big buck; that's one thing for certain, and when the moon is in the right position, and I take this goat weed, this catnip, this valerian, or whatever it is called, it will be the most effective at that moment and therefore in the best way absorbed by my body...'

'I must be right,' murmured the Count further while turning around and looking in a glassy, somewhat perplexed way through the great stained-glass window; gazing over the fields, beyond the meadows, and over the grasslands of Glancebury, which adjoined wholly or partly to his famous chateau, after which his field of vision suddenly remained stuck on infinity.

'But...,' as he said. 'Goat weed or catnip. Buck or no buck. There are plenty of more animals and people walking around in this immeasurable jungle called life... And sometimes they are even…' But he decided not to finish the sentence.

'But to completely come back to the earlier expressed

saying. To completely come back to the many compliments you have given me and my accommodation, and the many superlatives you have used for it. If you are so curious about the art expressions that can be admired here so plentiful. And if you are really that fascinated by the origin of this beautiful construction and plaster, then I might have something for you.'

And the Count got up for a moment, rummaged around in a chest of drawers that stood a bit further away, and came back with an even dustier book; even more dusty than the book scroll that—apparently for a very long time—had been lying under the sliding tile floor, next to the beautifully shiny ornament with the many cheerful cherubs and other gleamy decorations.

'Here, dear Marcus. Take this book home with you. Try to read it carefully and thoroughly, and try to take it in as well as possible. And the next time you're here, I'm very curious about what you thought of it and how much you exactly understood of it.'

'Because I just have the feeling that, when you have read most of this book, you will behold and admire this splendor of a chateau with even more awe than you have done so far...'

Marcus could hardly wait to be home. He held the book by his side without even having glanced at it and without even having understood its title. Actually, nothing seemed to get through to the boy at this point. Only the intoxication that made him, almost as if in a trance, put one foot in front of the other so quickly at this moment. Even the surroundings, which he could normally enjoy so much, passed him by like a blur. When he got home, he stormed up the stairs—and without informing his parents of his presence, as he had been doing more and more often lately—kicked off his discarded leather shoes, sat down on the edge of his bed, and then looked at the front of the present that the Count had given him about only an hour ago...

An illustrated book on Gothic

Splendid... was what Marcus thought. *Truly magnificent... Another new asset in which I can fully immerse myself.*

Another new book for my bookshelf... And Marcus quickly started reading.

With every sentence he read, he began to understand the words that the Count had spoken better and better. And with every word that Marcus mumbled, the castle began to become more and more alive:

'*An architecture of light that must elevate the spectators from the material to the immaterial...*' was what the book, among other things, told Marcus and what he—a few seconds ago—aloud had read to himself. Now, Marcus might have understood what this meant.

Because during that first time already, when he stood in front of the large wooden gate of the castle, and when he looked up via the decorations on the walls towards the towers that lay beyond, and he hardly could even see from that perspective, he already got the notion that he—by the architecture of this building—and by the building as a whole, was being taken to a place where he had never been before.

A feeling that almost made him experience what it would be like when one would be in higher spheres...

His finger slid over the pages of this newly acquired book again; an informative book which, despite the bone-dry material, was quite interesting to read. It gave Marcus the idea that he was becoming more and more of a connoisseur instead of a guileless spectator.

Almost a resident of such a magnificent structure, instead

of an outsider, just another unsuspecting visitor whose art and splendor of such a building largely escaped him.

Marcus began to read aloud again, so that the content could get through to him better, and hopefully, lifelike images would appear before his mind's eye once more:

'The Gothic cathedral of the thirteenth century differs clearly, and in many respects, from that of the twelfth century. Its architecture, therefore, broadly includes the following characteristics: It has pointed arches, buttresses, and translucent walls with internal spaces behind them.

It often has tracery, ornamental gables, pinnacles and crockets.

There are often finials as well as various forms of vaults.

And the aim is to obtain a uniformity of the space, rather than an addition to it...'

Great! was what Marcus had to think. *I have seen all of those characteristics pass by; pass by while shuffling through the fortress, but now I actually know their designated terms!*

What a special book! And how handy that almost everything is indicated with illustrations!

But a cathedral from the thirteenth century...? Could this mean that the Count has been residing in this castle for more than five hundred years? But Marcus shook firmly with his head.

Don't act like such a fantasist, Marcus! That way, no one will take you seriously anymore, especially not the big shots at the Gulden Gazette, a daily newspaper that values objectivity so highly. But maybe I could ask the Count soon? Maybe, if I bring it up in a neat way, he could tell me how the hell he got his castle...?

Marcus had read the book on Gothic thoroughly by now, and he felt confident enough to sit down with his good friend, the Count, again.

He told the man in detail about the many Gothic features of which he by now thought he knew so well and that he had just encountered again by walking through the castle.

He spoke of gargoyles and of pointed arches. He talked about buttresses, pedestals and of pinnacles. Marcus wanted to display his knowledge to the Count as best as he could so that the Count would know that Marcus had read the book seriously, that he had understood most of it, and that the Count's castle—which could easily be called a cathedral— was indeed beginning to come alive to him.

The Count was visibly surprised, of course, understood everything that Marcus was telling him, although he was wondering at the same time if Marcus had ever heard of flying buttresses, of the narthex, of arcades and the triforium, of archivolts or the rose window and of course, and not to forget, of the fan vault...

Marcus told the Count that he had not yet come across these terms in the book, but perhaps he would come them across eventually.

However, the young Glanceburie looked a bit disappointed. He thought he could finally equal the Count, perhaps even surpass him with some acquired knowledge, but the Count seemed to be able to waltz over his attempt with ease, and on top of that, even with two fingers in his nose.

However, the Count did not seem to miss this fact; he even found it somewhat touching, and he decided to give Marcus a tour through his illustrious castle...

'Look, Marcus,' said the man when the two had already started their artistic viewings. 'I don't have to show you the narthex because that's the long hall through which you came here, a corridor that you have gone through many times by now and that you can undoubtedly remember.'

Moreover, above that hall, or rather said, above the large wooden entrance gate, very well visible from the outside, and also one of the showpieces of this castle, hangs a very large rose window; a large circular window that you must have seen, because it is as wide as the entrance hall itself, as the so-called narthex. And if you haven't noticed it that well yet, then please take a good look above you, above the large wooden gate on your way out...'

'These things here are so-called flying buttresses, Marcus.' The two looked out of a large pointed arched window, out of a large elongated venster, while the Count told a short story.

'Architecture like this can only be built so high, can only contain such beautiful high decorative windows, because of that there,' and the man briefly told about these flying buttresses, about their function, and about their ability to absorb splash forces, the pressure created by the heaviness of the surrounding used building materials.

'As you can see, this chateau contains many different arch shapes...'

'Yes, I've read about that!' exclaimed Marcus in excitement. 'That one over there must be a crossed rib vault for example!'

'Very good, Marcus. Very good. A crossed rib vault arises from a perpendicular meeting of two half barrels. It is funny to mention that in Late Gothic, it was almost no longer present in this simplistic form. The vaults became more and more complex, but I will show you that in a moment.'

'But Count,' asked Marcus curiously. 'Then why is that the case in your castle? Why do Early Gothic and Late Gothic come together in your chateau? That's quite strange, isn't it?'

'Yes, most certainly,' said the Count. 'But the castle in which I live is quite strange, Marcus. It is a work of art!'

And Marcus shrugged his shoulders, he didn't knew anything meaningful to say to this, and the two walked on.

'This ceiling right here,' and the man pointed up, 'has one of the most beautiful vaults that this castle has to offer, with all its thin lines, which come together again into one center.'

'It, therefore, looks like the underside of a mushroom. If you look very closely, it looks like the bottom of a so-called fungus...'

'This fan vault is one of the showpieces within my accommodation, and I am very proud of it naturally.'

The Count also told some interesting facts about the many paintings that they passed along the way. He did this briefly, concisely, in an interesting way, and with his well-known flair.

According to him, buildings in the Gothic period became taller and taller and, therefore, apparently appeared narrower. This aspect could also be seen in sculptures, as well as in many paintings.

'Nice paintings, Count,' was what Marcus sincerely said.

'But those elongated figures aren't really realistic, now are they? There probably will always be people with a few extra kilos on their bodies.'

'And I believe some of them are called Rubens women if I'm not mistaken. But I personally can really appreciate such an appearance. Or girls with some extra pounds on their bodies, but the form is still visible here and there; they themselves often don't realize how beautiful that can be.'

'Not everyone has to be thin, you know, although morbid obesity is somewhat of an extreme on its own on the other hand...'

'Good story, Marcus,' said the Count sarcastically.

'Well….,' the alleged aristocrat continued. 'I don't like fat people that much, to be honest.'

'Oh?' responded Marcus in surprise. 'And why is that Count?'

'Well...,' the man said thoughtfully. 'Because they are always so full of themselves...'

And he had to laugh aloud about it himself, although Marcus didn't laugh with him this time.

'Don't you think my puns are funny, Marcus?' asked the man, somewhat disappointed.

'Well...,' said Marcus in return. 'That's not entirely the case, Count, only... It's just that I always feel a bit sorry for poor souls like that...'

'Oh?' responded the Count, and that with a serious face because he seemed to regret that Marcus didn't get along with his joke.

'And why exactly is that Marcus,' was what he asked, meanwhile looking outside a window in a bored way.

'Well...,' said Marcus, this time, however, with a big toothy grin on his face.

'Because those poor bastards are never entirely seen as full...'

And that afternoon, there was laughter, and also a conviviality, coming from the Count's stronghold, which people from the outside couldn't notice at all because these sounds were already softened by the thick walls of this splendid chateau, after which they diluted within the many corridors that this beautiful fortress had to offer...

Vampires...

The last period had been one of mysticism, of mystery, and also one of ambiguity.

For whenever Marcus had visited the Count, there seemed to be a certain truth between the two that could not be grasped, that could not be named at all, but that nevertheless seemed to exist at the same time. As if it were tangible in the air, constantly waiting for someone to come along and snatch it out of the void.

The Count was a mysterious person; Marcus' visits to his address were also shrouded in shadows, since no one really knew about these escapades, and Marcus seemed to be increasingly attracted to such an atmosphere.

It just had its charm: hidden knowledge, ambiguous conversations, secret compartments behind walls, doors hidden in the walls themselves, and keys for hidden lockers which themselves contained another key. Secrecy indeed predominated lately, and that was partly the reason why Marcus now took up another book.

It had been one of his very first possessions, together with the book about the ancient Indians. And it was also one of the two books he had received from his father during their very first trip to Light Town, and to its famous annual fair. Marcus remembered this trip very vividly, together with the small oral summary of the book that the bookseller had given him at the time, and also his father's negotiating method with the vendor that was not entirely to the man's liking.

Now, the time had finally come to go carefully through this uncharted book. It had been collecting dust on his bookshelf for quite some years now, and while Marcus' current phase of life could be labeled as 'exploration with a touch of enigma,' what fitted better with that stage than a following book that managed to connect so seamlessly with this?

Even though there was no title on the front of the manuscript, Marcus had labeled his acquisition as the Ultimate Vampire Book.

He had already skimmed through the book many times, just like he had done with the book about the ancient Indians, but for now it was really the time for some in-depth research, and also for some fieldwork, because who might know exactly?

There may be such an ominous and sinister person lurking around there somewhere; prowling through the nights, and wandering through the narrow streets and alleys of Glancebury...

Marcus quietly read on, trying to keep his imagination in check as best as he could so that it wouldn't fool around with him too much, while at the same time continuing his reading with the concentration span of that of a vampire hunter who held his silver bow and arrow already at the ready…

You have dared to open this book… said the unknown author.

You are about to enter a world of the undead. A dejected, pale, and forlorn landscape.

Where acquaintances from your immediate surroundings sometimes could wander. Without you ever knowing it, and without you ever realizing it...

And so the author went on for a while. But Marcus didn't like all that adornment, all that filling of the book, to make it more exciting for the reader. Marcus wanted clues, facts, or at least characteristics by which he could recognise such a shadowy creature, should he ever come across one...

This book also had a table of contents, but strangely enough, it was on one of the last pages of the book. Perhaps to reward the serious reader for his patience, for his decisiveness, and for his perseverance to go through the book completely, to be able to truly recognise a vampire, and thus perhaps even become a real vampire hunter himself.

Marcus shook his head, however. He was glad that he had found this page, even if it was by chance and certainly not by decisiveness.

He was just being impatient at this moment, and impatience was often not rewarded as a rule. Moreover, Marcus also knew how to turn this reference work, as was the case with the information about the old Indians, into a rather childish game. An infantile activity that actually didn't suit a young man of fifteen years old.

Nevertheless, Marcus shrugged his shoulders once again. It just fit his character. And whether he had found this table of contents by chance or by accident, it actually didn't matter that much. Because no matter how one would look at it, it would once again provide him with a world of experience which he could immerse himself in, with which he could increase his knowledge, and which could even give him the idea that he was already a bit submerged in this world but had to find that out through this mind-awakening information...

Marcus pressed his finger somewhere in the middle of the table of contents.

Here's where I need to be! The key features of the average vampire!

The key points by which he could recognise such a sorrowful being.

The characteristics of a vampire... was what the unknown author told Marcus, as if he spoke directly to the young man.

...traditionally it is a deceased person who, at night, rises from his grave to suck the blood from the living. Over the years, they have undergone many metamorphoses, although they all contain some elementary characteristics...

Right! was what Marcus had to think. Here's where I need to be! And he quickly read on.

Whatever the vampires look like, and how they have changed over the many centuries, they all have a number of things in common.

They all thirst for blood. They all have unusual powers and gifts. And besides that... They all have to avoid certain dangers...

Marcus did not really understand what the writer meant by the latter, although he would probably find out later on.

In addition…, the author continued, these creatures of the night must be careful that they themselves do not betray their deadly secret!

Marcus paused for a second to think about this, although at the same time, he seemed to shy away from it. This was a special book, he already knew that when he just got a hold of it, and when he couldn't read a single letter of the text yet. It radiated something exceptional; the design, the yellowish goldish colour of the cover, and the almost mystical knowledge that seemed to be hidden within its pages, which he didn't know anything about at the time, but which he had somehow sensed intuitively.

And now he did read this book, and it was indeed what he had expected of it, but this time he read it for a special reason. His heart began to beat louder, his hands became more and more clammy, and his mouth became drier by the minute, because...?

Because only this sentence alone revealed a lot, and he decided to read the sentence again and let it sink in for a moment:

Moreover, these creatures of the night have to be careful not to betray their deadly secret...

From day one, Marcus had the feeling that his good friend the Count carried a certain secret with him, and he also thought that he knew what this secret could actually be, because it might just be the concealing of his true identity...

Nevertheless, Marcus tried not to get too carried away in all of this.

His body started to calm down somewhat, and he tried to continue his reading with the attitude of an unsuspecting bystander.

After all, it was still too early for false conclusions and allegations. All this could be nothing more than an unhinged little fantasy, even though he couldn't help but relate all this information to the Count.

The writer continued talking, and the vampire was further explained:

These shy, even human-fearing creatures have supernatural powers and also very sharp fangs. And moreover... they often possess an ethereal beauty...

But Marcus was fifteen by now and he was almost certain that he didn't liked men. Did he? And he had to laugh aloud about it at the same time. No, that didn't seem to be the case with him. Nevertheless, his good friend the Count could not be called ugly either. The man was just very charismatic, that was definitely the case, at certain times that was...

They often isolate themselves, said the writer, without Marcus being able to respond to this. They often isolate themselves...

Gosh, thought Marcus, while the sentence housed through his constitution, and while some of his bodily fluids wanted to come to the surface of his skin, through the pores that is, and that wanted to act like little corridors to the outside world.

Marcus left the sentence for what it was, left it there for a while, because it wasn't going anywhere anyway.

There certainly would be a legitimate reason for all of this, and it couldn't be otherwise. And even though some characteristics could well be applied to the Count here and there, Marcus also had the idea that his own imagination was playing tricks on him again.

Nevertheless, he also felt a built-in fear creeping up on him. Perhaps not so much a fear, but more a built-in restraint. From now on, he had to stay on his guard for a while.

Because no matter how much he liked the Count, at this moment he didn't know all that much about the man to be frank, and one could never be too sure of course...

And even though they often hold high positions..., the author continued, they often remain tormented and reserved.

Marcus quickly walked downstairs, secretly grabbed his parents' dictionary, and was immediately richer in both knowledge and vocabulary.

He walked back up the creaking stairs with tired legs.

Maybe he got too carried away in all of this? Perhaps he should indeed have read the first pages of this book a little more consistently? Before plunging into this pitch-black landscape?

The writer had even warned him in advance, but Marcus had, of course, ignored this warning with competence, and he now seemed to pay a certain price for it.

It was therefore that a certain confusion crept up on him; somewhat of a second world that he—in addition to the world of the Indians—began to know and understand better and better, but which had nothing to do with his own world at all, with the real world out there; a world which Marcus seemed so eagerly to withdraw from on a regular basis.

Moreover, he now indeed began to see a vampire behind every word and behind every person he knew.

Marcus looked at the front of the book again, but there was still no title to be seen.

It was a very mysterious book that was clear by now, and perhaps not as lighthearted as the one about the ancient Indians, but equally as special.

Nevertheless, it was also a book that he had to watch out for, that could put him in certain danger, and that could drag him into its fall.

It was a wise thought that seemed to have a cathartic effect on Marcus. Exactly, Marcus! was what he had to think.

Read this book whenever you feel the need to, don't read too much of it at the same time, and always keep a healthy distance!

Marcus nodded to himself and then decided to read a few more lines before closing this book of size...

They often remain tormented and reserved, while exerting a strong attraction on people who suspect their secret...

This time, Marcus nodded attentively, turned the page, and a new chapter sprang forward:

The origin of these undead...

There are three important ways in which someone can become a vampire:

This can be done through birth. This can be done by death. Or this can take place through a bite.

The vampire always bites into a place of the body where a main artery is near the surface of the skin, and this is almost always in the neck or in the wrist...

Marcus ran his hand over his neck for a moment, gently touched his right wrist, after which he applied a small dog-ear to the page, and then closed the book gently and composedly again. Enough for today... was what he thought. He would probably never meet an authentic vampire in real life, but if he did, he would now be able to recognise such a frightening being from a reasonable distance...

'Say Count?' was what Marcus asked the good man again one day.

'Yes? Little friend?'

'What is that black object laying there so in front of you?'

'That black shiny stone on my desktop, you mean?' And the Count briefly ran his hand over the smooth surface of the object. 'This? Oh? Nix...'

And the Count erupted out of nowhere into a great burst of laughter.

The Count had such silly moments quite often, and Marcus often couldn't fathom whether he was being laughed at, the Count just had a very special taste of humor, or whether Marcus was dealing with a quasi-madman at such a moment...

But time passed nevertheless, the two had a nice time together as always, and one topic of conversation had not yet ended, or the next was already brought up.

'Well...,' the Count said again. 'Attracting and repelling people, karma, and the whole charnel play... Cold simply repels Marcus, and heat, in turn, attracts. Nevertheless, it is also true that heat, when touched fleetingly, can feel as cold. And that cold, if it is briefly touched for a moment, can appear as heat... Don't ask me how I know these things, Marcus, but I just know them. And I therefore call them universal values: the ambivalence of this dimension in which you, I, and so many with us, find themselves...'

And there went the Count again with his puzzling and cryptic talk. It seemed completely out of the blue again, although he told it with such persuasiveness that it almost had to be true, and Marcus, in turn, thought it was nothing but marvelous.

Marcus liked the statements of the Count, he liked the esotericism that seemed to lurk behind them, although there was only one pressing question that was burning on his lips at the moment; a question that the young man decided to ask, because the atmosphere seemed open to it and it was, at the same time, a chance to get to know the Count somewhat better...

'Where did you get all that persuasiveness from?' was what Marcus asked the man in a serious tone.

'Where did you get all that self-assurance from that you seem to display so boldly with every word that you utter?' But the Count kept his mouth shut for a moment, even seemed a little startled at first, and then thought carefully about his answer.

'Well...,' he said. 'Maybe it just seems that way... You know... Because... Sometimes I feel so sure of myself that I could walk into a room and let anyone in that space fall before me in awe...'

'But..?' asked Marcus, interestingly and curious about the sequel.

'But sometimes...,' the Count continued. 'Sometimes there are days when I feel so insecure about myself, so strongly in fact, that it almost hurts the eyes, and I would prefer to hide in a corner somewhere alone...'

'That sounds difficult, Count...,' was what Marcus said, and in a sincere tone. 'But you don't have to hide from me, lord. For me, you are as good as you are. You are simply a...'

And Marcus tried to come up with a suitable word for a moment, but then triumphantly stuck his index finger in the air. '...A real Count!'

And even though Marcus was not entirely pleased with the result, and was he even a little ashamed that his vocabulary was apparently so inadequate, these words seemed to have a greater grip on the alleged nobleman than Marcus could have initially suggested.

The Count stood huddled in the corner of his personal quarter. His shoulders seemed to shake slightly. And with a helpless, almost powerless face—an expression that Marcus had never seen in the man before—he looked at his young guest.

'Thank you, Marcus. Thank you very kindly for those intensely sweet words. You don't have the slightest idea how much you've touched me with those. Although there is probably no hope for me left...'

And with these words, a loud rumble was to be heard outside the castle. A flash of light that followed lit the place where the Count still stood so huddled, and for a very brief moment, even for less than a tenth of a second, Marcus thought that he saw a glimpse of a daunting monstrous figure standing exactly on the spot where the Count had just shown his grief.

Marcus' heart had now skipped several beats, and the room was now as it had been before that intense bolt of lightning; stuffy, dim, somewhat pale and colourless, while the Count still stood in the same spot.

As if the bright light from outside had created an optical illusion for a moment, playing with Marcus' perceptual ability, that somehow seemed so shaky in this questionable castle in the first place.

'I... I have to go!' exclaimed Marcus suddenly. 'I'm already way too late. Far too late for dinner at home!' And as quickly as he could, he fled the castle again.

The Count stood behind his desk for a moment in front of the large stained glass window, observing through one of the smaller pieces of the glasswork, and peering at a small green figure that had quickly pulled its vest over its head, and that quickly sought refuge back home due to the heavy rainfall.

'Yes… go little boy, just go...,' the Count murmured softly to himself. 'In the end, no one ever stays here for long...'

Marcus had plenty to think about during the walk home. Dusk had already risen considerably, and Marcus had the bright idea to not visit the castle again for the time being.

Perhaps the routine of everyday life would soon win over this idea again. And perhaps the Gothic structure would eventually beckon him again, with its architectural masterpieces.

But such visits in the late hours? No, the young Glanceburie preferred to pass those for the present...

At home again, and again alone in his room, sitting on the edge of his bed and with a burning candle right by his side, he couldn't resist taking a quick look at his illustrated book of the Gothic.

Gothic... said the book. An urge for verticality, and also an urge for light, which is brought in through high-placed vensters and large rose windows...

The first seemed indeed to be correct: a drive for verticality; an urge for high bulges and elongation. But an urge for light?

When something could be called melancholic… When something seemed to be hiding away; shrouded in the shadows of his own quarters, it had to be this resident of the chateau…

For even though Marcus regularly had uplifting conversations with the Count, and even though they often had a splendid time together, and there was even some regular laughter between them, the man also seemed to have something very sorrowful about him. What kind of things did this man have on his record, for heaven's sake? What did the Count actually seem to be hiding from?

Sub-Operations

Marcus couldn't resist opening the ultimate vampire book in the few spare hours that he had. He tried desperately not to involve the Count in this information too much, but the more he tried to repel the idea, the more it began to force itself on him.

But why did Marcus involve the Count so much in this in the first place? Was Marcus really plagued by a delusion that he himself had created, and which he himself thus maintained?

Had the information from the vampire book suddenly gone to his head? Simply because the knowledge it contained seemed to be completely separate from that of the world outside?

A certain reality that the young Marcus wanted to escape from in order to create his own exciting and also inner world of experience?

'It could all just be...'

And even though the young Marcus didn't seem to fully realise this fact, on top of that, there were also certain other suspicions, clues almost even, which strengthened his ideas on this subject only more.

Because from the very first day the two had met, Marcus had found the Count a special, almost illustrious person. A character who didn't seem to fit at all within the empty space between the earth's surface on which one walked and that of the firmament; that of the celestial vault far above it. The man just simply had something transcending; a knowledge of certain things that was way more refined than the rudimentary thought processes that existed on this earth, and which were so frequently applied on this terra firma.

Moreover, there were many other indications that the Count might be one of them; of being such a shrewd and also very cunning vampire who—without people even realizing it—lived unnoticed among his unsuspecting potential victims.

The Count had a great knowledge of esoteric matters. He was always on his own. He was very mysterious. And he always seemed to have something to hide.

On top of that, the Count lived in a large and beautiful castle. He possessed aristocratic traits. And he sometimes even had a haughty demeanor.

And Marcus thought he had already caught a glimpse of

his true appearance a while ago; some type of monstrous figure. An image that the lightning bolts behind the large stained glass window had played so eagerly with at the time.

And besides! Hadn't he heard the man say, right after their very first meeting, that he preferred to bite a woman in her neck if he saw an opportunity to do so? For Marcus, all this was nothing more than an accumulation of building blocks that, slowly but steadily, began to raise a certain fixed image in front of him.

Moreover, the Count didn't have a single mirror in his large abode. And religious symbols were also very hard to find. At least, certainly not the Christian cross, which made this skittish, bloodsucking species apparently so insurrectional.

No, all this simply couldn't be attributed to coincidences alone, and Marcus decided to continue his personal search; by exposing the true nature of a man who, not so long ago, had opened the gate to his chateau so hospitably to Marcus…

Marcus just had to know, though. He just had to know whether the Count was a vampire or not. But how exactly was he going to find out? He decided to take a strategic approach…

In the week that followed, he spent every night in his small bedroom. He carefully read the vampire's features, absorbed them, and then memorised them as if he was still in school doing some type of homework. Marcus then gathered all of his courage and went back to the chateau the following day to apply his cunning tactics...

Marcus carefully watched the Count while the man sat opposite to him like that, and while he once again was busy with some paperwork that lay on his desk.

Marcus dug deep inside his memory as concentrated as

possible and then decided to carry out his internal, and also devious, plan. He crawled back into his head —just as the Count was currently doing—saw all the book pages that he recently had so skillfully imprinted in his mind, and from there carried out his strategies...

Vampires had a certain style and class, although you could often recognize them by the following external traits: they had sunken eyes, they often had wavy black hair, and they had long black fingernails.

Marcus looked obliquely out of the corner of his eye, looking as inconspicuously as possible at the hands of the Count, who was still sorting out the piles of paper on his desk, but the only thing that Marcus could detect were the black fingernails from his earlier rooting in the vegetable garden.

Notice their marble skin, their craving facial expression, and their icy glassy eyes.

Marcus looked meaninglessly at the Count for a moment, and the Count looked back attentively but also questioningly. But when Marcus looked a bit closer at his eyes, they were not glassy or cold at all. The man actually had very bright eyes. He did have a harsh look, though. And the Count also looked quite pale, but that wasn't very surprising for someone who spent most of his life indoors.

'Is there something wrong?' the Count suddenly asked, and which was quite clear, because Marcus had been inspecting his face continuously for at least ten seconds by now, and without uttering a word in the process.

'No,' said Marcus very calmly, because he had already factored in this potential counter-question in his attempt to expose the Count.

'I just think you are a very special and also very fascinating person, Count. I don't know why that is, that's just how I feel about it...'

'Oh... Okay...,' said the Count somewhat dryly. 'Thank you... I guess...' And the man continued arranging his personal workspace.

Blood... thought Marcus. There was also a small chapter devoted to that. Is it perhaps the life energy that they themselves lack? A source of vital energy that they themselves can no longer produce because they have been cut off from the cradle of life, somehow?

Interesting... was what Marcus internally had to think. Let's try something with that...

'So... what I was wondering just now, huh, Count, is... what is actually your most favorite dish to eat? Because I hardly see you eat anything... And moreover... I also want to ask you what your drink of preference is, because, and also with that, I almost never see you consume a beverage...' But Marcus shook his head internally with these questions. Tactful Marcus. Very tactful...

'What do you mean, Marcus?' was what the man asked. 'You've seen my surrounding piece of land, haven't you? I myself grow the average crops, just like everyone else grows them in this country. And drinking? Well... I really only drink water, and the bottles of red wine that the grocer puts on my doorstep from time to time, only to run away quickly afterwards...'

'Red wine...?' said Marcus in a questioning tone. Hmm, interesting...

'What do you mean, Marcus?' asked the Count in a more irritated voice this time. 'Would you like to taste some red wine or something? You are behaving a bit strangely on this Sunday afternoon.'

But Marcus brushed it off as a form of interest in the man.

Moreover, Marcus didn't want to be fed drunk, because who knows what would happen if that were to transpire? Perhaps he would be led into the underground dungeons in a drunken state of being, if this castle contained such catacombs. And maybe he would be locked down there forever, so that blood could be tapped from him every day...

No, Marcus would decline this glass of wine in all politeness for the time being and certainly not drink from it. Not until he had a better picture of the Count, and not until he could trust the man some more…

Daily life went on as usual, of course, and so did Marcus' job as a newspaper presser.

However, the contrast began to increase between the things that he learned from the Count and those of the daily activities and their routines. The wedge between pursuing his inner dream, doing the right thing for his loved ones and environment, and living a life that he had envisioned for so long, now.

Sometimes Marcus was sent on an errand at work. He then had to go to the type-foundry, for example, to pick up new leaden letters for the platen presses. He thus began to map out Light Town better and better. And sometimes he even got respect from people from unexpected places; from people who also carried out their crafts in their way.

'Oh, dear sir, so you work for the Gulden Gazette? At such a young age, that is? That is admirable to say the least. Chapeau!'

And even though this made Marcus feel important and proud sometimes, those people were, of course, also unaware of the downside of it all: of the many drops of sweat that crept into his underpants every day due to the toil on the platen press, and that gave him annoying chafing marks in his groin.

Of the black hands of ink; a nasty stuff that he could barely get rid of, and because of which he had to go wash his hands at least twenty times a day to keep them presentable.

And not to mention the long endless commute between his hometown and that of Light Town; an undertaking that took up a lot of time every day, and because he sometimes wanted to visit the Count's address in his spare time, and he only got about four hours of sleep per night since a day only had twenty-four hours.

He still occupied one of the lowest positions within the company, but when he closed the door of the media company behind him, and he roamed the streets of this big city, he was often and suddenly seen as a real big shot.

And in the meantime, he may have gained a great deal of knowledge, and could therefore say that he had grown quite a bit intellectually. When he returned to the small town of Glancebury, he was often treated as if he wasn't that much at all…

All this was rightly a contradiction and therefore difficult to deal with, especially for someone of his age. And even though he was old and wise enough to understand all of this, to think it out thoroughly and eventually put it aside again, it didn't make things any easier...

One day, when he was sent on another task for his job and sat next to the coachman on the trestle of his carriage, he couldn't help but think about this stuff for a while.

Because even though he had the impression that he could put these things aside reasonably well, this problem seemed to sit next to him on the platform of the carriage, and he constantly seemed to carry this problem around with him, wherever he went...

Nobles, aristocrats, gentry... was what he had to think for

a moment. They all just had it easy... Highborn and therefore automatically a foot in the door when it came to high positions. Perhaps they had known much less hardship than Marcus had experienced in his life up until now? And maybe they also knew much less than he did when it came down to certain knowledge matters? Yet, these people were always looked up to in a way.

In the end, it was nothing more than a false form of recognition, which Marcus thought in a sour way.

A raised bubble that seemed to contain no substantiveness at all. Nepotism in its purest form…

Marcus thoughtfully rubbed his chin for a moment. Maybe he should also gather a crowd of like-minded people around him? In order to form some sort of power bloc, something to display his dominance with, and to make people bow to him to show them eventually how things actually should be done?

Marcus suddenly laughed loudly while the coachman looked at him in surprise. Marcus could imagine this picture already. Or should he form a guild, perhaps? Maybe even a secret society? A mysterious group of individuals with their own language, hand gestures, and customs? As mysterious and enigmatic as the existence of a true vampire? It would really be something...

The carriage had arrived at its destination in the meantime. Marcus pressed some coins into the man's hand in a trance and then stepped down from the platform via a short staircase.

His own personal society... It would really be something... But what would he actually call it?

He finally looked at all the black ink on his fingers, then walked into the type-foundry's shop, after which the shop door closed behind him with a tinkling bell. Let's just keep it with the order of the black hand for now...

One day, Marcus just couldn't keep it to himself anymore. The work he had been doing for three, almost four full years now, was just too simple. And he simply couldn't stand it anymore. He just simply couldn't stomach the fact that the head printer in charge was always so adamant about it, and that he praised the work always so much.

Anyone could do this work eventually. Even the paupers in the back streets of Light Town; wandering around stinking and with an endless smell of booze around them. According to Marcus, this work was far too simple, far too mind-numbing, and perhaps even a mindless activity to be called...

But was it really all that simple? Was there perhaps more to this work that he hadn't realised before? And was the underlying knowledge towards the final end product indeed that simplistic?

'We produce a beautiful daily newspaper, Marcus,' was what the printer in chief said to him. 'Sturdy paper with a beautiful relief and a font that is really impressive; by means of relief-printing and that with a distinguished beaded edge...'

Marcus decided not to go against the man and to accommodate the head printer in his tale. He even wrote down the used terms on a piece of paper.

At home, and all alone in his locked-up room, he looked at the scribbled piece of paper for a while: relief-printing, beaded edges and different types of fonts. He wanted to familiarize the people around him with the craft that he practiced.

He looked at his small bookshelf with some despair. Vampires... Gothic... And the knowledge that the ancient Indians possessed... There is still so much to do, still so much knowledge to gather, and also so little time... He looked out of the small bedroom window for a moment: at the lands and fields that had to be cultivated, at the animals that had to be taken care for, and at the entire running of a farm that he could still choose for. A hardworking, fruitful, but also excruciatingly slow existence.

At least a lot less hectic and chaotic than the urban life he had now chosen for. The letters, the words, the many choices... They all began to dance in his mind's eye again, and they already seemed to tire him with their playful, yet compelling, rhythmic steps.

What was actually most suitable for him? What did he actually feel most comfortable with?

Marcus straightened his shoulders the next morning. He had chosen his own path in life, and it was important that he fought hard for it. In the meantime, he had regularly expressed his dissatisfaction about the monotonous, long-winded work at the platen presses. He had also received quite a few comments about it, but all this time, he was still allowed to keep his job; something he should actually be grateful for.

One day, he decided to do his own research. A trip along all the sub-operations of his craft; how paper eventually became a newspaper, and how a newspaper eventually became readable...

It was indeed a very simple operation what Marcus had been doing all of those years, but in the end, of course, there was more to this work than simply pulling a lever. The printer in chief had persuaded Marcus indeed—without the man fully realizing this—with his earlier summed up terminology. It had been Marcus indeed given the idea of being part of a larger, more specialised, whole; something he was now starting to realise better. A train of thought that was previously lacking because he had thought too black and white about his own activities, and was consumed by the routine of his own suboperation, and the dissatisfaction that resulted from it.

Marcus had absorbed the terms of the chief printer meticulously, and now he actually wanted to know the follow-up processes. So when he saw the opportunity for a short break, he decided to take a look at the papermaking business.

Coincidentally several rag men just drove by with their pushing carts, or with their horse and wagon, and with their fairly large beam scales, their so-called unsters, in order to hang the rags on, weigh them in that way, and in that same way enabling them to come to a reasonable price - in consultation with the housewife in question.

Marcus walked, therefore somewhat cheekily, into the paper mill, located against the river Thimes; a waterwork that had made the city of Light Town so grand through its water power.

Marcus stood in the doorpost with a certain self-assurance, in order to immediately make his presence known; a character who thought he would make a big impression, even though no one really seemed to notice him.

The boy took a good look around and soon recognised the process by which the paper was made; the main reason why he was visiting this place.

He had already seen the rag men driving by with their carts, and with their large scales on top of them on which old discarded clothing was being weighed, and now he saw how these rags were sorted in the paper mills.

He quickly walked to another mill and saw how the now-wet, rotten textile was taken out again, how it was cut into narrow strips, and how these were then put in other tubs of water.

Large wooden mallets, powered again by water power, pounded these soaked, half-decayed pieces of fabric into small fibers, which were then mixed with the water in the tubs.

When the wooden hammers had finished stamping, this suboperation was also finished, and the old discarded rags—once worn by a citizen of Light Town—were then grounded into a pulp, and the so-called paper mash was ready.

Marcus was truly amazed by all of this. He understood this process by now, as it was clearly carried out before his field of vision, and it was almost as if he had stepped into this place at the very right time. The processes were therefore very obvious to follow, and it was, therefore, a constant cycle that was executed with precision.

Marcus was still looking around with self-confidence. One moment he stood at the paper mills, and another moment at the large water tubs, actually without noticing that he was now being closely observed.

A man, with a somewhat grumpy expression on his face, walked up to the careless boy because he simply couldn't stand the fact that one of his employees was eating out of his nose so ostentatiously...

'Say, why are you standing still, boy?' asked the man in an irritated tone. 'Go to work, now!' And Marcus quickly explained his momentary presence to him.

'Oh…,' said the man. 'That's indeed different... And now you would like to know the follow-up processes?'

'Yes, very much,' said Marcus with enthusiasm. 'I now understand where the raw materials for making paper come from, but where exactly can I see how this actually leads to a sheet of paper?'

'Well,' the man said very clearly. 'Then you have to go to the papermaker...'

'Oh,' said Marcus in return. 'And let me guess, this one can be found all the way on the other side of town?' But the man looked at him with a silly expression for a moment.

'Yeah… I don't think so. That, of course, would not be very convenient from a logistical point of view, Ey? No, this person is located in the room next door. Just take a quick look, but preferably not too long, because I'd have you rather not keep my employees from their work, or have you distracting them with your presence...'

Marcus thanked the man exuberantly, assured him that it wouldn't be too long before he would be on his way again, and then stepped inside the room that the man had just pointed out to him.

Marcus had seen how old garments, discarded rags, were grounded into a certain paper mash, and now he had arrived at the subsequent process; at the papermaker who knew how to make real paper from this so-called pulp.

Marcus stood still for a moment and then thought carefully. Even now, he could stand and watch around him, and follow all the intermediate actions that would help him find his way within this paper-making industry. But what if he just ask the papermaker for an explanation?

Of course, that was not allowed; he simply wasn't allowed to keep the employees from their work. After all, the supervisor had told him that very clearly. But what if the papermaker just quickly explained the process to this suboperation? If he quickly would point out a few things to Marcus? Then Marcus would have become much wiser in one fell swoop, it would take up a lot less time, and Marcus would be able to leave here much faster, so that he no longer had to bother other employees with his momentary presence.

It would be the killing of two birds by means of one stone, as it was always so beautifully said within the ever-flourishing nation of Ingland.

The papermaker agreed with this. He understood Marcus' presence. After all, Marcus had explained his purpose to the man, and the man also understood that he couldn't be kept from his work for too long. And besides, Marcus' break was also almost over.

The man, who was called a papermaker, simply because he carried out this craft, put a finger in the air and said that Marcus had to pay very close attention.

'This doesn't have to take long. Open up your eyes, prick up your ears, and behold... Step one! First, we scoop up a sheet of paper.' And the man dipped a shovel form; a wooden framework with a bottom of fine mesh consisting of something that looked like copper wire, at the bottom of the tub with paper pulp.

'Step two!' was what he said very matter-of-factly. 'In this step, I take the framework out of the mush again, shake it a number of times very well and with a certain tact, so that the pulp is well distributed over the shape of the frame. Then!' exclaimed the man.

'Then I walk at a reasonable pace towards this man here: the so-called brusher. This gentleman right here,' and he patted the man in question on the shoulder, 'makes sure that the wet layer of paper is brushed off on a layer of felt. By brushing each sheet on a layer of felt, a pile is created that is then pressed, so that the remaining water can drain away.'

Marcus nodded enthusiastically as he began to understand the process better and better.

'Finally!' the man exclaimed again. 'Finally, the sheets are hung on drying sticks in order to dry them.'

And he pointed towards a long row of sheets of paper that hanged out to dry.

'But be careful! You now, may think that the paper is

suitable for printing or writing? But that is by far the case. There are now two more sub-operations involved and needed, and they are perhaps the most important.

After the paper sheets have dried, they are immersed in a bath of bone glue, after which the sheets have to be dried again. When these sheets are finally completely stripped of moisture, they are pressed again and then cut to size.

And behold, best young man, one has a beautiful sheet of paper; highly suitable for printing and writing...'

Marcus thanked the papermaker perhaps a little too exuberantly. He also shook hands with the brusher. And then smugly walked out of the papermill again.

His mother asked why he was so late again that evening, and Marcus explained the whole story to her. About the whole walk he had gone through today, and the knowledge he had gained in the meantime about the profession that he practiced.

His mother seemed impressed, but his father had his reservations, of course, and he couldn't resist to let his displeasure shine through, albeit under the skin again.

Marcus decided to retreat to his sovereign abode upstairs, to his small bedroom, with his three books standing on the wooden bookshelf that hung high against the wall above his bed. He mused about his parents' reaction to his self-initiated research, an initiative on his part that should have been applauded.

He now knew the many applications, the many sub-operations, which eventually led to an actual newspaper.

From the rag man to the papermaker. From the type-foundry to the paper pulp. He knew it all by now! The inking process, the printing process, he could almost write a good article about it...

And one might think that, since Marcus now knew a lot

more about this whole process, that he would also appreciate his craft somewhat more, which had actually been the whole underlying idea for this approach, all this seemed to be counterproductively, strangely enough.

He now knew so much about this specific line of work, and he now had so much more insight into the intermediate steps that led to the creation of a daily newspaper like the Gulden Gazette, that he began to feel more and more like a drudge, and also felt an increasingly clear realization that he had way more to offer, and clearly performed below his level.

A normal person, in quotation marks, might have drawn a certain hope from this: a certain satisfaction, and also a certain enthusiasm, that he could be a part of, could be a cog, within the creation process of a prestigious newspaper like the Gulden Gazette. But Marcus was simply not normal. He simply saw how things were in front of him; with a sharp and also clear mind, and he just knew that he could contribute way more to his environment than he had done so far.

An average person might have kept his mouth shut about this and would have gone on with his daily activities, and probably wouldn't even get involved in such an imposed delusion that suddenly knocked on Marcus' door again. But Marcus was simply not normal.

And so he had no choice but to show his displeasure again, simply because it would eat at him otherwise, and because otherwise he would just keep sabotaging himself; with a routine that he would keep imposing on himself, simply and supposedly because it was expected of him somehow...

Marcus made his dissatisfaction very clear at work, even more than he had been doing in the past couple of years. He simply had much more to offer. He just simply felt that way. That realization ran through every vein of his body. And it was time that his superiors would notice that, also.

Nevertheless, the printer in chief suppressed this rebelliousness of Marcus very purposefully.

He knew of Marcus' whims by now. He knew that the boy threw his butt against the crib sometimes. And he also knew that this often blew over on its own.

The man confronted the boy once again with a sober reality that Marcus, how much he felt in his right on this point, could not argue with whatsoever…

'Don't whine so much, Marcus,' was what the man said to him in an almost playful way.

'We don't like that here that much. No matter how terrible you think your work is, we still expect a certain smile on your face. Or just go and look for something else, otherwise, understand? Besides, you only work ten hours a day, so you really don't have that much to complain about, hm...?'

Bertus had been even more grim towards his son lately. And if he got the chance to place subcutaneous remarks, he seemed to do so gladly.

However, the man also did his best. With all his might, he still tried to convince his son that he was in the right, but Marcus remained stubborn.

It seemed to hurt the man: his only son, his once so small sprout, who had walked so often with him across the fields, who seemed to look up to him so, and who was destined to follow in his footsteps, had now suddenly become a stubborn little fellow who seemed to know everything better. Someone who, according to Bertus at least, thought himself greater than he actually was. And who now seemed to prefer to avoid his old father, rather than to seek a certain rapprochement to him.

The man seemed to be in a certain pain over this, had suffered a certain sadness because of this, and Marcus simply dismissed it all as a form of selfishness of the man that he himself would rather not be confronted with.

Bertus loved his son. He granted him a better standard of living than he had always known. And this was his way of making that known to the boy; at a time when they were once again engaged in a heated discussion and when their egos, as had happened more often lately, seemed to clash with each other once again…

'And then I'll tell you another thing, son!' his father shouted. 'Everything is not only science, everything is also a cycle!' His father stopped for a moment, took a good look at his only son, and then walked away, shaking his head again.

'Everything is not only science, but everything is also a cycle?' And Marcus seemed to be looking for his father for a moment, even though the man had disappeared through the back door of their farmhouse and had already crossed the yard.

I'll be darned! thought Marcus. And with a frown, he looked in front of him for a moment, with thick wrinkles on his forehead and also with big surprise in his eyes.

That was exactly the remark that the Count could have made!

Marcus was a little embarrassed—by now. Not because he had stood his ground, but that he kept believing in his boyhood dream. And also not of the fact that he might have had the potential to damage the family honor with his youthful excesses.

No, actually more because of the situation that had managed to play out again before him, and that had occurred so many times before during his upbringing: his mother who took his father Bertus to the small side room of their farmhouse again, and who tried to talk out a discussion that

Marcus, as a growing man, would have liked to have spoken out directly with his father.

But this was simply how certain things were dealt with in the Pritchard's family: actually an infantile way of communication, and also something that maintained a certain detachment between the members of this family, but what the instigators of this rogue method just didn't seem to realise...

His father angrily stepped away from the small room, then looked at Marcus in exasperation, after which Marcus realised that it could now go either way, but probably, and as often, via the way of the least resistance...

'In the 17th, and also in the first half of the 18th century, it was a cold and also, bleak mess in the world, Marcus! And in my time, things were also anything but easy!

Your generation is largely raised with a silver spoon. Ha! Even the climate has improved tremendously! You don't know half how good you have it, Marcus! You don't know half how good you have it!'

And that was basically all that came out of his father's mouth, as he walked away in anger again.

Bertus thought carefully about the things that he had tried to make so obvious to his son lately.

Marcus had clearly changed since he went to Light Town almost every day. And maybe he had to take a different approach this time. A final helping hand to get through to Marcus' blunt head and to hopefully bring him to other thoughts, to other priorities, and also to other insights...

Everything is Science

'How to divide the plots of land, what to cultivate, and what formula to use...'

'What formula?' asked Marcus.

'Yes, I'll be there in a minute,' said Bertus in a somewhat presumptuous tone, as if he was far from finished with his story and this therefore could take a while…

'What kind of barn are you going to use for the cows? Will you secure them all winter? Or will you let them run free on some days? Where will you get the manure from? And the dry feed? And what kind of storage place are you going to use…?

These are just the little things, the few things, that make an agricultural business stand or fall, Marcus.

Even your friend, the little chicken farmer, uses a certain formula in his work, it can hardly be otherwise. Just ask him soon, because I've heard that you wander around there on a regular basis...'

But Marcus didn't want to talk about the other villagers of Glancebury, who were apparently following him with their gazes.

He was very curious about the formula that his father had just hinted at him, but that he hadn't told that much about yet up to this point.

Nevertheless, his old man seemed to be on a roll, and he seemed to derive some pleasure to put Marcus finally in his place when it came to certain agricultural knowledge matters.

The pigs and piglets could be heard from a clear distance, with their high-pitched screams and their low-pitched grunts, and coincidentally, Bertus was just looking in their direction.

'The pigs...,' he said composedly. 'Even when setting up their bed barn, some form of knowledge comes into play. There must be an outdoor climate going on inside their barn, and it is a good thing if the walls of it contain cracks and crevices. In that way, it shouldn't be too hot inside for them because that's something they don't like. And if they do get cold in some way, they snuggle up against each other because that's in their nature, while keeping each other nice and warm through their own body heat, which is also good for their mutual social bonding...'

'But...,' said Marcus, because he wanted to add something to it.

'Indeed, but...,' was what his father said in return. And he deliberately didn't let his son finish his sentence because he himself could now finally have his say.

'But it is important,' he continued, 'to divide this so-called bed barn into three sections.

In my case, that means a central place where the pigs can relieve themselves, and where I also can get a large part of my manure from. Within their personal living space, a free-range area with straw in which they can root and toss and turn.

And in the back part of this pig hostel, as I always jokingly call it, a raised curtain with behind it a kind of bedstead in which they can retreat, in which they can sleep, and in which they can feel safe...

Ah, my dear son, I could tell you so many facts and things about the ins and outs of our farm, but it is actually a subject that a person can never stop talking about. And I hope that you will develop a certain love for it yourself one day, so that you will discover this formula on your own and thus derive a certain pleasure from it...

I know you have plenty to do, Marcus.

And I also know that you are busy with your job, with commuting between here and there, and that you sometimes even get an assignment home with you from your work at the printing factory. But this is my personal assignment to you. A learning method from father to son. A teaching assignment from a seasoned farmer to a young farmer in the making...'

The small chicken farmer was also standing in his yard, near the large chicken coop that Marcus hadn't seen in a while, and Marcus decided to get straight to the point.

'Is it true that you also have a formula?'

But the chicken farmer didn't really understand what young Marcus was saying.

'Well, just,' said Marcus. 'A certain method of how you approach everything here...'

But the man had to laugh out loud.

'Of course, Marcus,' was what he said. 'What do you think?!'

And the man calmly and in a controlled manner explained his formula to Marcus.

A word he actually had never heard of before, but of which he could understand the context.

'Look,' said the chicken farmer. 'You don't have to be an educated person at all for this, or know all the scientific facts or details. You can also learn a lot from others, like I did from my old man in the past.

But what's even more important is to simply look at the animals that you are working with, while at the same time observing their behavior.

I have been working with these creatures for quite some time now, and I am almost certain that I know some of their tricks by now; tricks that my father didn't know yet, for example.

For example, I know that chickens like to sit on a perch.

And even though that doesn't sound very stilted, I've really found that out by myself.

Okay, maybe not quite, and maybe I'm lying a bit right now, because I remember very vividly that my father experimented with this back in the day.

He thought that the chickens might like that. That would make them feel safer. And that it might even increase their egg production. But nothing could've been further from the truth...

It was a smart move by my old man, without a doubt, but this trick didn't seem to be working for him, and I finally understand why.

My father bred a heavier chicken breed, and that actually says it all: his chickens were simply too heavy to sit on a perch! Haha, funny right? And even though this is just a simple fact, it is also something that you have to find out for yourself. And even though I am patting myself a little on the back with this right now, I nevertheless got the vast majority of my knowledge from my father.

Do you want to know the rest of the... what was it called again...?'

'Formula…,' said Marcus.

'Right!' exclaimed the man delightedly. 'Now I have learned something from you, too!

Do you want to know the rest of my formula as well?' And the man seemed to be beaming for a moment.

'Yes,' said Marcus somewhat dryly. Because even though all this wasn't high-level knowledge, and certainly not something that knocked Marcus back steeply, it could still be funny and also slightly interesting to hear the rest of it.

Moreover, there was little for him to do on the farm today. He wouldn't really know what to do with the rest of his day anyway. And there was almost never anything to do in the center of Glancebury, which was actually not even worth this designation.

'Let me hear all about it!' shouted Marcus this time and also in a sort of delighted way; arousing a certain enthusiasm within himself which probably would not be fulfilled, but that would give him a certain perseverance to be able to spend some more time here on this piece of land of the chicken farmer.

'Good!' said the chicken herder. 'My formula! A science largely passed on through my father...'

Yes, yes, was what Marcus thought to himself. Hurry up, please!

And he felt how his self-generated motivation, to be able to hear all this in this way, quickly began to plummet again.

'I have learned...,' the man continued.

'Yes, from your father,' added Marcus sarcastically.

'Yes!' the man exclaimed. 'Ehm, how do you know that?' And the man looked at him with a silly expression on his face.

'Because you've said that at least three times by now!'

'Yes, yes, okay...' And the man doubtfully scratched the back of his head.

'Anyway, where was I...'

And Marcus sighed deeply again.

'You had learned from your father...' And Marcus almost wanted to walk away, annoyed. Simply because this man's slow way of thinking seemed to even lag further behind the stagnating development that this town of Glancebury had been going through in the past decennia.

But as if struck by lightning, as if struck by a firm kick of a stallion on his behind, the man suddenly and rapidly started to talk about all the ins and outs of his small-scale chicken business...

'Look,' the man said in a sudden smooth tone of voice.

'A chicken coop, and mine is of medium size, is best built out of wood, and should never contain too many cracks, crevices and openings. And do you know why that is, Marcus?' Although the man didn't let the young lad answer.

'Because lice, parasites, and other pests can nestle in it.

Chickens don't like these critters that can hide in their plumage. They are clean animals, you know, and they are very careful with their feathery jackets.'

The man looked at the sky for a moment, seemed to think

carefully, and then triumphantly raised his finger in the air.

'Rain and wind! Very important to take into account!

It is therefore important that the entrance to their coop is largely free of these weather conditions.

The entrance to the coop is therefore best placed towards the east or the south...'

And Marcus wanted to ask why that was, although he could imagine the reasons for this.

Wind, of course, provided a certain coolness, and apparently these winged friends of his needed a constant dry, maybe even somewhat sweltering, temperature.

And rain? Well, rain caused cold, or but better yet, caused moisture.

And moisture, in turn, could cause mold, and that seemed somehow disastrous for these animals.

Marcus nodded with a sincere interest this time, he wanted the chicken farmer to continue talking, and that was indeed what this man did in a tacit, but nevertheless, reciprocal consensus.

'The nest box!' the man almost yelled.

'Also very important! And where the influx of eggs takes place, and thus also the largest part of my daily bread.

It is very important, Marcus...,' the man now said in a serious tone, '...that it is dry and also warm and dark in there. And even though my old man once said that sunlight is actually good for egg production, and our dear Lord may know where the good old man got that knowledge from, he indeed seemed to be right in that respect.

Because even though these creatures like a certain darkness in their nesting place, they really produce the most eggs when the sun shows itself more often; especially in spring and summertime, when the days get longer again...

No, that old man of mine was certainly not retarded, not at all.

And finally! The free range area! A very crucial part of this chicken coop, of which I will gladly reveal the secrets to you, and absolutely a necessary addition.

Because how would you like it, Marcus? To be locked up between four walls all day long, and never be able to see the light of day?

That is simply unhealthy, Marcus, for both body and soul, and that is no different for animals in any form, size or shape.

Chickens love to scratch, to run around, take dust baths, chat a bit with one another, and occasionally flutter around, if they can get themselves off the ground, that is.

Yes, a free-range area is very important; a crucial appendage to the coop.

And in my case, it is also quite large, because I have quite a few chickens. But anyway, what was I trying to say again?

Oh yeah! It is very important to cover this open area of the coop with chicken wire, otherwise they can flutter out of their shelter, and they may never come back.

In addition, this open part of the coop must be tightly closed, otherwise foxes or weasels can get in, and we don't want any more clucking in the chicken coop, as it is, of course. The man walked around the large pen, which could almost be called a complete barn, and then stopped for a moment at the wooden fence that gave this free-range area its shape, while a number of hens curiously looked through the cracks of it to watch their observers.

'I deliberately left large openings between the wooden planks, which together form the fence of this free range area, so that the girls can still look outside the coop for a bit, and thus do not have the feeling of being completely locked in.'

Marcus felt a certain respect for this. He thought it was noble that this man was so committed to his running and also a fluttering source of income.

And whether this was for a certain self-gain or because of a certain animal friendliness, Marcus could not quite figure out, but the chicken herder clearly seemed to realize that their mutual relationship was a matter of give and take and that they were both dependent on one another in a certain way. And Marcus gave the man a thick, fat, and also feathery plume in his mind for that.

'Has anyone ever escaped?' was what Marcus asked with now even more interest, as he looked at a chicken that was gazing back at him through one of the cracks in the wooden fence.

'Certainly!' said the man with a smile.

'What many people don't know is that chickens, if they really want to, can get fairly high off the ground.

Of course, they aren't real high flyers, but I have seen them on the roof of this large chicken coop before, and I have even found them in the tree next door.

But these little rascals have it good here, so they never go far away, they just keep hanging around here. Look,' the man said in an even more serious tone as he suddenly looked at Marcus with a glint in his eyes and - instead of grains of wheat - began to throw terms around that Marcus had never ever heard of before, but which immediately managed to put the boy in his place in terms of his earlier looking down on this seemingly ordinary chicken farmer.

'Look,' said the man for a third time by now.

'I've kept an eye on these scurrying land fowl for a while, and I can tell you with utmost certainty that these beings are a lot more intelligent than we people realise.

They have a very clear hierarchical pecking order, and they have social conventions in use of which many we are unfamiliar with, of course, but that could really make our heads spin.

It would be funny wouldn't it...,' continued the man, who suddenly seemed to put on an academic hat, '...that while we as Homo sapiens stand on both our feet, and in this way look haughtily into the world around us, and look down on all those frolicking little life forms that supposedly get in our way, while those same crawling creatures may have their own language patterns, have their own way of complex thinking, and may adhere to social norms which we as humans can actually learn from. And that they might look up to us instead and may be thinking: Hmm, maybe we should keep those lanky people on good terms, with their fickle behaviors, and their chaotic way of living...'

'In other words,' added Marcus suddenly. 'Maybe we are the real idiots here? And not the other way around?'

'Indeed, Marcus,' said the man. 'I could not have put it in better words.'

'But dear sir,' added Marcus suddenly and respectfully.

'I don't want to downgrade your beautiful theory, but...don't chickens actually walk upright also? On both of their feet?'

And the man paused for a moment. 'Yes, you're actually quite right now that I think of it.'

'So what can we conclude from all of this?' asked Marcus in a wise, but also somewhat pedantic tone.

'That animals and humans may be closer to one another than we think, and that we'd better keep things friendly among each other?' said the man, as he removed his woolen cap from his head while scratching the top of his head for a moment.

'Nicely said!' exclaimed Marcus in return.

'I couldn't have put it in better words either. But I think the mutual relationship is going well so far, right? Doesn't it?'

'Yes, yes,' the man said a little hesitantly. 'But maybe I could be a bit nicer to them every now and then, to my chicken friends that is...'

Marcus nodded one last time with enthusiasm, then decided to walk away, although he did say something to the man in the meantime:

'Because we don't want to fly into each other's feathers now, would we?'

The chicken farmer couldn't laugh about this at all, although he did watch how Marcus walked away so suddenly, and how he finally disappeared from his sight.

That dubious, somewhat vague, but also wise young man, whom the Pritchard family could proudly call its own...

'I know you have an ambition to be a journalist, Marcus, to be a reporter,' was what John McAllister said to him when the young man sat next to him again on the platform of his cart. 'And now that I've had lots of conversations with you, I just might have the feeling that you may succeed in that one day. In any case, you have read the newspaper very regularly already. You have read several books with strange stories in them that can only appeal to my imagination, and you can also write on top of that.

I think it's quite clever, Marcus, very clever even, especially for such a young guy like you.

And even though I'm just a simple worker, an illiterate even, although not everyone in this town has to know that, of course, even I could teach you a thing or two...'

And even though Marcus wanted to interrupt the man at this moment, simply because he already thought fairly highly of John, he decided to let the man finish.

It was something different for a change; a compliment out of an unexpected corner, and at the same time a small revival of Marcus' self-confidence, which had suffered so many dents of late. And even though he wanted to tell John this, that Marcus had learned a lot from him as well, especially in the field of driving a horse and cart, or how a person should live their life in general, Marcus didn't want to shout down John's gesture this time. Even though Marcus really wanted to, and especially in these types of areas, speak from his heart so much. Again...

'Look,' said John.

'Even though I know little of journalistic life, or about authorship for that matter, I just have the feeling that you can never know enough for that kind of profession.

And that's why I have, and maybe you could use it someday, somewhere in your writings, a fun fact for you.

We may always call my wagon, the means of transport that we are sitting on right now, a farmer's wagon, but technically it is a farmer's cart.

An actual farmer's cart has only two wheels, almost no suspension, and you may notice that during a trip, especially if the road is bumpy.

So a farmer's cart has only one axle; one axle, with two wheels. A farmer's wagon, on the other hand, has two axles, four wheels, and is also often equipped with leaf springs...'

John scratched his head for a moment because it was quite a plain story, but he still thought that Marcus might like these little facts.

Marcus liked sitting on a farmer's cart, from all that shaking feeling, although he was a bit disappointed that John had made him so curious just now.

It wasn't high-flown knowledge after all. No, not at all.

And it was indeed just a funny fact; a funny fact which he could always use to put someone in his place with, with which someone could be lectured:

'Hey, there goes another farmer's cart.'

'No, that's not a farmer's cart, that's a farmer's wagon, because it has four wheels, and a farmer's cart only has two...'

'Oh, that's pretty funny to know...'

'Yeah, isn't it?'

No, Marcus preferred real knowledge; stilted knowledge.

And of course, someone could also be lectured with that, but that person just had to comply with it, simply because it was a favor granted to him or her. That was simply Marcus's way of thinking about subjects like these.

He had always thought that way about such matters, and he probably always would...

A Further Exploration of the Vampire Book

Marcus was at least halfway through the book on vampires now. He had read all their previous characteristics thoroughly, and he began to become more and more of a connoisseur of these shadowy beings, at least in his own opinion...

About these beings who were bound to the darkness, who nevertheless continued to yearn for the light, and who seemed to wander around on the earthly plains with an aesthetic value that they still carried within them, but who also walked around with an emptiness in their souls from which they, with all their might, tried to escape.

It was something that they were constantly reminded of in their steps, and which kept them discouraged, frustrated, and bitter at the same time.

Marcus began to identify himself a bit with these creatures. At least, he began to understand their incentives and backgrounds somewhat better, and he also understood that they were actually victims of themselves, and not necessarily and completely malevolent.

It was a given for which he began to feel a certain sympathy, a certain kind of pity, or rather said a certain compassion.

It was a certain melancholy that he also carried within him, although it was probably to a much lesser extent.

It was a bit similar to a wall of dark clouds in front of the sun; the light still seeped through here and there, and the spectacle was beautiful to see, to say the least, but at the same time, it was also a sad and somewhat ominous scene.

It was like a painting that everyone could identify with, although it was also a state of being that people preferred not to aspire to.

And it was also a painting that appealed to the imagination, but that people preferred not to hang on the walls of their personal living space, because they would be reminded too often of this potential state of mind.

It nevertheless seemed to be part of the ambivalence of life, a term that the Count had often spoken of before; being trapped within the contradictions of this dimension; a fact that, if one could withdraw from it, or rather said, rise above it, only then one could escape from it, and thus truly be free...

Wonderful... thought Marcus for a moment. Really beautiful...

And for a moment he felt a certain pride and also a certain euphoria, because he suddenly, with the Count in the back of his mind that is, thought he had uncovered a certain universal value which could wipe out all the peripheral earthly issues around him; the things that had been so firmly taught to him from birth and that had almost been rammed in...

Nevertheless, Marcus had thought and philosophised about this enough, at least for now.

And even though he actually learned the most from this all

just by thinking about it so deeply, the time had now come to further expose this ultimate vampire book, and to hopefully find out if the Count was actually a vampire, and how Marcus could best handle the man's exposure.

Marcus ended up on a series of pages where the gifts of these night creatures, or rather, where their abilities were better revealed.

By now, he knew about their physical characteristics in broad strokes, but these here were aspects that he had not encountered in the book before. His body started to warm up again, the tension increased once more, and so did the contractions that the chambers of his heart produced.

It was an effect that this book often had on him, especially when he thought he was on to something. Could he perhaps find something here that could give him a decisive judgment? He began to read in a voracious but also concentrated way:

Vampires can suffer from a deadly frenzy…

Although the book did not say whether this was due to a lack of blood or whether they were just very touchy...

And if a vampire does get hurt, he doesn't feel any pain, and heals immediately...

Marcus thought about this for a second, mused about it for a moment, and instantly thought that he detected a small opening in this.

It was a potential opportunity to learn more about the Count, and thus about his alleged identity, although he immediately realised that he had to abandon this option.

Marcus didn't want to intentionally injure the Count, even

though he might have been able to substantiate his theory right away with this...

They never get tired. They are particularly difficult to defeat in physical confrontations. And their strength only increases with time! So they become stronger as they get older...

Marcus left this quality for what it was.

After all, he had often seen the Count in person, he had often spoken to him, and he had also observed him on a regular basis.

The man didn't look particularly strong. He didn't seem to hide excessive muscle mass under his clothes. And he was actually just quite slim, somewhat thin even, and almost to be called bony. Moreover, Marcus had never seen the man lift anything heavy in an easy way.

On the contrary... He had seen the man move a pile of heavy books the other day, and the man had visibly struggled with it at the time.

No, this fact didn't seem to be applied to the Count at all.

And it even seemed to shake Marcus' theory a bit...

They are often endowed with some extraordinary powers called the dark gift.

Each vampire has different special gifts, but they do have some of them in common.

Magical abilities: mastering the elements, enchanting or bewitching, and turning base metals into gold...

Hadn't the Count talked about that before? Alchemy or something? Certain alchemists?

But Marcus didn't know that much about it, didn't understand this whole concept that well, although one day he would ask the Count for a further explanation.

Spiritual strength; a hypnotic power of the eyes to be able to direct the thoughts of people and animals, and thus force them to carry out orders.

Mind reading, and also telekinesis...

Telekinesis... No idea what that word meant... And Marcus didn't really feel like going down the stairs again to consult his parents' dictionary about this word.

Because one: he lay far too comfortably currently, a position that he would undo by standing up now.

And two, and actually the main reason, he just had the idea, a hunch, that such a word wouldn't even exist in a common dictionary like the one his parents had on their bookshelf. But a hypnotic power of the eyes? A force with which they could control both animals and humans? Well, the Count fitted quite well inside that category. The Count could look very directly out of his eyes, in an almost penetrating way, and this could give someone, at du moment, the idea that he was looking into one's inner self.

It wasn't something he always did, but at times, he definitely portrayed that act. Especially during occasions when he displayed his knowledge so exuberant, while he pretended that they were fixed facts; something that was impossible to argue with.

As if he immediately put someone in his place and didn't want to know anything about one's ignorance.

Simply because this would defy his own mind through a

form of going astray; a going astray which he himself perhaps wanted to be reminded of the least.

However, it wasn't a particular look that made Marcus feel like he was losing control of his own mind. It was a certain way in which the Count tried to take such a deep look within his state of being that it could make Marcus feel a bit nervous and uncomfortable at times.

Yet, Marcus was well aware that he himself did this too sometimes, and with him, probably so many people. Perhaps it was just a form of observing someone's facial features more deeply, even though Marcus didn't always find this decent behavior, and sometimes he even found it an intrusion into someone's state of existence.

But perhaps all this was coloured by the fear that someone might find out something vulnerable about a person like yourself; something that a person preferred to keep to himself, about something that could evoke shame, or something that could be taken advantage of in a certain way. Marcus didn't know exactly. He only knew that the Count used this trick regularly. In any case, more often than the average person did that Marcus encountered in his daily life.

Nevertheless, Marcus could accept this from the Count somehow. As if the man, by having all his knowledge at hand, and by the wealth of information he possessed, had a certain right to it.

Moreover, since the very first meeting with the Count, Marcus had also experienced a certain reciprocity, a certain equality between them.

Something that Marcus liked very much, something he didn't encountered that often in daily life, and which softened the man's sometimes penetrating gaze.

Because Marcus knew that the Count wouldn't take advantage of it, and also because they got to know each other better and better lately, and certain social and also emotional barriers seemed to fall away with it as a result...

Marcus suddenly awoke from these striking series of thoughts.

Profound, and almost intellectual pieces of thought, which he had never known he could recall so easily at regular intervals, but which at the same time were also a bit coloured by his own insecurity.

Marcus had stayed with the skills, with the - as the book described them - dark gifts of the vampire.

And even though he began to enjoy thinking about peripheral matters, about life itself, and about the Count, almost even more than reading this book itself, he also knew that it was actually this book that gave him the tools to come to such ideas.

So he started to read further, even though his eyes were starting to get weary, and his stomach somewhat grumpy and rebellious.

Flying speed, was what the book read.

They move extremely smooth and elegant. Sometimes they are so fast that the human eye cannot even follow them. As if they appear out of nowhere...

Ha! thought Marcus. Ha! for a second time. Well, that was something the Count seemed to have a hand in. Several times, he had startled Marcus with his sudden appearance. Marcus could almost never hear him arrive.

And Marcus always had the feeling that something, or someone, was watching him when he walked alone through the chateau again; alone through the narrow corridors, and through the wide entrance hall with its large rose window high above it, which would always lead him back to the entrance again.

A portal that seemed to connect this erected bubble of both knowledge and mysticism with the gray, pale, and somewhat insignificant world outside...

They defy gravity by clambering up and down steep walls, or by jumping vertically up from a standing position. And some vampires can even fly...

Now, Marcus had never seen the Count fly or jump very high.

The only thing he did see the Count once do was jump out of his skin. Almost, although at the same time, it also couldn't have been.

Nevertheless, that was also something that Marcus preferred not to evoke in his old friend.

Because even though he had never seen the man ignite in a real frenzy, Marcus also had the idea that the Count carried a certain wrath within him that Marcus would rather not be confronted with…

Sharp senses… They have an extremely sensitive hearing, and sense of sight and smell.

Their hearing is as sharp as that of a wolf, even in a noisy environment, and with their hypersensitive eyes it is even possible to see in total darkness...

The only way to apply this, as Marcus thought, was to make a lot of racket in the Count's personal quarters, while asking him a number of questions at the same time.

But first of all, he wouldn't know what kind of tool or instrument he would use for this without raising it questions in the Count's mind.

And secondly, it would probably look ridiculous, it might irritate the man on the spot, and it might prevent a next visit to his castle, to his chateau.

And to gauge whether the Count had hypersensitive eyes, and to see him wander effortlessly through his quarters without bumping into anything, would mean that Marcus would have to visit the castle at night while hiding in one of the many rooms of his stronghold.

Something that was almost impossible to do, because his parents would expect him to be in his bed around that time of night.

Moreover, the Count might be very good at blindly strolling through his halls, simply because he knew the shape of his quarters so largely by heart.

And an additional factor… If Marcus could carry out this plan in all its impossibility, how could Marcus observe the Count in the pitch black in his turn? While he himself wouldn't be able to see anything? No, this internal scenario was both stupid and reckless.

Moreover, Marcus wouldn't even dare to visit the chateau in the twilight of night again.

The stronghold aroused a slight fear in him in broad daylight already. And if Marcus were to sit there like that, in the dead of night, looking for the movements of a man who, of course knew his quarters way better than Marcus himself, it would be quite possible that the Count would notice him first and not the other way around...

Transformation. A remarkable ability to move around unnoticed.

They can shapeshift or adjust their appearance when they are in danger of getting into trouble in their human form.

This can also mean a different age or gender, or even a complete transformation from human to animal.

As a bat, it can flutter unnoticed to its victim's bed. And like a wolf, by means of its speed and its keen senses. Vampires can also turn into dust, fog, or steam, to slip through small cracks or keyholes...

Marcus decided not to go into this, because it was a too-far-from-his-bed show anyway…

He probably let his imaginative mind play tricks on him again; let it take a pointless path again, while he continued to build on it, but at the same time lost sight of reality in the process.

Pointless? Maybe... But still, Marcus also had a healthy and also well-founded doubt about this whole matter.

A doubt that Marcus had felt regularly in his life, and which was not to be taken lightly, simply because he had been in the vicinity of the truth for so many times by now.

Marcus actually had little to lose, and he knew how to make an exciting game out of this. And if he was close to the truth despite all these fantastic excesses, it would undoubtedly become clear soon…

The life of the undead.

A lot is said about them. And a lot is also written about them.

But they seem to have some similar traits in common.

Marcus tapped his finger on the page. Maybe I can find some more clues here...

Maybe here I can find what I am looking for...

They follow a strict diet, which largely consists of blood.

Older vampires, however, are better able to resist the urge for it, and they last longer between feedings.

They are nocturnal creatures... When darkness falls, they start to move and prepare to look for a victim. They seem to lead a normal life during the day, but it is simply in their nature to go out at night...

Marcus thought about this for a second. Nevertheless, the Count always seemed busy during the day, with whatever he was doing. Maybe he should just ask about it?

Perhaps Marcus didn't have to enter his fortress at all in the middle of the night? Perhaps he could just hide near the gate? In order to detect a sign of life?

A flying man, perhaps, or a wolf, or an unmistakable form of mist?

It could give this story a lot more strength.

But what if the man caught sight of him at that very moment? Maybe he would fly Marcus at his throat? In whatever form he might be at that time?

He could plunge his razor-sharp fangs into Marcus' arteries. He could feed on his little comrade, whom he might not even recognize in that moment, in all his bloodlust and rage.

And at that moment, he could endow Marcus with a curse; an affliction that Marcus may have been partly to blame for because of his reckless form of curiosity.

Marcus saw this picture all in front of him. He grabbed his neck at the same time. And then felt the gag of despair that went down his throat through swallowing.

And what if the Count had disguised himself as a bat?

There could be numerous bats residing on, and flying around the chateau. How could he ever recognize the man among them?

It would be a needle in a haystack; an awaiting of a certain death sentence that Marcus would have imposed on himself so vigorously...

Isolation... They are constantly looking for new victims, and they try to keep their identity hidden as much as possible. That is why they are constantly wandering around, from here to there, because they simply live longer than the people around them.

As a result, they can often lead a lonely, and also desolate life...

Well, thought Marcus, if this doesn't refer to the Count, then I don't know what does! But Marcus didn't really know what to think anymore.

One time, he came across things that he could relate to the Count, and the next time he found something that completely proved the opposite.

It was therefore a certain separation, a certain schism, between a constant 'indeed' and a constant 'maybe not so after all.'

And that fact alone was a perfect hiding place in which a vampire could move freely. No one would ever believe the phenomenon of nocturnal creatures, and that, of course, worked very much to their advantage.

It was a schism between a constant yes and a constant no, and the truth had to be somewhere in the middle.

A truth that Marcus had been looking so stubbornly and almost so obsessively for all this time, even though all this was starting to take a run at him and even though he all started to dislike it more and more.

A ray of light... read the book further.

It's not all doom and gloom when it comes to the vampire. Because of their hypersensitive senses they can fully enjoy beauty.

Many of them have a distinct artistic aptitude. For example, they paint, or they play a musical instrument at a high level...

Hadn't Marcus seen such a particular instrument in the castle once?

Hidden away in one of the chambers of the Count? A kind of piano-like object?

Would the Count sometimes entertain himself with it at night, perhaps? The production of sad, but also very beautiful sounds and tones, which were supposed to elevate his own melancholy to a form of liberation for a while?

Marcus really had no idea. It was just guesswork. And he wasn't even sure if he had actually seen the instrument or if reality and fantasy had intertwined in his head once again.

What he did know with great certainty, however, was that the Count had a whole range of works of art hanging on his walls.

Marvelous illustrations of scenes that, even with Marcus' underdeveloped artist's eye, were often supposed to represent religious snapshots.

How did the Count actually got a hold of these paintings? Had he made them himself?

In any case, this was a good topic of conversation to talk about with the man, to show some interest in a friendly way, and in a playful way, to find out whether he actually carried this vampire trait within him.

Nevertheless, Marcus was starting to get tired of this game; a game that started to become a bit of a burden, and which sometimes made him even feel nauseous.

It was all a bit too cunning and underhanded, and if anyone could be cunning, it was a night creature like this one.

And if the Count was really a vampire - and Marcus started to feel embarrassed again, because he was doing nothing more than guessing - then of course the man had already figured out his game, and it was really Marcus who was being watched by now, and not the other way around.

Yet, this book continued to beckon him.

He just had to know; perhaps an answer to a suspicion that he was not a complete and also utter fool, and that he was finally right this time.

For now, however, he had read enough, he thought.

He therefore nonchalantly, but also somewhat

despondently, shoved the book off his lap so that it fell next to him on the bedroom floor with a thud, but it still lay opened.

He leaned forward for a moment, at the same time in an intriguing way wondered which pages had been exposed to him this time, and to see if his obsession, which was still raging strongly beneath his skin, was accommodated by this small twist of fate.

Evil-Resistant Aids... read the heading of the page.

Amulets and tricks that can ward off a vampire...

Yes! thought Marcus. This may be what I've been looking for all this time. This is something I could work with.

Marcus picked up the book again, read the first evil-repelling aid, but decided to keep it to himself for now, and not to say it out loud.

He had read enough for today. His eyes were even more tired now, his head was packed with silly facts, and by now, the time had come for a well-deserved purifying sleep.

In the not-too-distant future, he would find out what was actually going on with his good friend the Count.

Before long, he might be able to confront the man with this potential truth, and then he would see if this revelation would stand between them...

Marcus' parents discussed their grown-up conversations always in a small separate room of their farmhouse. Conversations that he and his little sister were never allowed to attend. Marcus suddenly had to think of this again, and his thoughts were coloured by contempt. He really didn't felt any hatred towards his father, and they got along quite well most of the time, although he seemed to lean more towards his mother in some way, and that had two particular reasons.

Reason one was that he could talk better with this woman. And reason two… And that's where that retarded little consulting room came into play again, for as long as he could remember disputes between him and his father were always discussed between him and his mother, which she then discussed with her husband Bertus.

When Marcus came home tired from work that late afternoon, he happened to be in for a big surprise, and it was almost as if the devil himself was playing with the matter.

His mother took him by the hand for a moment and, to his father's great surprise, took Marcus this time aside in the small consulting room and not Bertus.

'Son…,' his mother said in a solemn tone.

'You have to listen very carefully to me now. Your father has indeed been a lot more grumpy towards you lately, but that has its reasons.

Your father is very disappointed by this all. Not necessarily in you, but more in the fact that no one will take over our dairy farm now. After all, you are his only son, and what should happen to this house in the coming years?

According to your father, you aren't taking your responsibility, and you're living with your head high up in the clouds…'

'But you supported my decision, didn't you?' said Marcus in a sad and also pitiful tone.

'I've shown you my dream a long time ago, haven't I? You stood largely behind it, didn't you?' But his mother looked embarrassed at the ground.

'I thought it was a short-lived thing, Marcus. A good way for you to spread your wings some more, to get to know urban life somewhat better, and that you soon would notice that big city life is almost even harder and more uncertain than life in the Countryside, and that you eventually would realize that you are in the right place; here with us...'

'So you've never believed in me at all?!' shouted Marcus angrily, disappointed, and also somewhat indignantly.

'I did, Marcus,' his mother said. 'I truly did. I have always believed in you, but just not so much in your...'

'In my dream?! In my passion to become an established reporter?!' Marcus added, embittered.

'It's hard out there, Marcus...,' was what his mother somewhat soothingly said.

'I'm afraid they are keeping you on a leash and that they will never give you a real chance to...'

But Marcus had heard enough by now, and he quickly sprinted towards the living room to finally confront his father-something that Marcus, instead of this man, dared to do...

'I'm not living with my head in the clouds, Father!' was what he shouted.

'Because I just know that I will be a respected man one day! And that I will end up in a big, nice house somehow! I just know that it will all work out one day! I...'

But his father turned up his nose again, taunting...

'Ha! What do you know ass crumb! You may be starting to get the facial features and also the outward features of a man, but deep down inside, you are basically still a child. My biggest mistake in this life is...' And he angrily pointed a finger at Marcus.

'....is that I gave you those damn books!'

But this stung Marcus deeply. How could his father kick, that which was so dear to Marcus' heart, down so low?

How could someone, who said that he loved him so much, hurt him so much at the same time? Marcus just couldn't understand this given.

Marcus continued to pursue his dream, nevertheless.

And even though it wasn't really nice at home anymore in terms of atmosphere, his mother kept giving him some money on a regular basis so that he could at least pay for the ride to work, and he wouldn't do anything crazy in the meantime like fulfilling his mother's worst nightmare; of becoming a drunkard, or an unhinged pauper, languishing somewhere in a back street of the city of Light Town.

'Don't worry, Mother,' was what he regularly said to her reassuringly.

'It will have to take a very long time, and also many setbacks, before I will take such a route!' And his mother then often smiled for a moment, but whether she was completely reassured with this answer was, of course, another matter...

The platen press, which Marcus had stood in front of so many times before, seemed to be a welcome change for a change to be able to think carefully about things that were going on in, and around his life, in the small hamlet of Glancebury and beyond.

He had no connection at all with the work that he did, and was even fed up with it, but the many noises around him; the printing presses that were pressing their plates into the sheets of paper, the rustle of piles of paper sheets that were constantly dragged in, and the footsteps of colleagues that swayed around him all the time, often put him in a certain trance mode in which he seemed to forget everything around him for a moment, and as a result of which he could think concentrated and clearly again about the many life issues that were constantly defying him.

Sometimes friends were even more valuable than family members, was what he had to think about for a moment. Sometimes these seemed to be closer to a person than the blood bond that one shared with one's loved ones.

True friends often stimulated a person's personal growth, while family members sometimes tended to slow it down, sometimes even worked against it, and sometimes even had the tendency to break it down meticulously. And why it often worked that way, Marcus didn't really know, and whether they did this on purpose, he didn't really know either, but for the young Marcus this fact was in any case a given.

After all, he experienced this more and more lately, and it started to frustrate and disgust him to a great extent. Many a person might capitulate to this.

Many a person might surrender to the social pressure and abandon his or her ambitions and ideals for the common good because of this, but then they didn't know Marcus yet.

No, not Marcus. Because even though he almost died spiritually sometimes, and the opposition of his parents made him hurt a lot inside, it also seemed to strengthen his conviction at the same time.

In the conviction that he was all alone and by himself up

to this point, still walking a certain path in life that seemed to have been mapped out for him.

The only thing he had to do now was what he had managed to put off for far too long.

All he had to do now was to stand his ground, set certain things in motion, and thus prove to his parents that he knew very well what he was doing from the very first start...

Marcus had had regular conversations with the editor-in-chief, and the man had said the same thing very often as if he wanted to teach everyone who worked at the *Gulden Gazette* the basics of journalism.

The man had said it many times by now, and even though it often had something irritating, it still seemed to work.

The voice of the editor-in-chief, at least his short message, played through Marcus' head once again, and it always sounded the same:

'The freedom of the press is a wonderful thing, Marcus; our fundamental right to make feelings and thoughts publicly known.

A democratic society can only function properly if freedom of the press is properly regulated, after all, that is a core condition for the society in which we find ourselves.

Nevertheless, you will always have to be careful with what you write, because even though there is a certain freedom of the press, the responsibility of what's written still lies with the publicist. One can therefore be prosecuted for this, provided, of course that one has crossed certain boundaries.

This can be an incitement to hatred, slander, or spouting falsehoods, for example.

These are the limitations that a real reporter needs to know, Marcus. This is the number one rule in the authors' handbook. And if you hadn't known this by now, you'd still have a very long way to go...'

Marcus had remembered these words vividly, he'd understood them perfectly well, and now the time had come to confront the editor-in-chief with the promise he had made him so long ago. The promise that Marcus could apprentice as a reporter; provided of course, that he would come up with a very good story...

One night, tucked away in his small bedroom, with the soft glow of a burning candle right beside him, he thought that he had finally found his story. He was going to write a piece about how difficult it was to move up the ladder within a journalistic company like the *Gulden Gazette*. And about the pros and cons of awarding someone without experience, but with the right dose of motivation and abilities, a position within a company like this one or any other company for that matter.

Because even if the piece would be somewhat coloured by Marcus' own opinion and therefore not entirely objective—an important journalistic lesson that he had heard many times before and had also managed to remember very well—he could well create a small social movement with this article…

However, when Marcus had largely finished the piece and wanted to show it off to his supervisor, he received the unfortunate announcement that the editor-in-chief, and also the man with whom he had made this arrangement some time ago, had been fired with immediate effect. Marcus, therefore, left all his work for what it was, paused with his own suboperation for a while, to ask the fired editor-in-chief what was going on exactly, and whether the rumor was actually true; a rumor that Marcus had only just heard...

'Oh,' said the man somewhat stoically. 'It's just you. Marcus is your name, isn't it? Promise? Promise...? Oh, that promise! Yes, I'm sorry, lad, but I'm afraid that arrangement can't go through. I have been fired by those bastards, you know, because I've tried to expose certain abuses within this company. After all, I thought at the time, and that with my silly head, that this would promote a certain business efficiency eventually, but they took it as a form of threat apparently. They kicked me out lad...

I've bitten the hand that has fed me for so long, apparently, while I was only trying to do the right thing, that which seemed to me to be the right thing to do for this company.

This is quite unfortunate, boy. And in addition... And sorry to have lied to you a bit... I'm actually not the editor-in-chief at all.

Everyone here with a somewhat higher position calls themselves that way. There is a fight for this position, you know, and I thought you too had figured this game for yourself out by now...

Anyway... and I'm thinking aloud right now...

Maybe you can lead your one-man quest in a different way? Maybe you could try it with another editor-in-chief?'

Marcus followed up the man's advice, and as soon as possible, went to another figure who awarded himself such a title.

There was simply a need for haste. Marcus had carried this plan—and also his only plan for the future—with him for years now, and he could no longer bear to put it aside unused;

like a sigh in the wind, after which it would evaporate, and his skills, and perhaps himself as a whole, would vanish in thin air, and nothing would ever be heard of him again...

Marcus tried to express his first sentence as well as possible to this man; a sentence that had been gnawing at him for at least three full years now.

He explained his story to the new editor-in-chief as clearly as possible, and also expressed the heavy burden that weighed on him from his home front.

He talked about the reporter-ship that he had aspired for so long now, and that he even had a real article in the pipeline; an article that could well be worth publishing.

Marcus was allowed to explain his article somewhat, although his new supervisor didn't seem entirely convinced of the chosen topic.

Nevertheless, he thought it was a nice piece of investigative journalism, especially for someone who was just starting, and who came from a small farming hamlet where people generally couldn't see farther than beyond their own noses.

Yes, there may have been a small talent slumbering in Marcus after all; with his inquisitive gaze and the way he looked at his surroundings. It was a capability that a writer, no matter how talented or how skilled he was, had to carry within. The so-called new editor-in-chief actually thought this was an entertaining conversation, and he found the assignment given to him by the man that they had just shown the door, also comical.

At the same time, he was also as transparent as possible with Marcus, and he didn't beat around the bush at all over this:

'Dear Marcus,' was how the manager started his speech, somewhat excitingly.

'The man who gave you this assignment was wrong on many fronts in terms of business operations, although I can only agree with him on the journalistic points that he pointed out to you. I really don't have time for this. And actually, it's also quite unprofessional to give someone like you a chance like this one; someone without any prior education, or without even a certain procedure that has to be followed in advance.

Nevertheless, I also see that you want this with all your might, might even give everything for it in the process, and apparently have already had to make a lot of sacrifices for it in the meantime. I'll try to be as honest with you as possible, Marcus.

And this will probably lead to nothing at all, and you'll probably never become a real reporter eventually, but I will give you this chance anyway.

Solely for you, so that you can experience for yourself that it's actually impossible what you're longing for, and that it can therefore give you an awareness of which life direction is the most sensible for you to take, and that you can also say to those around you that you have been an apprentice reporter for a while.

That you haven't succeeded at it in the end, but that you at least have tried with all your might, and that you have done your utter best for it.

Don't expect too much of this, Marcus, because all this will most likely come to nothing, but go and take a look around.

Go and take a look around for the story that can make our ears ring.

Something that is topical as well as newsworthy, and which can also shine on the front page of our high-quality newspaper.

You'll only get one chance, Marcus. And only one story.

Now get back to work, lad, because the good citizen out there wants to be able to open up a newspaper again tomorrow, in order to stay informed of all the urgent news that our fine nation has to offer...'

Marcus was ecstatic, of course, shook hands with the new, or perhaps, only real editor-in-chief in this building a little too exuberantly and perhaps also a little too long, and then went back - but with lighter steps than a half hour ago this time to his awaiting platen press to do exactly what he had been doing for so many years now; inking leaden letters and then printing them into infinite sheets of paper.

The editor-in-chief shook his head when he was back in his office, and while he was still pondering over the previous conversation that he had with Marcus:

What have I gotten myself into again? That poor bastard...

So driven... but also with so little sense of reality...

Well, at least I didn't present him with false promises like the last person did. I just gave him a little hope again, and also a boost of energy and motivation, which he can use on the platen press again for the time being.

Soon, a misfire of a story will appear on my desk, I will tell this idealistic rookie the truth once more, and he will thus be an illusion richer, and that charade will also be over.

The man shook his head firmly once again, although he had to laugh to himself at the same time. Oh well, all this is actually quite funny; entertaining, however, also a somewhat childish game. Something that could break the daily monotony a bit, and that would make up for an amusing story; a story that will circulate within the walls of this company, of course, not outside of it, let that be very clear...

Marcus thought of nothing but finding a good story in the weeks that followed.

He was thinking about writing a piece about vampires, with his own kind of twist on things, but...

But that, of course, was anything but front-page worthy.

It wasn't even worth mentioning. Unless half-dead creatures suddenly rose from the graves of the cemetery a little further on. Then it would be something else, of course.

Maybe he should take a good look there soon? To see if there was some nocturnal, undead scum around?

Who were looking for an unsuspecting passerby whose meat they could feast on?

But Marcus shook his head once more, and in doing so, also shook away this ridiculous idea.

He couldn't prove the existence of vampires anyway. At least not yet. Maybe one day, but for now, he'd better keep things objective.

A good story about Indians, perhaps? He could definitely say something nice about that. Information that he had managed to get from the Indian book, and also some ephemeral facts that the Count had sometimes used to argue about.

Nevertheless, Marcus' knowledge was also incomplete in that area. He knew something about it by now, but most of the information really came from the Indian book that stood on his small bookshelf, and didn't come from his own hand.

And to indiscriminately copy an already existing book would not only be a form of plagiarism, it would also devalue his talent for writing and could destroy his only chance at a true authorship.

Plagiarism... Also something to take into account...

It would be difficult to come up with a good and also worthy story in this way. Pursuing a dream to become a reporter was more difficult than Marcus had initially thought. And so was the writing process itself...

Marcus sat opposite to the Count, in a spot where they had sat so many times before.

Marcus on a chair in front of the teak wooden desk, and the Count behind his favorite workplace with a meters high stained glass window behind him, which gave this room a bit of an ecclesiastical atmosphere.

How this showpiece had ended up here, who had actually made it, and how the Count had come to own such an entire castle in the first place, was something that Marcus had to ask him again. But for now, for this particular moment, the now somewhat more cunning Marcus had the Count something else to ask.

If Marcus wanted to come up with a good story, perhaps and ultimately an entertaining piece about Indians, then the Count was the right person to instruct Marcus in this.

After all, the Count had a wide array of knowledge at his

disposal about such topics.

Not only in his personal library but, and so it seemed, also in his mind.

The Count turned out to be an ideal source of information, and Marcus, opportunistic as he also could be, eagerly took advantage of this...

'Dear Count...' as Marcus often began his questions.

'I found that conversation about Indians that we had a while ago very interesting, could you tell me more about it, maybe?'

'Telling indeed...' was what the Count somewhat sarcastically said.

'Because in the end it was more of a monologue than a dialogue in the first place, wasn't it? But you can't help that either.

Indians... Indians... What more can I tell you about them... Well, let's see...

It probably hadn't escaped your notice that we're living in quite a turbulent world, Marcus.

There are many people walking around on this globe; people who often take a different point of view of things but who always, in one way or another, try to impose their own points of view onto that of someone else. If you, as a human being, fall somewhat by the wayside, or you do not fit within a certain type of framework then people, or rather said groups of people, will rally behind their own certain points of view and at the same time try to exclude you if you don't fit in with that particular form, shape, or framework...

You have probably noticed that before Marcus, what I have understood from your stories.

After all, your way of thinking didn't fit in with the social boundaries that the residents of Glancebury have imposed on themselves either...'

Marcus nodded because the Count was absolutely right about this, but what this had to do with Indians had to be seen from his story.

'Indians seemed to be a completely different breed of people in this respect.

They therefore seemed to be closer to nature, and they therefore would never taunt an individual or question his or her true essence, simply because this essence is prompted by nature.

However, sometimes it happened, and maybe this is all a bit too far-fetched for you, that a person wasn't happy with the body in which he or she was located.

Sometimes a man was born as a woman, or a woman was born as a man, and the spirit didn't seem to be in line with the body in which it resided. The Indians have known about this phenomenon for a very long time, and they faced this socio-emotional dilemma with charity and with patience.

After all, they didn't want a soul to go through life miserably. After all, that was not what life was intended for.

Because human nature is a force to be reckoned with, and an unhappy individual not only functions flawfully within the life stream in which we all find ourselves, but such a sad and unhappy individual also functions poorly within an entire tribe of Indians.

If something like that was noticed, Indians kept a close eye on one another within their tribes after all, an emergency situation was invoked and they entered into a joint conversation.

A meeting was then organised, the person in question was of course involved, and his or her life issue was thoroughly discussed. After all, the Indians as a people were great enough to place the well-being of a single individual above that of an entire group.

Simply because they were wise and grand enough to realize that such an act made a group only stronger and closer in the long run.

Yes, Marcus, I think that really has something magisterial, you may definitely know that.

I therefore consider such well-considered decisions to be of paramount importance. And even though there were also violent and bloodthirsty tribes among these Indian people, of course, this is a given that I strongly embrace.

And which our somewhat distorted, and somewhat estranged urban world, could learn a lot from...

The Indians were certainly not ignorant or dumb people! And Marcus could almost jump for joy with enthusiasm over this given.

Extraordinary! I have another gem standing on my bookshelf!

But just as good as the vampire book? And Marcus shook his head firmly for a second. No, it certainly wasn't as good as that one. But definitely a close second! Of the three books that were now standing on his bookshelf, it was definitely a close second!

Marcus Forges a Plan...

Marcus may have been nice to the Count, and this behavior was definitely sincere, he was at the same time also busy with his own agenda.

Marcus had never met anyone like the Count, and the immense pile of knowledge that the man had amassed would take a normal person at least a hundred years to gather...

The book about the Indians was indeed special but not as special as the book that now rested on his lap.

This illustrious package of sheets of paper was now almost at its end, and Marcus was apparently on the right track in his investigation. Because even though Marcus had already read many pages of it, and he had almost gone through the book completely, he had finally found something that he could use. He had stayed with the ominous Evil-Resistant Aids: the tools that were needed, or at least could be put to good use, in unmasking a shadowy creature like the vampire. It was one of the last headings of the book, the page where he had put a crease after which he had closed the book again with some reluctance, simply because his eyes had become too tired to continue with the reading. Marcus put his finger on the first word while all kinds of potential plans were already unfolding in his mind, plans that he could carry out soon. *Fire...* read the first word. *Something that could be seen as purifying in a symbolic sense...*

Marcus, of course, thought about this, even though the book said nothing more about it. Marcus knew that there was nothing more purifying than fire. Nothing as sterile as this particular element as the schooled ones in this universe knew. Marcus tried to imagine a campfire, then thought about the great bonfire that was sometimes lit in Glancebury; usually once a year and that at the end of the calendar. Marcus also envisioned the fireplace in the living room of his parent's farmhouse; there where robust blocks of wood were being laid in wintertime. A fire that warmed both his house as well as his body and limbs, and of which the sometimes annoying smoke formations were largely sucked up through the open chimney on the roof of their residence. Marcus knew that you could throw anything into the fireplace, and he had done so many times. The fire would scorch everything in its path and in the end, nothing would remain of the objects that underwent this torture, except for a remnant of ashes and their typical smells.

Fire was indeed a purifying phenomenon, and it took everything with it in its fury, without any concessions, good or bad. You could throw anything into the fireplace, really.

But to throw the Count into the fire and to see his chateau go up in flames entirely in order to purify his alleged malice? No, that seemed a bit too rigorous, even for Marcus.

After all, only some fragments would eventually remain; a ruin of a beautiful piece of architecture of which Marcus didn't even have the knowledge or the skill to build, with a thick layer of ashes laying on its foundation in between the poor Count had to be somewhere. A sad pile of dust that Marcus could never find again and to which he could never ask another single question... Marcus quickly read on and left this self-conjured specter of doom for what it was; a cleansing, yet also excessive approach, to the exposure of a certain kind of truth.

A truth that Marcus more and more began to believe in, and that kept him under a certain kind of spell, but which he also had to watch out for, because otherwise he might end up with impulsive, perhaps even destructive tendencies.

Garlic... read the following word. Good... was what Marcus had to think. In any case a lot less extreme than fire, and also something that was easy to obtain.

One can hang a strand of garlic in front of the window, or wear it as a string around one's neck. The smell is simply too strong for these nocturnal beings. They will not want to stay in the vicinity of it, and it will eventually drive them away...

Marcus wrote this fact as minuscule as possible with a pencil on a slate that he still owned from his school days and then quickly read on about the third Evil-Repellant Aid that was mentioned in the book. *Silver, iron and lead.*

All are metals, and all are also usable if they somehow get into the vampire's bloodstream...

Hm, thought Marcus. Unfortunately, I can't do much with this. Metal was something he could get a hold of, that was for sure, but it would also mean piercing the Count's skin while poisoning him at the same time. Doing great harm to the man or inflicting a certain form of pain on him was simply not in Marcus' intentions. He just wanted to be able to demonstrate - and that in a playful way - that his good friend was actually a shadowy being, although and at least he was already on the right track with a strand of garlic.

Rice and seeds read the fourth repelling aid. *Counting is often an obsession for these dangerous creatures. They simply cannot resist counting all the grains in front of them, even if there are a thousand of them!*

Yes! thought Marcus. I'm going to try this out soon! No problem at all! After all, there are plenty of seeds and grains to be found on our piece of land and in our barn!

Sanctified water: one of the strongest weapons against a vampire, and also a substance that immediately burns their flesh. However, this Evil-Repellent only works in the hands of a true believer...

Marcus thought about this for a moment, but at the same time also had his doubts. Perhaps this was a doubt located somewhere deep in his heart, a form of doubt that he had always carried within him, a certain feeling of inner insecurity that would probably give this weapon no chance of success. *In addition...* the author of the book continued. *These nocturnal creatures cannot step overflowing water either: a flowing river is a hellish blockade for them, but so is a small flowing stream that can block their way...*

Hm, thought Marcus again, I could definitely work with this.

And he also added this possibility to the slate, to the shortlist that was to form the backbone for the devious plans that he was already concocting in his head.

Knotted rope: this actually has the same effect as seeds and grains. A vampire simply cannot resist untangling a tangle of rope. They will be obsessively absorbed in it, because the knots have to be untied, even if it costs them many hours of work... Try it out in your immediate environment, you of course can never know...

And that's exactly what I'm going to do! Was what Marcus

thought. He looked at the black slate with the four small, but nevertheless, clearly written guidelines with complete satisfaction, then hid the writing board far under his bed and left the other ominous tricks for what they were. He had already read them cursorily. They were a little too far-fetched for his taste anyway, so he couldn't use them for his small but, and that, in his own words, genius plan.

The next few days would be entirely devoted to collecting these aids, the tools that would help Marcus unmask his good old friend. However….the long list of ominous tricks had yet another appendix: a small piece of text that seemed to belong to it, that was printed in a somewhat smaller font, and that had to provide the serious vampire hunter with a final chord for the tragic opera piece in which he soon would play a part…

How to destroy a vampire...

Marcus carefully read the sentence a number of times, let it sink in as well as possible, and then noticed how his gaze wanted to read the text underneath it in an almost compulsive way. He left the text underneath it for what it was and instead looked at the page number in question and then placed a small fold at the bottom of the page.

Maybe he would need this information again one day, although it was clear by now that Marcus wasn't looking for a complete erasure of his good old friend. Because even if the Count were a true vampire, then Marcus would only respect that given, would even be very proud of it, and his secret would be safe with him. Hopefully, the man would never lash out at him, and they could just talk this matter out, exactly as it would befit two decent gentlemen. The book was now at its end, although it would make Marcus lift one last veil on this concealing phenomenon. A veil behind which another lowered curtain would remain; a darkness, but also a mysticism, in which such a phenomenon could remain hidden, and that anyone who would cross its unfortunate path somehow would leave in a certain delusion.

The book therefore, had an open ending, which hardly could be otherwise, although it gave Marcus nevertheless a clue that strengthened his intuition, and thus also his ever-growing suspicion.

The history of the vampire: a belief in blood-drinking creatures that goes back for at least 5000 years...

And for the last time for the time being Marcus tapped on this page of the book again.

A belief that goes back for thousands of years? That can't be a coincidence, can it? This information must come from somewhere, right?

The ultimate vampire book had now finally come to an end. Marcus had learned a lot from it, and had also enjoyed it intensely. It had revealed a new world to him in which he had been able to immerse himself, and now the time had lastly come; a time in which everything he had learned so far, and all the knowledge he had gathered about this elusive phenomenon, could finally apply to the environment around his little person...

The day, on the whole had arrived! Marcus looked under his bed, slid the slate from under it, and looked carefully at the four notes again, at the four key points that he so convulsively had been looking at in the last couple of days.

He had managed to collect all the right supplies and had hidden them in a paper bag, a paper bag that he had found on the central square of Glancebury, and he now gathered all his courage to come into action. He looked at the slate for one last time, and this was what somewhat sloppily was written on it:

1. *Garlic... Who knows how the Count will going to react?*

2. *Plan with a glass of water, see garlic...*

3. *Strand of rope that holds the bundle of garlic together. Let's see how that will work out...*

4. *And last, but certainly not least important, grains and seeds...*

I'm going to drive the Count nuts with this! Thought Marcus almost manically. I'm looking forward to it already! I love this man! But don't go around and play games with me! I'm Marcus for Pete's sake! Marcus from Glancebury! A force to be reckoned with!

Marcus had a day off today, or at least it was a Saturday.

Although lately, he had not been asked to help on and around, their farmland. Maybe his parents saw that he was so busy during the week, and they allowed him his well-deserved rest. Perhaps they mistook Marcus for a lost cause, they already mourned about him in silence and looked with sorrow in their eyes at where and in what sort of place Marcus would eventually end up. Anyway, Marcus was currently frank and free, and he wanted to use this day to implement his - as he liked to label it himself - genius plan. He decided to walk to the chateau. It was only five kilometers away from his home, so that was doable. And he simply didn't want to burden McAllister on a Saturday. And perhaps the good man himself had a day off today? Moreover, he could use the sparse money that he possessed for other purposes.

Marcus walked along the fields, along the grounds, and under many tall trees, and with a sun already quite high up in the sky because they were heading towards summer again. There was no wind at the moment. A clear blue sky adorned the celestial vault, and it wasn't exactly a scenario for the shadowy matters that Marcus was currently engaged in.

Maybe he was acting somewhat infantile with all this. Perhaps he was concerned with matters that a normal mortal shouldn't interfere with at all. And maybe an alleged vampire was very dangerous to begin with, and it was better to stay away from them as far as possible. And to make matters even worse, they maybe even had a link with a certain underworld where there was no peace to be found at all and where only sadness and melancholy predominated. Nevertheless, Marcus seemed once again strengthened by a certain line of thought.

For evil, no matter how dirty, filthy, or vile it might be, and with a chance that it would want to pull a person down into its sinister grottos, those kinds of beings should also feel a certain leniency towards a certain form of mutual understanding. After all, and whatever the sort of creature in question, and no matter how good or bad it may be, everyone ultimately appreciated being heard and could appreciate a certain mutual rapprochement that could eventually even transcend universal and opposing values...

Marcus strengthened himself with that soothing thought while he held the paper bag tightly under his arm. Soon, the ultimate truth would shine through. Good or bad, right or left, above or below, Marcus would accept the Count for who or what he ultimately was, and he hoped that this man would be able to reach out to Marcus and, of course, and even better, that he would be able to appreciate and accept Marcus' intentions in the end...

Marcus opened the gate, for it was never closed during the day, although some force always had to be exerted on it to be able to open it. He walked through the narthex with the large, broad rose window parading high up behind him. He then walked through the atrium, went through a door on the right, climbed the stone spiral staircase to the top, and thus ended up in the Count's most favorite quarter. Marcus had gotten rid of the paper bag in the meantime. The bulb of garlic now rested in his right pocket, and the grains from his father's storeroom lay in the left one. The Count would undoubtedly have some water in a carafe on his desk and an empty glass probably standing there too, although Marcus could eventually get a hold of one somewhere. He was now holding a string in his closed palm and that shouldn't form a problem either. The moment of truth had now arrived...

It was a fraction of time, and that also within a moment of time, of which Marcus could never have imagined, not even in a million years, that he would ever be a part of it. He hadn't even known the Count two years ago. And a few years prior to that, he was still mastering reading, writing and calculation as a little unsuspecting and somewhat otherworldly boy. Meanwhile, he thought he knew so much on the other hand, and had made such giant leaps personally that it was almost too much to comprehend. He felt happy in that regard, sometimes even felt blissful, and that had all started with meeting the Count. He tried to expose a certain entity but with the realization that this person, one way or another, would never ever be inferior to Marcus. Vampire or not, creature of the night or otherwise, this man had made him retain a certain joy for life, and Marcus just hoped that he could return the favor one day...

'So Marcus, are you back again?'

'Yes,' said Marcus, holding the string in his hand even tighter. 'Listen up, Count!' was what he exclaimed a little too enthusiastically. 'I had a good conversation with the grocer the other day. You know, the one in Glancebury? The village I come from? This guy claims that garlic is a great medicine! Packed with all sorts of antioxidants! Although I don't exactly know what he meant by all that. But in any case, as the man said himself, apparently very anti-inflammatory and also beneficial for the removal of bodily waste!

Bring me a glass, good sir!'

And the Count scratched his head for a moment, grabbed the carafe of water which stood next to the carafe of red wine that also always stood on his desk, and then handed it to Marcus.

'Do you have a glass with that, perhaps?'

'No,' said the Count, 'is that necessary?'

And Marcus nodded. 'I want to immerse a clove of garlic into the water so that its medicinal effect comes into its own...'

'Fine,' said the Count, and he handed Marcus an old and also dusty wooden chalice.

Marcus took a clove from the garlic head, from the bulb from the rest of a whole strand that he had thrown into the bushes on his way to the chateau. He then peeled the clove, put it in the wooden goblet, occasionally immersed it with his finger, waited for a moment, and then took a sip from the brewage.

'Hmm,' he said, overdone. 'Truly wonderful, healthy and

also very refreshing at the same time. You should try it too...'
And he handed the cup to the Count at the same time, and that
with an expectant look. The Count took the cup, then took a
sip, and then coughed and sputtered it out. 'Damn it!' he
shouted. 'What a nasty stuff! And I almost choked on it too!
No, please keep this stuff with you. I'll stay with this here,'
and he tapped on the glass cap of the other carafe with the red
wine in it. Marcus frowned for a bit.

The Count's reaction to this garlic stuff was justifiably
debatable, while he was already plotting his second plan
beneath the worktop of the Count's desk: to make a tangle out
of a string, and that should bring out the Count's annoying
compulsions.

'Look,' said Marcus again, digging deep inside his left
pocket, pulling out his hand, and then spreading dozens of
grains over the Count's worktop. 'A fraction of the harvest
from our field of last year. Aren't the grains beautiful in form?
Big, fine in shape, and also splendid in colour?'

'Yes, yes, I guess so...' the Count muttered, somewhat
surprised. And he shoved the grains together with both hands
in order to take a closer look at them. For a moment, it seemed
as if his gaze was fixated on the group of seeds. And for
another moment, it seemed as if the man couldn't stop this
gaze at all.

Nevertheless, he pushed the group of grains back to
Marcus and then started rummaging through the pile of
paperwork that lay in front of him. Marcus was not yet
convinced. He got up, said that he had to go to the toilet, and
then deliberately knocked over the goblet of water that stood
between them on the desk. The Count startled when the
massive wooden chalice bounced a number of times, and with

hard blows, on the shiny marble floor beneath them, which also caused an annoying echo in the hollow interconnected rooms of the castle.

'What are you doing, Marcus!' the Count shouted, irritated. 'You just keep messing around!'

'Yes, sorry, Count,' lied Marcus. 'I really have to go to the toilet… If you'd just step over this water here, then I will lend you my clean handkerchief so that you can sweep it up yourself and so that I can go to the restroom. I'm really in need…'

'Hmpf,' was what the Count replied. And he looked at the puddle of water that lay between him and Marcus.

'Quickly go to the toilet, boy and then clean this mess up when you get back here, including all these seeds…' And he picked one up and then shot it demonstratively between two fingers in Marcus' direction.

'Okay,' said Marcus somewhat resignedly, after which he looked at the Count for a moment and then walked away. *Darn it!* was what he thought during his steps through the chateau. This man is just impossible to catch! Either the man just does stuff out of the blue, and I'm completely wrong with all my suspicions, or he knows exactly how to avoid things in a devious way…

It doesn't look like he tolerates garlic, or at least, he seemed to give that impression. He wasn't counting the seeds very attentively. Nevertheless, he immediately swept them together, which could also indicate a form of compulsion. And he didn't seem to want to step over the puddle of water either. Maybe because he was too lousy to clean up my mess, but still…

No, Marcus didn't seem to be able to make a definite answer out of this. It all lay completely in the middle again, as was always the case with the Count. He just simply couldn't lay a finger on it… And let that precisely be one of the greatest attributes of a vampire!

Marcus was now more enthusiastic, now more than ever, simply because of the important finding that he'd just made. Of course, a shadowy creature like the vampire was not easy to catch! Of course, they didn't show their vulnerabilities too openly! Marcus had played this game way too simple and on top of that much, too showy. And if anyone was a master of games, proficient in bending a certain truth, it was a creature as described in the ultimate vampire book...

Marcus therefore turned around, pretended to have been to the toilet, dried the marble floor of the Count's study with his handkerchief, and then sat down opposite the Count again.

'Look,' said Marcus one last time. 'I want to ask you one last thing before I leave you be again. This here is a tangle of rope. None of my colleagues at work have yet managed to untangle it so we've made a funny bet around it. Each of us gets two days to get it loose, and the one who succeeds in the task gets a penny from each other participant. Would you like to help me with this bet Count? I will share the prize money with you, of course...'

But the Count had to laugh heartily about the proposition. 'Well, now, we're talking about real pennies here? Now, that's what I call a fat pot! But it's all right, Marcus. And who knows? A few extra pennies here and there are always welcome, of course. And maybe I'll earn enough with this bet to buy myself a new bottle of wine. Count me in! Put the ball of rope on the corner of that table over there and come back tomorrow to see if I've succeeded. After all, tomorrow is Sunday, and I'm not off the impression that you are a churchgoer, so I expect you here in the afternoon around the stroke of twelve, at a time when the sun will already be fairly high up in the sky. Go now! And we will see each other again tomorrow!'

Marcus walked back home, somewhat defeated. You couldn't call it disillusioned, but that he hadn't become any wiser was a fact. He had never encountered such a mysterious person like the Count before. Someone who was so completely and utterly elusive. But hey! Maybe Marcus himself was such a person, too? After all, his own parents didn't seem to get a hold of him and that seemed to frustrate them extremely also. He didn't seem to fit in with his fellow villagers of Glancebury, and he also didn't fit in with his colleagues on the work floor. What, or who, was he actually himself? A simple newspaper printer who took a shot at being a reporter? No one seemed to be able to place him correctly and neither did he himself sometimes.

No place seemed the right one for him and that made him somewhat elusive, something of an enigma, but at the same time also somewhat lonely. Marcus also walked around alone on this terra firma. And even though he had, in a way consciously chosen to do so, the universe also seemed to push him in such a direction deliberately, and which made him walk with his head bowed down underneath the common sun. Actually, he was not that different from the Count at all in that respect. Or was this just a form of how one could live his life? Something that a person could consciously choose to do so?

Elusive, unfathomable, not being able to place someone... He definitely knew more of such people. He himself maybe, the Count for certain, but perhaps also a John McAllister, the cart driver, or the small chicken farmer who always seemed so content of being all alone on his small piece of land, with nothing more than his chickens that the man could talk so enthusiastically about to this day. Or even the cloth weaver... A man who never cared about social conventions, who did his work undisturbed, and who didn't care about what other Glanceburies thought of him and who couldn't really be pigeonholed.

Maybe it was something to be proud of, a certain distancing from the masses because the masses often just did things without a bigger meaning behind them. And while they didn't properly understand the long-term consequences of their actions, in the process they often dragged so many others with them into their blind pitfalls.

No, it wasn't that bad at all to stand alone in life and in the world. After all, and in that case, you could only fall back on yourself, and you could only blame yourself when things went wrong. Nevertheless, it didn't seem to be a form of loneliness that tormented young Marcus so much. No, it was more a feeling of indefinability, the feeling of not knowing where one belonged, where one could fit in, and he had always carried that feeling within him, ever since childhood. Would he ever be able to shake off this feeling? He had no idea… Although only time could tell...

Tomorrow, around twelve o'clock sharp in the afternoon, he would confront the Count with the suspicions that he had been carrying with him for months now. The result wouldn't really matter to him because for now he seemed to have lost enthusiasm for this silly little game. Tomorrow, he would have his final answer. Tomorrow, he would really know the truth.

And if not, then not, and if so, then so. And then he will move on with his life, trying to seize his place beneath the common sun with hopefully a destination in which he could finally find a certain real peace, and which hopefully could, and that for a longer time, soften his indefinable feelings...

'Here, your rope,' said the Count when Marcus stood the next day around noon in his now lighted room again. I completely untangled the ball of rope. In other words... We're getting money from your colleagues!' And he gave Marcus a playful wink. 'But do tell me, Marcus, because you've acted quite strangely yesterday...

You had all kinds of weird stuff with you. You were constantly messing around. And you were throwing things on the floor all the time...

Were you having a bad day or something? Were you still sleep-deprived, maybe? Or had you secretly drunk some of my red wine?'

And the man looked at him with that characteristic glint in his eyes again, but Marcus had had enough of this tug-of-war. And if the Count was playing him for a joke again. If the Count already knew about Marcus' earlier exposure plans, then the man didn't seem to have minded it at all, and then now was for Marcus the ideal time to have his say and to point out to the man what Marcus had wanted to tell him for months now...

'Wow...,' said Marcus in a controlled manner, in order to give the Count a brief moment for the revelation that was about to follow.

'You are... Dear Count... And that, according to my calculations... Nothing more than a real vampire! I mean...

You seem to have a hard time tolerating garlic. You are noticeably afraid of religion. And you have almost no mirrors in your chateau…

Not because you are afraid of your own reflection, but simply because you cannot see your reflection in a mirror at all! I've read about these things somewhere, Count!'

The man seemed to be startled by all this candor and for a moment his face seemed to distort. Marcus wanted to add something to this tale, and even though this didn't seem entirely wise to him, he decided to do so anyway; in a bold but also moderate tone, 'You are…,' said Marcus calmly and also understandingly, 'just a restless soul…'

The Count's face changed back to a somewhat gentler version, and with almost something of an awe in his voice, he spoke to the young boy, 'Restless… Yes… I think that's the right word, Marcus. Restless…'

The man seemed somewhat sad, while Marcus looked in his turn at the ground out of a form of shame.

'It has been enough for today!' said the man suddenly in an elated way. 'I shall retire to my chambers. You will find your way home again, won't you? And don't go wandering around my halls and rooms again…'

But when Marcus looked up from the immaculate marble floor from underneath him, the Count had already suddenly disappeared… Marcus felt an imposed impulse all of a sudden. The Count had gone up in smoke again, and his rooms stood now wide open to explore, almost as if they belonged to young Marcus himself in a way.

He desperately wanted to search around for a while, to see if he could find and discover puzzling, perhaps even sinister, things for a second time on his own, and so hopefully be able to study them if he got another chance. But even though this thought seemed to force itself on him once more, he decided to shake it off on the spot right there. Moreover, he had already done this sneaky searching at the beginning of his escapade with this castle, and the Count had been sharp enough to have found it out the first time, so a second discovery wouldn't be too hard for the man either.

Marcus didn't want to risk his friendship with the Count. Moreover, these were the man's affairs and not those of Marcus. And sometimes, personal affairs were simply too personal to mess around with. And even though he believed that this whole building was beautiful and majestical at the same time, at the end he decided to walk in a straight line towards the large arrival hall in order to get home again...

That night, Marcus sat alone in his small bedroom for the umpteenth time and as always in the vicinity of a burning candle of which there was not much left but a little stump. With a beating heart, he took out his most favorite book again.

This time, his gaze remained on the front cover however. The colorless front suddenly drew an image of a castle, entirely shrouded in shadows and with a mysterious figure staring lonely out one of the tower windows. Lightning flashed across the sky, and bats made their flight back to their dark hiding places.

Marcus looked at the spiritual drawing for one last time with attention, after which he put the book away again with a deep sigh. After all, the information that this book contained was already deeply embedded within his head.

He blew out the candle again and then lay thinking in

silence as his eyes slowly began to adjust to the dark.

He had to think of the Count, of course, while a certain pride ran suddenly through his body. *Darn it!* he thought. *Almost all the characteristics match up! I've actually made friends with a real vampire!* And while his thoughts rattled on for a while, and while he dozed off in a certain sleep at the same time, he wondered for a moment whether he should tell this all to his parents or not. Such a special man... And such a special friendship...

However, also another thought slumbered through his mind, while the young farmer's son had already and almost made the inevitable crossing to the warm embrace of sleep: *Don't do it, boy,* was what this soft little voice told him, *your parents won't be open to it anyway...*

The White Death

During Marcus' next visit to the chateau it seemed as if nothing had transpired between them the last time. The Count behaved quite normally, not any different than usual, and he even seemed a little cheerful. As if the unmasking that Marcus had wanted to bring about during his last visit, had brought some relief to the man. Marcus actually understood less and less of it all. Because if this man was truly a vampire, why didn't he just say so? After all, his deepest secrets would be safe with Marcus, and his true identity definitely guaranteed.

Now, and for the umpteenth time, there had another gaping hole arisen between them; one of conjectures, of unspoken thoughts and ideas, and of a guessing by Marcus' behalf that he was getting more and more tired of by the minute. A gaping hole of something that could very well be, but on which Marcus just didn't get an honest answer. An evasion of a certain truth that the Count turned out to be very adept at, just like all the other adults seemed to be that Marcus had encountered in his, so far, short life...

Maybe this all should be put to rest. Perhaps this all was no more than a learning process that Marcus had to go through somehow. Indeed... Not everything needed an investigation. Sometimes, one just had to take things as they were.

After all, there were a lot of people who didn't like to show the back of their tongues during daily encounters, and that apparently had to be respected as well. Nevertheless, Marcus felt rebellious again, somewhat powerful even, for even the great omniscient Count; the man who thought that he knew everything always better, and who always knew how to put Marcus in his place so cleverly, suddenly didn't seem so powerful or grand anymore, or even man enough to prove Marcus in the right, or to compliment the boy on his ingenuity.

It started to annoy Marcus even a bit. In this way, he could also pretend to be an alleged nobleman, to be a well-schooled intellectual; self-taught of course, but still...

Simply by spouting all the knowledge that he carried within him, but leaving knowledge matters of others in the middle, so that he himself could feel like the most important party in the room. Marcus still felt a certain rebelliousness bubbling up inside of him, and he wanted to put the Count in his place for once, and to let him know that Marcus might be miles behind him in terms of knowledge matters, but that he might be able to trump the man in terms of intelligence.

Nevertheless, this was also an infantile train of thought, of course, a feat of pride that could cost Marcus dearly again, not in terms of consequences or even of losing face.

No, because of the fact that the Count was a person not to be messed with, and a being always had to acknowledge its superior - on an intellectual level or on any other level for that matter, if one thought he could recognise the difference in quality...

'I can see how you look at me, Marcus,' said the Count. 'You are so transparent, so incredibly lucent, and you move through life so openly that it can almost be labeled as naive. I can see how you look at me, as is also now the case, and that's exactly how you've watched me during our last couple of meetings. I just let it come over me, and I accept it to some extent, because the only thing a real gentleman can do is laugh at ignorance, but for now I've had a bit enough of it…'

'Hmm,' mumbled Marcus softly and a little under his breath. 'Or… or are you perhaps tired of having to listen to yourself all the time…?'

'Ha!' exclaimed the Count loudly, while it startled Marcus somewhat, afraid of a certain mental outburst or afraid that he might be risking his friendship with the Count through this form of pride or admittedly through this stab under the belt.

'Ha!' exclaimed the Count for a second time, this time even louder, with a grin on his face, but also with a pedantic finger. 'Your jokes are even more outdated than the Humours Theory of Claudius Galenus!'

'Claudius! Who?' asked Marcus, bewildered.

'Claudius Galenus! The Humours Theory of Sir Claudius Galenus! The belief or opinion that every person can be categorised into four specific types. And that the corresponding mental state is caused by an excess of certain bodily fluids within the human body! And even though it is an outdated theory, it is still a doctrine that I continue to embrace because it still gives me a certain satisfaction, and also a certain insight, into the characters of my fellow human beings, a certain perspective on the many lives that I have encountered during my long, very long, wandering through life…

You, my dear Marcus, seem to have an excess of all the humours within you…

You are somewhat choleric, carrying an excess of yellow bile within you, and that is why you are often so angry and irritable with your surroundings, simply because they don't seem to hand you the opportunities that you've had in mind for so long by now, and of which you deep inside know that you could fulfill them...

You are also sanguine, with an excess of blood running through your body and with a certain enthusiasm that burns through your whole constitution because you look at life with a certain knowledge eye, and you desperately would like to make changes to your surroundings with that life energy...

You also seem to be melancholic, with too much black bile in your thunder, because you are discouraged, you just can't let go of the past, while you are also being hindered in the pursuit of your own ideals…

And finally, you are also a phlegmatic! Phlegmatic because, and despite everything just mentioned, you sheepishly observe your life from the sidelines. You seem to be fine with all that, and you are just passively waiting for others to give it a certain turn...

I know you Marcus, much better than you might realise, and I think you are a very special person, special because you seem to carry all these human states of mind within you. But don't ever think that you know more than I do, Marcus, and I'm not talking from a form of pride here.' And he gave Marcus another playful wink. Because the Count also knew that he was dealing with a hint of youthful opportunism here. Marcus had clearly been intimidated by all the knowledge that the Count managed to shake out of his sleeve so effortlessly. And Marcus, when it came to these kinds of knowledge matters, really only knew two types of people up until now.

People who knew a lot about very little. Or people who knew very little about a lot. And the Count, on the other hand? Well, the Count actually knew a lot about... Well… A lot...

Marcus, coming home to his small bedroom again as, where he almost always found refuge after his secret visits to the Count's address, thought for a moment about why he had attacked the Count with his earlier ignorance and foolishness.

Against a man who had offered him a great deal of hospitality, who had taught him a great deal of knowledge, who had even made him think differently about his surroundings, and who was also the reason why Marcus now stood in life in a certain way.

A man who in the end, even politely laughed at ignorance and who always seemed to offer his guests another shot at it, to let them try again. Marcus started to feel a bit nauseous, he really felt like an idiot at this moment, and he swallowed a small wad of despair once more that his previous ignorance had caused him. Only now, as he calmly reflected on the true motives behind his almost jealous rebellion, it began to dawn on him somewhat.

Marcus was just frustrated, irritated and also despondent, that he could hardly do anything or achieve anything in life. Exploring suspicions, making certain connections, digging through knowledge matters of which he thought they could be of use to him; all these things always seemed to fail with him. It always started with a form of enthusiasm. He then invested all of his life's energy in them. He eventually even put his heart and soul into them, after which they always came to nothing. He began to think more and more that he was basically just muddling along, running around like some type of headless chicken, while chasing exciting and sometimes even infantile inspirations, which eventually turned out to be nothing more than typical fantastic boy's adventures...

Did he actually have it in him to be a real reporter? Could he actually look at things in an objective way? Could he actually organise the connections that crossed his path? And could he save himself from staring at coffee thick? Marcus really had no idea, although he was now beginning to seriously doubt himself. But maybe he could still learn from all of this. Perhaps, with a certain dose of experience and with the passage of time, he could still master this all reasonably well?

He would simply have to learn to take his naïve and impulsive excesses into account and think at least twice before he would act on something. In any case, that at least was a given that he had learned today. He had to work on his negatives. His strongest qualities, his eagerness to learn, his ability to absorb knowledge, and ultimately also his intelligence should eventually prevail and for the time being, mask his lesser points until he had gained sufficient experience and he could establish himself on a certain intellectual plane.

But would he eventually become a real, local news reporter? Actually, only the future, very hard work, and a lot of pain and effort could ultimately tell...

Marcus had been a bit bullied at work lately, and why that was, he didn't really know exactly.

Perhaps it was because of his attitude that, especially during the last working year, had changed somewhat. Perhaps it was the fact that he had experienced a certain growth on a spiritual level in the last couple of months and that he therefore, became a potential threat to others and thus also a certain target. It could also be because he was just doing his job and never showed less, but he also never showed extra commitment to his work. With, at first glance, a kind of lack of motivation that started to dislike his colleagues more and more.

Perhaps also because Marcus hinted in this way that he actually felt too good for this line of work and could thus give his co-workers the feeling that they too, were less to him. Marcus didn't know where the wringing point lay exactly, and it didn't interest him very much either, although, of course, this change of approach had to come from somewhere. More and more often, it was like, 'Hey! Keep working, boy!' Or, 'How slow can you go, Marcus? Is the White Death coming for you again?'

But Marcus often replied in a somewhat haughty tone that the White Death largely concerned infants and toddlers and that he himself had hung up his pacifier on the willows a long time ago. Yet, this small bullying, these subtle jabs underwater, seemed to carry a certain usefulness with them. Marcus had now something to think about again, and it was, therefore also a subject that he could put to the Count on his next visit to his chateau.

'I was thinking about the white dead Count the other day,' was what he said when he once again delighted the Count with his own presence.

'Where does that folktale even come from? And why does this disease suddenly seem to have jumped from teenagers and adolescents to children and young toddlers? That's quite bitter, isn't it? Where does this phenomenon even come from...? Or rather... Where does this whole rotten disease actually come from...?!'

'Well, dear Marcus,' replied the Count.

'It's actually not a folk tale at all. Strangely enough, this disease actually exists, and I have seen it happen in all its manifestations...'

'Are you serious?!' exclaimed Marcus excitedly. 'So it's true that people who suffer from this disease also suffer from a...'

'Indeed,' added the Count. '...they suffer from a pyoderma gangrenosum, for example, from a flatulency of the abdominal region, and malabsorption of the entire intestinal system. But also from fissures of the skin and from annoying, painful pipe ulcers. To explain it a bit better... This nasty disease can cause cavities in the body annoying little tunnels that can be interconnected, and these are called pipe ulcers, also called fistulas in medical jargon if my memory is correct. Poor souls who are affected by this debilitating disease often look pale and lose weight very quickly, and this is due to a certain withdrawal of vitamins from the body. This is called, with a fancy word, malabsorption Marcus.

In the past, many adult patients, and now unfortunately also younger people, could've been seen with an unnatural bulging of the belly. This is due to an excess of gas accumulation, due to an excess of air in the intestinal region, of farts that can't make their way to their ass to put it somewhat irreverently. And I might just have the idea why and how that is...'

'How?!' asked Marcus, mesmerised, sitting on the tip of his wooden chair opposite to the Count's work desk of course, because he wanted to know everything about this frightening but also fascinating subject.

'Well, actually, it's not that complicated at all. In one way or another, there seems to have been a certain imbalance created within the human body. It's therefore often seen that certain foods that one could tolerate at first are suddenly no longer digested properly. I just have the feeling, Marcus, that these foods that are left behind in the intestinal tract undergo a rotting process because they cannot be processed properly, and thus, a surplus of toxic substances is created with all the negative effects that they entail; for both the body and the brain; for the mind as you will.

Don't pin me down on this Marcus, and the medical science field still seems to be in the dark within this area, but I just have the idea that I am in the right direction with all of this. Sometimes, I even think that the cause of all this misery lies on a mycobacterial level, and that a very annoying bacterial form is responsible for all this, and that it knows how to bind to the DNA of the host and thus can protrude its annoying effect.

And because it can even present itself as a gene and so can bind to one, it can remain hidden for years on end, even for decades, even for a whole life long, while it occasionally, or on a regular basis, continues to have its annoying effects when an unfavorable living environment within the intestinal flora - at least that for the host, but favorable for this biological intruder occurs within the abdominal region...

In that way this bacteria can feed itself and remain strong, while the body and mind of its desperate host slowly and chronically deteriorates and becomes weaker. Is the intestinal flora not in its favor but that of the host? Then this bacteria will go back into hiding and will remain in the background for a very long time, somewhere hidden within the immune system of the host, within its DNA, to resurface once more again when the odds are in its favor. And so this invalidating cycle keeps on continuing…

I'm not going to bore you with too many details Marcus, and it's just a hypothesis on my part, but I believe that I'm pretty much in the right direction with all this. I have studied the symptoms of this disease extensively, a process that I've followed meticulously, and even though it is very clear to me that this disease can be an outright horror, it is nevertheless also fascinating to experience it up close because it has taught me a lot about the functioning processes of the human body.

How to cope with this disease is now for the most part clear to me. And even though the general public still doesn't know where this disease exactly comes from and what origin it precisely harbors, and it still remains one big mystery for many, I just might think that I have found the culprit of this affliction somewhat. Finally… After years of study…'

'How do you know all these things, Count?' was what Marcus asked in surprise. 'Simply by pricking up your ears? Or by reading a lot about this kind of matter?'

'No, Marcus,' replied the Count. 'Simply because I've had this disease myself. I don't think very highly of people, Marcus. You may definitely know that, but I do have a great admiration for certain kinds of professions. For surgery, for example, and for the people who perform such a specialism. Such people are worth their weight in gold, Marcus. In my opinion, such people deserve a statue…'

'You may be right, Count,' said Marcus. 'But aren't you

talking a bit in your own alley right now? I mean... I just get the hunch that you're speaking from experience right now. Moreover... Worth their weight in gold? I've got the feeling that people like such already have enough gold in their bank accounts and that they can buy as many statues as they really want to...'

But the Count had to laugh heartily at this. 'I don't think you fully understand, Marcus. What you are right about though is that I, indeed, have had to deal with this. And that doesn't mean that I've held the scalpel in my own hand, but that they had to put me under such a tarpaulin at some point also...'

Marcus had become hungry for knowledge once more, a certain appetite for information that the Count had once again managed to arouse in him. He took out his vampire book again. And even though he'd thought that he had finished it by now, that he had read this piece from front to back, and that he had turned his back on it, there was a special reason that he had now opened it again. He sifted through the book, took a look at the many subjects, and then finally found what he was looking for. His heart pounded in his throat again, his urge to become an investigative reporter was rekindled with this, and his slightly trembling index finger followed the words that gave Marcus the feeling that he had finally found the right angle…

An angle that could be potentially groundbreaking but also a trial so dangerous that he could put his own life at risk at the same time... His trembling finger followed the following text:

How to recognise an unfortunate victim...

Although only two small holes betray the vampire's ritual, the prey will soon recognise the signs of their fate... For example, their breath starts to smell. They look pale, shy away from religious customs, and become more active at night. Most of them languish until they die, only to be reborn as new vampires themselves...

A stinking breath... thought Marcus. Which, of course was due to a malfunctioning intestinal tract and so a surplus of toxic substances, which the Count had explained to him so clearly a few days ago. Seeing pale and white... That couldn't be a coincidence either... And finally, a general malaise, one getting sick and wasting away, after which the unfortunate soul soon would die…

Indeed, Marcus was reminded of the symptoms of the White Death, characteristics that seemed to be very close to the consequences of a vampire bite. Was there perhaps another vampire living in their midst? Did Glancebury recently have a vampire as a resident, maybe? Or perhaps even much longer? Marcus' heart started beating faster again. He had to think deeply for a moment, after which he seemed to feel a certain euphoria. Marcus was now finally on a case! A case that was definitely newsworthy provided he could come up with certain proof. After all, he still handled the platen press at work, and he still went to his job reluctantly every day, even though he was right here right now and, in this very moment, almost a real local news reporter. What did he say now? A real investigative journalist! Marcus quickly abandoned this delusion, although, at the same time, he thought deeply and carefully about the village in which he was brought up and also of its inhabitants.

Because who could it be, exactly? Who had actually come to live here just after the end of the war overseas?

It could be anyone, of course, one of the returned soldiers at the time, the most obvious choice. Could someone abroad perhaps have been bitten? But Marcus felt his enthusiasm soon wane. In this way, it could be anyone, and this guessing already seemed to take a run at him because the possibilities were literally limitless... Moreover... he had an additional problem on top of that. Because Marcus was only four when 'the boys' came home, and he could remember little to nothing of that whole timeframe. And if he wanted to get to the bottom of this, then there was only one thing for him to do; then he would be forced to go back in time... He should ask his parents about this one day. Yes… during dinnertime or something. Very soon he would question those two parents of him carefully...

'Count?'

'Yes, Marcus?'

'Are you actually aware of the war that had occupied our country so many years ago? And which largely had been fought overseas?'

Although the Count had to laugh in his head for a moment. 'Of course, Marcus, what were you thinking?'

'Well...,' asked Marcus. 'What is your opinion on that case?'

'Well...,' said the Count in return.

'I adhere to the philosophy of Pallas Athena, you know, I'm not really of the approach of Ares. Warfare will probably always exist as a phenomenon, but in my opinion, the best thing, in my experience, is to bring a dispute to a standstill via a mutual consensus. Diplomacy is what it's called, Marcus! I believe that's the most beautiful thing there is! Because only in that can one truly detect style and class!' But Marcus had no idea what the Count was talking about, and he was also disappointed that the man didn't automatically make the link with the White Death or something in that line.

'Something seems wrong, Count,' said Marcus. 'It seems as if the war at the time, or at least the return of the troops, coincided with a rearing of the White Death. Could this perhaps be true? Did the soldiers accidentally bring an exotic disease back to their homeland? Or...'

But Marcus decided not to finish his sentence. What he was trying to do was to make a possible link with vampires; that a soldier, or several soldiers, had been bitten overseas, thus were passing on this sickening baton, and that they were unknowingly causing a real pandemic within their homeland of Ingland. But Marcus had long since swallowed the sentence. He had been tiring the Count too much already with the somewhat strange stories that he had been preaching lately, and maybe it was time to stay serious and realistic for once.

'Could this be right, Count?' repeated Marcus again. 'Did the soldiers accidentally bring back a disease to our country? And has it gone dormant in the meantime? With all the consequences that it entails?' The Count hadn't said anything for a while. He looked around suspiciously for a moment as if the two had potential eavesdroppers and then still said nothing. He just looked at Marcus searchingly, with that characteristic glint of him in his eyes, and he even seemed to smile at him for a moment, although his face then also got a more serious expression, and Marcus just had to make do with that apparently.

'That could very well be...' was the only thing the Count had to say about this, only to stop talking about it in all its entirety...

Marcus thought about the situation for a while during the long walk back home.

Why was the Count so shady about all this? Did he know more about it, perhaps? Why would he conceal certain things for Marcus? And why was Marcus not confided in this...?

Bertus' Long-Awaited Formula

'Okay, where should I start?' said Bertus thoughtfully. 'I have one deep litter barn, and in my case, that's one with pigs in it. This is a stable, and the word says it already, in which the manure is potted up. I cover the manure with a new layer of straw on regular intervals so that my pigs stand higher and higher after a while. And when the mixture of straw and manure has reached a certain height I go and empty the barn. I load this ripened, well-compacted manure, onto the manure cart, drive it towards the fields, and then spread it over my farmland. We have a combination of cows, pigs and one workhorse, I don't have a bull. The neighboring farmers occasionally come by with their bulls so that these animals can impregnate my cows so once in a while, and when necessary. Because you know, Marcus, a cow can only produce milk when a calf has been born. We have a number of ten cows. We use their milk ourselves, but most of it is for trade.

The calves are usually raised from yearlings to heifers, provided they are females, of course. The males are, in turn, bred again, and they either go to the slaughterhouse or they are raised to become powerful 'donors,' so to speak... You probably know what that word means, don't you, Marcus? With that smart head of yours...,' Bertus shook his own head sarcastically.

It was simply another form of contempt for Marcus, a

certain form of contempt that he had seen the man never show so openly...

'Six pigs...' continued Bertus undisturbed, and that with a certain compulsion in his voice.

'With their deep litter barn with manure for the land, while most piglets go to a neighboring pig farmer to be bred further for slaughter. The manure from the cows is generally collected on a large manure heap, which I then sell on to neighboring farmers for next to nothing.

We also have a piece of uncultivated land for crops to grow on, of course: our medium-sized field for own usage. We regularly take vegetables from it if the harvest has been kind to us, and which we also eat from ourselves sometimes. But most of these vegetables; of this green food and thus also vegetable waste, go straight to the pigs because these animals simply need a versatile and also fiber-rich diet...

Can you still follow it somewhat, Marcus? Because I'm far from finished... The grass of our land is mainly eaten by my cows and my workhorse, although that may have been a point that you'd already understood.'

Marcus almost wanted to nod along enthusiastically and at the same time, talk animatedly with his father about the ins and outs of working in the fields, but at the same time he also felt a certain sneer coming up and so also a sob within his own soul; a palpable tear deep inside him because his own father pretended to be a stranger to him. As if it was Marcus who had abandoned him, although the boy had never meant to do so in that way, at least not so explicitly. Marcus was just trying to live his life and shape it to the form that he had best in mind, although he seemed to lose all his loved ones in the process...

'Ha!' exclaimed Bertus, just as the Count had exclaimed so many times in such a manner. 'Grass...! Well... there's much more to it than just its vibrant color; to those green blades that a farmer doesn't have to do anything for apparently, simply because nature always seems to renew them on its own. Or is that perhaps the kind of farmer that you wanted to become, Marcus? One of those farmers who could just sit back in his wooden rocking chair while all the animals, all the crops, and even the soil would take care of itself, while they cultivate, feed and renew themselves, so that a new cycle would arise that you wouldn't have to do anything for at all? Is that perhaps the farmer you'd like to be, Marcus?'

'Ha!' the man exclaimed again. 'Children's stories! Child's play! Nothing more than empty fantasies and fabrications! And yes! Idleness is perhaps the right word for it! No, Marcus... Cows also need straw, to lay on, for example... And what about hay?! Something that has to be taken off the land every year, and that in every time of summer? A very precise process that mustn't fail at all? And wherein (the) fungus mustn't get too deep because then you won't be able to achieve your entire annual routine? Well, you can have a lesser year, of course, like mowing the grass a bit too early in the season for example.

That can definitely happen, and it has happened to me too once before. But it doesn't make you happy. No, not at all. And it's not very efficient either. And if you have three of such consecutive years, while at the same time making even more mistakes, then you can close down your business very quickly, Marcus, believe your old raving father...

Laziness is an eyesore within our profession. And

punctuality and perfection are things one should always and constantly try to strive for. But the very best thing is to be constantly ahead of one's own formula. Cows like to eat grass. That makes sense. But they also like to eat wheat straw and hay for a change. The horse also likes hay and wheat straw from time to time, so that's also something you should take into account.

My pigs prefer to eat green food, but they also like to eat wheat and oat grains, for example: two types of grain that you have to grow on your own specific piece of land. Can you tell me Marcus, in which months it is best to sow wheat and oats?

No, you can't Marcus, and I'll tell you why. Because you've never really paid attention during your tasks. You were always daydreaming, invariably closed in in that own head of yours.

It can be called a miracle that you've never hit us over the head with the flail during the summer months. You are often so inattentive, so extremely introverted, and so not keeping reality in mind; it's a foolish form of dealing with reality that could cost you dearly one day. After which you'll wake up one morning and open up your eyes eventually, but by then, it will probably be too late...'

Marcus felt some tears welling up and he wanted to walk up to his father and hug him fondly; a certain caress like the man had done with him so often – especially in his days as a bumping little toddler - although Marcus also knew that it was foolish to think that this man, at this given moment, would appreciate such a form of rapprochement.

It was again an infantile and also naïve thought; of a somewhat unworldly boy who was actually still a child somewhere deep in his heart. His heart felt broken when he noticed how his father continued with his story uninterruptedly. All the words fell silent, and the world seemed to pass the two by for a brief moment. Now, all there was left was an ongoing struggle between two generations that just didn't seem to understand each other. At the same time, a love bond that had cooled down intensely, and that would probably never be the same as it was once before...

Bertus continued his relentless speech, not at all paying attention to the sullen expression on his son's face. Something that had to caught the attention of the seasoned farmer, it couldn't be so otherwise, but it was also something he decided to do nothing with anyway…

'We have four hectares of land,' continued the man. 'Two and a half acres of pasture land for the horse and cows, one acre of agricultural land for the crops, and half a hectare to lay fallow. We only have one hay wagon, which also serves as a manure cart.

We have four wooden pitchforks, four hay rakes, a number of scythes and flails, and also a lot of wicker baskets; baskets of which a lot of them, albeit somewhat unfortunate, were cobbled together by your little sister. These are all the tools and aids that must be used within one's formula Marcus, within the never-ending cycle of farmwork that rears its head during every season and over the entire year. A cycle which also needs to be 'read', since we farmers are very dependent on the climate around us, while not a single year is exactly the same weatherwise...'

Marcus actually wanted to add something to this, he thought that he had discovered this aspect on his own by now already, but he kept his mouth wisely shut.

There was no more honor to be gained from Marcus after all, and he let his father's stream of words wash over him even further. Indeed, there was much more to this farmwork than he had initially thought. And now Marcus seemed to be too far behind in the knowledge that one needed to run such a farm independently. Marcus was now fifteen, sixteen almost, and that was an age frame in which an adolescent had to have a certain profession behind its name. Preferably a craft that he'd already mastered, and with quite some years of experience already. But Marcus had remained stuck with his head in the somewhat soggy clay soil on the other hand, and that also a little too skillfully...

He had carried out his imposed work a little bit too inattentively and also a little bit too half-baked from a very early age on, and this form of laziness now seemed to catch up with him. He had developed into a compromising soul by now; not knowing which direction to steer his life in, and he had taken two waterways as a result. He was now half a farmer at almost sixteen years old, and he was also half a reporter. At least… He felt that he stood with one foot in that profession by now. Marcus was basically half finished; actually as he had always felt during his yet short-lived life. Somehow not quite complete, and in his own opinion, never quite belonged anywhere. Now, he had to hear the almost angry story of a man that he had always looked up to. A man who seemed to treat him like some meaningless servant by now; like a person who was tolerated on his property provided that he tacitly did what he was told, and who had to find refuge elsewhere at the closing of the day when all the work was done again...

Was it really too late by now? was what Marcus pondered. *Is this family bond really unrecoverably broken? Has it indeed suffered such irreparable dents, scratches and also cracks? And has my so-called rebelliousness now become irreversible?*

Marcus had no idea for the umpteenth time, and he also felt confused; a state of mind as he had so increasingly experienced in the recent years. Would this man, who spoke to him in such a pedantic way, want to extend him a helping hand once more?

Could they ever have a healthy father and son bond again? Without their subcutaneous struggles all the time? And with a common vision that they both could support with a certain satisfaction...?

'A cycle that is not a year the same...,' continued his father again. 'Nevertheless... the routine work does recur every year; provided that one can read the weather elements, and provided that one can apply an instinctive estimate of a number of days to a number of weeks.

Such a routine goes a bit like this, Marcus: in autumn, we sow the wheat so that it 'overwinters,' and in spring, it grows into a complete plant. The summer is therefore, dominated by the wheat harvest. With our flails we attack the whole thing, beat the grains out of the ears, and then the wicker baskets and the wind come into play; to separate the proverbial wheat from the chaff. The remaining wheat stalks are then collected, they are bundled, and they are then stored in a dry place, so that they can serve as straw feed for both the cows and the horse. But beware!' And Bertus looked at his son with a haughty look. 'The summer months are also dominated by haymaking. Something that you've also helped with a couple of times but that you probably didn't quite get your head into.

We join forces as soon as the grass is high enough and when the razor-sharp scythe goes over it again. We then lay the cut grass in long rows so that when the sun rises, it makes it difficult for dew to creep in. After that we let these rows of grass dry on the land for a couple of days.

Provided, of course, that one has felt the weather somewhat and one can gauge whether there will be no rain looming in the atmosphere. Finally, we drive into the land, we load these rows of dried grass onto the hay wagon and then unload them again in the hay barn in our yard. Endive, beets, and cauliflower are usually sown around mid-spring, so that we can remove them from the land around autumn again. After all… it is nutritious food to get through the vicious winters, these crops have a long shelf life if stored properly and in a cool place, and it is also excellent green food for the pigs. A bit of the same story applies to kale and kohlrabi. Spinach is a very easy vegetable on the other hand, and it can be sown in all seasons, except in winter. Something that is very easy to remember, and also a vegetable that requires very little care, and which carries a certain laziness with it that will probably appeal to you to the fullest…

The remains of the vegetables that remain, largely due to personal use or otherwise, go to the compost heap behind the pigsty. A brownish belt that you have probably come across before when strolling around our yard. This so-called compost breaks itself down slowly, and so it becomes a black, crumbly substance that can be very well used to enrich the soil structure of our agricultural land with, and in this way, to do even better justice to the crops that grow on it...

Our cows are twice a day milked; the first time very early in the morning, and the second time somewhere later in the afternoon. The milk then goes into large milk cans that I put in front of our house and which are collected by a milk porter every day, except on Sundays.

It may already be clear to you, Marcus, that a person in a profession like this is—and that's certainly so in my case—partly dependent on others. From the cattle farmers, for instance; those surrounding farmers who occasionally come by with their bulls to get my cows impregnated.

I'm dependent on the milk porter, of course, and also on the abattoir, where I bring my animals sometimes and when I'm really in need of money.

But I'm also dependent on the surrounding farmers whom your mother regularly gets her vegetables from, to be able to put them on the table for us in the evening, cooked and well. Or from the vegetables that I get from them myself if I'm once again short on green food for my pigs. Other people are dependent on my milk, Marcus, but myself for green fodder, for example, because my arable land is not that big, and the biggest part of this land is really intended for grain; grain to maintain this cycle, this routine, this formula…

You are partly dependent on others, Marcus, in this profession, you shouldn't want to do everything on your own always. You shouldn't want to be all alone in the world always…'

And Bertus looked at his only son with watery eyes for a moment, seemed to want to hug him right there on the spot, just like Marcus wanted to do so earlier, even though nothing seemed to happen between them in this area.

It could've been a small chance of reconciliation, and that they both might have cut off simultaneously simply because they couldn't read each other's minds. And it was perhaps also too early, or perhaps even too late, to bury the hatchet now that lied so gleamingly between them so seemingly. Nevertheless, his father—albeit in his own down to earth way—seemed to take the first step forward in this regard: 'You could do all this...' said the man but in a somewhat melancholic tone, '...all this that I've just told you Marcus, write down in your own spare time and for yourself, and perhaps even categorize all this information.

And it might even become a well-selling book In addition to your farm work... Focused on the still young and also still somewhat inexperienced farmer. And since with the passage of time, all these agricultural processes will also change, you could choose to include all of this information in your own writing; a book that you could always work on! A book that is never really finished! Wouldn't that be something, Marcus?!'

And Bertus finally walked away, although he did say one more thing in his steps; a razor-sharp conclusion to a very lengthy story: 'But don't you ever think that farmwork is not science, boy. It is science! Pure science!'

It actually had been a very boring story that Bertus had managed to serve up to his son.

Marcus may have acted a little bit silly, but he also understood that his father was trying to put him on the spot a bit. In the end, everyone was in the right again, except Marcus of course. Apparently, there was science behind everything whether it was applying knocks to leaden seals to qualify high-quality cloth. Whether it was the shuttle with which spun yarn was chased through the warp. Or even the way in which a horse was harnessed to a farmer's cart. There was skill and knowledge behind everything so it seemed.

Maybe he could use this fact for a good piece in the newspaper soon? To create some type of awareness among people who thought that everything went by itself? That everything was a matter of course? But who was Marcus actually fooling? He himself had always been a person who had never thought about such things before. He himself had to learn such things from the people around him; from people who had pointed them out to him so explicitly when he was moaning and groaning again, while walking with his miserable soul under his arm for the umpteenth time.

And to publish their life experiences and also their life insights as if they came from Marcus' own hand would almost be a kind of appropriation; some kind of mental plagiarism...

No, he would certainly keep all this in the back of his mind and perhaps use it again someday, but not before he himself had tasted some from these life lessons.

Not before he could say, and that in all good conscience, that he had mastered some form of science himself, just like all the other Glanceburies had once done...

The Gulden Gazette

Everything was science, which was quite clear by now, but did that make the things that Marcus was dealing with anything less? Marcus knew about things that his father, for example, knew nothing about, but he, on his turn, didn't talk to this man in a pedantic way, now did he?

Marcus was also concerned with a certain science, and how to interpret it exactly was difficult to say, but perhaps it was the science of life? Marcus would notice it all in the near future. He would eventually find out where his own ship would run aground. He had to hold on to this boldness for now and not let go of this belief in himself—something that he had always carried deep within—not for anyone...

Marcus aspired to be a reporter, and whether he would succeed in this only the future could tell, although Marcus was also a reader above all; a skill that shouldn't be underestimated.

It was a second ability, in addition to his supposed writing skills, and also a quality in which he could always continue to take cognizance, which could give him the feeling that he didn't fully belong to the plebs. Not only did a lot happen in Marcus' small, perhaps somewhat meaningless life, but at the same time, a lot also happened in the country itself and social developments began to follow each other up at an increasingly rapid pace. Marcus therefore, read his own newspaper, *The*

Gulden Gazette, with a certain eagerness. He didn't want to miss any of the information, and he wanted to stay informed about everything in the meantime. He was now of the opinion that he wasn't that different from the Count at all.

For even if everything were to fall away from Marcus, and the ground was to be pulled out from under his feet again, he would at least have that which the Count had so frequently instructed him within the last couple of years and which no one could ever take away from him: the great knowledge that Marcus had gained in the meanwhile, and what he pursued once more by opening his own newspaper, and by reading her articles carefully. The newspaper articles read the following: they spoke of a strong wind blowing over this great and also strong nation and of changes that were felt by all of its citizens; of all of those who came from its wind corners:

A Shift in Prosperity; A Shift in Power?

It should be very clear to all that powerful noble families still undisputedly occupy the first place in state and society. However, with the rise of the affluent bourgeoisie, the power between the two seems to be increasingly blurring. The gentry, also known as the landed gentry, seems to be gaining more and more respectability. This mainly concerns professions such as doctors, lawyers, rentiers, and rich merchants. Real landlords still enjoy the most respect, but for how long?

This is a development that the Crown and its relatives are currently considering. Appropriate measures and laws will therefore, be implemented to accommodate everyone in this, and to keep Ingland in the saddle as a monarchy; a Royal Order that has made this country what it is today and that should never be forgotten...

Marcus nodded enthusiastically at this. He now understood that there was a power struggle going on in the country; one that would undoubtedly be settled by the ruling and also incumbent power, and he then greedily began to read the next newspaper article:

An Embellishment of the Cities of Ingland

In the larger cities of Ingland there is more and more a revival going on of the streetscapes.

Whether it is in Cinterbury or in our own Light Town, we can see a certain advancement everywhere; a certain modernization of the surrounding infrastructure. More and more often, and in more and more parts of these large cities, we see lighting appear, sewerage and water pipes are being installed more often, as well as the construction of decent paving, and even something as simple as house numbers to replace the old wooden signs with.

The government, but also the population, is increasingly aware that such civilized developments come with certain advantages. For example, people seem to be more aware of their own behavior within these streetscapes. People experience the increasing hygiene that comes with a cleaner living environment. And people feel more and more connected to social and cultural life. It is therefore not surprising that more and more artistic and learned societies pop up like mushrooms. In more and more coffee houses, one can read the newspaper, many new clubs are opening their doors for some nighttime entertainment, and in more and more centers, one can attend lectures or immerse oneself in other forms of liberal recreation. These are all developments that will only continue from here on, and which will make Ingland's capitals a refuge for all of those who want to enrich themselves socially, culturally, and also intellectually...

Marcus found this a nice development; cultural and also artistic gatherings in which he would also like to get involved someday. One day, his time would surely come. One day, he too would join such a self-developing audience, but for now, he read the third headline of this revealing newspaper. One that was a lot more simplistic, actually no more than a statement, but which was also exciting to read and which conveyed a social risk that always had to be taken into account to some extent, unfortunately...

Shameless Pickpockets!

Be on your guard! Venerable, and also noble visitors, who are visiting the seaside resorts of our illustrious coasts, as well as those who visit the hot springs that lay deeper within the country. It is well known to you all that, moving within these higher social circles, one appears here 'naked.' That is, without the swords belonging to your particular ranks, in order to create a friendly atmosphere and to be free of etiquette for a while.

Now, this fact is also known to shameless thieves and pickpockets, who move within your circles without any embarrassment and who are lurking on the priceless possessions that you are unsuspectingly carrying with you, awaiting for a moment to snatch these away from under your white smeared noses.

This warning may apply to the visitors, but even more to these unwelcome bathers:

Be very wary that thieving and theft are still punishable by death! Anyone caught red-handed will be hanged from the highest tree or eventually end up on the scaffold! We can't, will not, and won't tolerate this kind of behavior! This message also applies to young adults, as well as to children; to anyone who cannot keep their hands to themselves!

To all the decent beachgoers among us: keep your eyes open and your bags closed.

Keep the coastline as clean and as pleasant as possible; for everyone to enjoy in the near or distant future!

Marcus didn't really have a thought about this. Well, actually he did. He himself would never stoop to such an uncivilized level. What was actually going on with these types of people? Didn't thieves realize that, by stealing other people's possessions, they were immediately duping these individuals? Didn't they understand that these obnoxious behaviors also brought negative and destructive chain reactions with them? That they could put people to shame? And that these victims could gradually lose their trust in their fellow man? And thus, eventually, everyone was affected by this? No, Marcus had not a single good word to say about these kinds of people, about these kinds of culprits. And if he ever got into trouble himself, and maybe even ended up homeless, then he would just hold up his hand, maybe steal a loaf of bread so now and then, but never ever the jewelry or any other important or valuable possession of a person.

Thieves evidently didn't thought thoroughly about their misconducts. They evidently didn't thought deeply about the consequences of their own actions. And Marcus wouldn't be surprised if the emotional intelligence level of such people lay somewhere within the lower reaches of the human mental spectrum.

A Reduction in Metropolitan Excesses

The wave of alcohol abuse, which in recent years has taken place in our unimaginably growing capital, now seems to have finally reached stagnation. Partly by regulating the number of inhabitants, as well as by implementing the law of 1751, a treatable point has finally been achieved. Alcoholic sales points have also been tightened up. And with the introduction of both coffee and tea, alcohol consumption has been reduced and infectious diseases have largely been suppressed, because the water for all these pleasure drinks must first be boiled before it is processed into an end product, and thus can be consumed.

We would therefore like to draw everyone's attention to keep your own alcohol consumption in check, and to behave yourselves on the streets of Ingland. Extreme public drunkenness is subject to a local ordinance, as well as a fine, and sometimes even a prison sentence if repeated offenders do not care about the written - or unwritten - rules that apply within the public order.

Marcus couldn't agree more with this and he closed his favorite newspaper again, simply because he had finished reading it.

Mother Takes Marcus Aside in the Small Side Room

It was clear by now that Marcus was going for a certain authorship. Time was running out more and more, and a tension—actually more a form of panic—began to prevail within the family of the Pritchards. Mother pulled Marcus by his ears into the small side room once more; into the room where 'grown up stuff' was always discussed, or certain matters that concerned the whole family. Marcus began to feel a certain aversion to this small space; for this small side room that used to be able to raise a certain mystery within him, and which he was even a bit shivery for in earlier times, but which he now only found childish. His mother spoke to him with a certain desperation in her voice, and just like with his father the other day, Marcus also let this parental story wash over him…

'Don't you understand Marcus…,' was what his mother said. 'Don't you understand that this is his biggest nightmare?! His only son who keeps refusing to take over the family business? To take over the legacy of the Pritchard's? A legacy that has never been broken in the last two hundred years? Think carefully, Marcus! Our family branch might end up with you…' His mother cried big tears of grief, and Marcus did the same that night in his bed.

Why does it all have to depend on me?! He thought with frustration. *Why can't I not, just like so many others out there, dig my heels in the sand and then wait and see when all the tumult blows over again?! It is unfair, I tell you!! Unfair!!!!*

Marcus picked up the vampire book from his bookshelf, took a good look at it, and then threw it against the wall opposite to him with a loud bang. The book fell apart into several pieces, and many pages were now scattered on the floor of his bedroom; a place where his boyhood dream had once started, but that by now had become a nightmare.

He nevertheless still gave himself some courage; only audible to himself, somewhere deep inside the epiphysis, deep inside the pineal gland, there within the so-called seat of the soul; a very small piece of brain tissue for which current brain science didn't have a name yet, still knew nothing about, let alone about its workings. Many thoughts echoed through Marcus' constitution. They seemed to take over his brain partially, they were carried along through nerve pathways with lightning speed, they then flowed through his veins and muscles, and they finally made his fists bulge into weapons of decisiveness. No one had ever been able to hear these words, about these thoughts of him, or notice this whole flow of energy.

Not even the bats fluttering outside that, with their ultrasonic sounds and through their use of echolocation, were trying to pluck the insects out of the air in their hasty manners.

Yet, Marcus' decision was very clear by now, and anyone who thought they knew Marcus a little, might have been able to pluck these words out of the atmosphere in one way or another. This inaudible, and very refined train of thought, sounded a bit like this:

Always stay true to yourself, Marcus, because hardly anyone can touch the truth, even if they wanted to. But if you think you can, then you should just go for it, and do it! Even if it costs certain sacrifices! Even though if everyone will vilify you for it! And even though if you eventually will succumb to it!

Marcus cried himself again to sleep that night, secretly hoping that the next morning would be different and secretly hoping that the next morning would not come at all...

The next day, he thought about the conversation that he and his mother had had the night before. He and his father were farmers, not miners, and apparently they, and that for a very long time, had been taken for granted within the small town of Glancebury.

Of course, farmers were also necessary in the area after all, and their products were definitely very welcome and also indispensable, but they also and often had the idea of just dangling around somewhat; like the third wooden spare wheel mounted on the back of a farmer's cart. Weren't they seen as real men within the village, perhaps? Bertus seemed to have been less bothered by this all than, for example, his own father; Marcus' grandpa. Bertus had simply inherited this inferior complex from his own old man, and now he tried to pass it - unconsciously probably - onto his own son, so it seemed. The cloth weaver had called this the 'dejected tradition' years ago, but Marcus wasn't planning to fall for such ignorance, and he was now very close to actually saying this to his parents, and then especially to his father. Although, in the end this would also be somewhat unreasonable, and also too easy a way. And Marcus just wasn't like that, Marcus simply just wasn't that false and vicious, and at that very moment, Marcus suddenly realized that he and his father had much more in common than they could ever have initially suspected.

They now both seemed to be pioneers in the midst of a pack of yes-men. His own father had also managed to hold onto his own, to have managed to keep his back straight in all of this; within an environment where he actually wasn't welcome at all, and in that respect no one could have understood Marcus better to this point than his very own father. It was like a boat that had been completely missed, that now had even drifted unmanned, and that in the distance - as if all this wasn't worse enough - had also sailed on the cliffs with creaking sounds of splintered wood...

Glancebury's Hidden Secret

'Is there anything wrong, Marcus?' was what the Count asked him, because he seemed to be able to read the boy's despair from his face. 'You look so sad.' But Marcus didn't react to this, didn't say anything at all, and he was actually just staring into infinity.

'A while ago, we talked about four types of people Marcus, about the humorous teachings of Claudius Galenus, and to be fair, these four types can actually be divided into three subclasses. Well, actually into four subclasses because the so-called alchemists are also a part of them. Do you still remember this, Marcus? That we've talked about this a while ago?'

Marcus nodded, while still staring into a certain abyss; with a look on his face that was smeared with this oblivion; a certain state of mind that life, with its often confusing and also unpredictable twists and turns, could regularly evoke within a person...

'Now, let me tell you about the first three types of people, Marcus. People in all their manifestations that you, myself, and all of us, encounter so often within our daily strolls.

Look, Marcus… life is quite magisterial; truly ma-ster-ful, and it is such a shame that this goes unnoticed so often, simply because there are so many dimwits walking around.

In my experience there are three branches of people on the other hand: people that can see the bigger picture. People who don't see the bigger picture or who deliberately close themselves off from it. And people who deliberately oppose this entire line. The first type of people have the hardest time, Marcus because they are constantly being pushed to the ground by the second type. And the third group of people, you ask yourself now? Well, this group is eventually the laughing third, and they just stand by and observe because they are somewhat maniacal. They seem to feed themselves on schadenfreude, and they also seem to carry little to no compassion for the two prior groups. Life is a game within all of its intrinsicality, Marcus, within its core, and it is a blessing when you realize that, but it is also a curse at the same time. Because if you understand this fact through a certain wisdom, and you try to bend the rules of the earthly game in a more positive way, then it is evident that you will be thwarted in your steps. Or that you may end up all alone simply because you don't have any fellow players within your team. That's how earthly life works somewhat, Marcus; that's how life, which unfortunately has become a game over time, is somewhat structured. And loneliness is ultimately the prize of a true whistleblower; that is ultimately the true destiny of someone like you or me...'

It didn't seemed to be going very well with the Count lately. The man hadn't been feeling very well for a while apparently, and Marcus tried to cheer the lord of his castle up a bit with some substantive conversation and with his own, now again, cheerful mood.

'Can you tell me something about the problem that apparently has been going on in Glancebury for years by now?

And that largely has been brewing behind the scenes?

About the apparent feud between the former miners and that between the farmers? Of whom most of them have settled in this village later on? Is this problem perhaps really there? Is it perhaps a matter of territorial demarcation? A taking of the land by the farmers that the original residents believe only they can claim?' But the Count slightly shook his head.

'The only thing I can say for certain about this incident, Marcus is that...' And the Count tried to choose his words carefully. 'Well, let me put it this way... It seems that the miners are trying to cover up their own guilt by shifting it off to the peasants, although no one really seems to be blamed here eventually, and in this matter, Marcus. Some people are simply somewhat weak. And real people, real personalities, can often be recognized by one thing and one thing only.'

'About what then, Count?' asked Marcus with interest.

'Those that from time to time can acknowledge their own mistakes... because if everyone would do that on a regular basis, Marcus, oh boy then...'

And the Count suddenly stopped talking about it, because the entire sentence simply didn't needed to be continued. Although Marcus could nevertheless notice the follow-up sentence on the Count's old, somewhat steely, and now also haggardly pale face:

'...Oh boy, then you would not only get tolerance, but also a mutual understanding, and that into infinity...'

Marcus found it a somewhat woolly story, nevertheless one full of wisdom, and he himself seemed to have figured everything out by now. 'You don't have to tell me anything anymore, Count,' was what the boy said. 'Because I know by now what, or who, you are... You are an educated genius! The well-read aristocrat who sits high above in his ivory-decorated tower! But also a restless soul! A person who could wrap any person around its lank finger, but also one who will never find true love himself!'

And Marcus reinforced this statement by resolutely extending his own index finger to him.

'That Count! That is what you ultimately are!' And the Count in the end? The Count in the end could do nothing more but nod, slightly smile, and only confirm to this sharply put saying by Marcus...

Things were going very badly for the Count by now, a plummeting of his health that seemed to have taken place overnight. Marcus was very worried about his good old friend. He tried to cheer him up with some good conversations, with some jokes here and there, and by making him warm cups of tea, but it seemed as if the man was no longer receptive to this all. He looked pale and gray, was severely emaciated, and there was suddenly an emptiness behind his eyes that Marcus had never noticed in the man before. The Count looked up one last time from behind his desk, he then looked straight into Marcus' eyes—with what seemed to be his last strength— and Marcus' eternal companion then said the following:

'I don't have that long anymore, Marcus… I can just feel it... I... I need someone to take over from me... To pass the baton to… I don't have that long left, I'm afraid... The burden has become too heavy... Unbearable even... I am tired... Dead tired...'

And the Count decided, right there on the spot, to share his spiritual inheritance with the young Marcus. A legacy that consisted of telling one of the greatest secrets that he'd carried with him for so long now. It wasn't his inner soul stirrings this time or his deepest, darkest secrets, which he undoubtedly carried a lot within. Nor where the alleged nobleman got his title exactly from, how on earth he could own such a vestibule; such a splendid chateau, and why he actually was who he was. No, none of that. He would now give the little reporter in the making a revelation that would leave this young scion from the Pritchard family tree knocked back steeply.

About something that had always haunted Marcus and those close to him and that could shake the small village of Glancebury to its foundations. Marcus pricked up his ears, his eyes got wider and wider with every word that the Count spoke to him, and at that very moment, a little piece of history had actually already been written...

Marcus now stood in front of the Count's grave. In one hand he held a master key, and in his other hand a black rose. Marcus thought deeply about how he would bring all this.

His potential choices were well-considered, and he finally decided - and after much deliberation - to just go through with it. The Count was now dead, and Marcus now finally had a real story. He wrote and wrote, and he wrote even some more, until his left hand could do no more. But no matter how many sheets of paper he had used, the pieces of text never seemed quite good enough. Not good enough was perhaps the wrong word for it; not worthy enough.

Because his experiences of the last two years had the potential to become such a good story, that he didn't exactly knew how to tackle it properly. Should he reveal the Count's personality to the fullest? A man who had only been reviled and taunted by those in the outside world? Did Marcus actually grant the reader this favor? And was Marcus' ambition to become an established writer so grand that he wanted to reveal the special bond that he had shared with the Count unquestioningly? It could've been a posthumous abashment of the close covenant that they had shared together. Marcus' hand was still itching, the sheets of paper continued to ogle, and the ink in the small jar never seemed as pure as it did now, although he decided to leave it at that for this evening. Marcus lay on his bed, somewhat depressed. It was a wonderful story, potentially, but at the same time also a dilemma. Why couldn't things come to him by chance? Just as it did so often with Sunday's children?

He shook his head firmly and then sighed very deeply for a moment. He had to come up with something for this...

Marcus knew a lot by now; a whole lot. And even though it was only a fraction of what the Count had known himself, and not everything that Marcus had heard from him fully grasped, it was nevertheless a lot more knowledge than many other contemporaries of his possessed. Marcus finally felt important for once. Not necessarily better than anyone else, but that he too could finally take a certain spot; that he too deserved a certain place beneath the communal sun. At first glance, a figure that wasn't very special, perhaps even somewhat meaningless, but also someone with more to offer than one could suspect from the outside. Someone who - if it really came down to things - could be looked up to, who could be learned from, and who could perhaps even be built on.

And even though he was still that somewhat lanky farm boy; a character that someone could just walk past by on the streets, and a figure perhaps not even to be greeted in his or her steps, slumbered in him also a realization which suited him. A realization that he had always embraced and that he had always felt in his still young life; from that very first time when he had noticed the smoke of Light town in the very distance against the horizon, and when he sometimes—if the weather permitted on that particular day—could even catch a glimpse of its looming and towering structures.

Marcus was content with the life that he was leading now; still caught up between two fires somewhere; between the two ropes that were pulling very palpably at him and that were still calling him some kind of harlequin. It seemed to be a satisfaction that was growing on to him recently; finding himself within a society that seemed to look down on him, and which he left in a certain disillusion but which he nevertheless looked at from high above like how an ibex—the Count's favorite totem animal—that would do when it stood on a mile-high rocky outcrop once more.

Marcus now felt a certain satisfaction in all the setbacks that he had experienced so far; realizing that being looked down on from time to time didn't necessarily make a person weaker. And that could provide a human being even certain insights that could never be found so easily within the conventional masses. Marcus was now finally satisfied, that was clear for now, although he still wasn't completely satisfied with the communal place in which he occupied a spot. After all, he would never feel better than anyone else, that wasn't simply in his nature, but he did feel himself too good for the craft - or rather said - for the production process in which he had become a small cog in for almost four years now; always toiling away at the platen press; with a head full of knowledge, wisdom and also interesting facts, which seemed to fall so silent with every thump of the heavy top plate on the smeared iron base.

Marcus was more, could more, and wanted more. And, of course, a certain respect for the resilient soul that could resign to such a monotonous and discipline-devouring task, but young Marcus could no longer. No, young Marcus could no more. A young man who was pulled out from under the clay and who simply wanted more than just mud and soil in his existence. And who symbolically craved the minerals and the other deep materials that lay hidden within this sediment. Marcus had already opened a lot of newspapers by now. And he knew that time, its developments, and so also its changes, thundered on ruthlessly and inevitably. A lot was happening in the country by now, although Glancebury seemed to miss all of this. As if this small hamlet was still cut off from all of the national problems outside; resting in her own little bubble of friendly simplicity; a calm however, that was soon to be disturbed…

'Extra! Extra!' It sounded from everywhere in the busy courtyards of Light Town.

'Come and read it all! Come and read it now! For only three pence you too will find out about this grave incident!' A very well-dressed man, who might even be of nobility, walked up to the newspaper vendor in a controlled manner. He pressed three small coins into the boy's hand, looked at the front page of *The Gulden Gazette*, and then greedily began to read.

The front page of the newspaper read the following In large bold letters:

The Deception of Glancebury!
A Pretext Like No Other!

Due to the war that was waged overseas roughly forty years ago, and the coal that was so desperately needed at the time, there has been a shortage of raw materials within the acreage of Ingland. After all, cokes can be made from coal; cokes that are so desperately needed for the production of steel, and steel that could be used in the arms industry again, of course, and thus in war.

Now, this may not even be such a big revelation - after all, many of you may know about this subject - although it is true that the smaller ones among us are often weighed down by the larger ones, and that hasn't been any different for what happened to a small, almost meaningless, remote Inglish hamlet. Meaningless, I hear you think? Indeed...

A used mine is often pumped dry and thus stripped of its water as a rule, although this never seemed to have happened in the mine of Glancebury.

Probably because this would've been a time-consuming job, and also because it would've cost a lot of money.

A necessary measure that has never been implemented because there simply wasn't any more honor to be gained from this mine. The raw materials were simply consumed and used up, they had served their purpose within the war well, the mine no longer had any priority, and the small miners' village next to it was therefore left to its fate...

Now, this isn't even that special at all. And a laziness of the State that has probably happened before. What is very bad, however - and the ruling government at the time must have known this - is the following: Everyone knows that during the mining process, and this is certainly the case with coal, harmful substances are being released.

A logical continuation is therefore that, when a mine is no longer used or needed, it must be pumped dry in order to not let these harmful substances run freely. Unfortunately, this has never been the case for the mining village of Glancebury, and of course for its mine itself...

Not long after the mine had been vacant, and not long after the war with foreign countries had been fought and the troops had gradually returned home, a phenomenon had suddenly arisen that was named the white death.

A terrible and also debilitating disease that first mainly affected the elderly and middle-aged, after that adolescents and teenagers, and not much later even very young toddlers and infants.

This whole incident was dismissed as a curse. It had become like a folktale. And some even attributed it to the battle that had been waged—as some punishment from above—by waging a war that should never have been fought in the first place. A few dared to say this openly, but many played silently with these thoughts in their minds.

The white death had thus become a taboo; something that people preferred not to talk about, and which managed to push the unfortunate victims of this disease even more into isolation.

It was also not talked about, and it was also covered up by means of a social prohibition, because some actually knew where the problem came from, and this could've caused certain embarrassment or could've duped certain people— people who were holding high offices at the time, but also a number of prominent Glanceburies probably—names that I cannot mention, simply because I do not know them—and which is of no importance whatsoever, because it isn't in my intentions to discredit certain people, but more so because I am simply trying to raise a problem that needs to be addressed and that eventually needs to be solved...

I can tell you with fact, dear readers of this article, that the white death isn't just some made-up folktale, and it also isn't some shadowy punishment imposed from above.

It behaves very real within in our midst, and it can even be substantiated in a scientific—and also in a logical way.

The problem for all this lies with the abandoned mine itself. The problem is, therefore, with the groundwater, with the crops that come from the surrounding lands, and therefore also with all the cattle; especially with the cows that eat from these grounds. They eat from the ever-growing grass which is so saturated with this moisture filled with toxic substances.

It is therefore, not surprising that this disease is increasingly affecting infants. After all, there is a social development going on within society in which mothers are also increasingly working outside of their homes.

They seem to breastfeed their children less and less often, while at the same time switching to the bottle; to a warmed-up bottle of cow's milk; A substance which is actually meant for calves, not for growing human infants.

In addition... milk which is therefore also quite contaminated.

If one would do random checks, and if one would investigate the groundwater in—and around Glancebury, one would find out that it contains huge amounts of sulfur and phosphorus; certain chemicals that are the byproduct of coal mining.

This also implies that the mine itself wasn't completely empty and dried up at the time it was abandoned, so there must still be large amounts of coal hidden somewhere...

And even though these chemicals aren't necessarily that toxic in small amounts, and can therefore only cause some abdominal pain, nausea, and also vomiting, a constant exposure to these substances can, of course, be disastrous for the human body over time, especially for the young and sick. These are the substances that the residents of Glancebury have been ingesting for many decades now, and therefore, also gradually.

And if one isn't strong enough. If one doesn't have enough biological resistance. Or if one is receptive to these substances in some way then a certain susceptibility, a certain vulnerability, can be seen that will only increase over time and with age.

Then one could see symptoms as paleness, an annoying distended abdomen, an increasing fatigue, and finally, a serious intestinal malabsorption which will often result in death...

The government must have known this all along. However, she has meticulously covered this up because finances simply take precedence over human well-being, and there is little credit to be gained from a small and also insignificant town as Glancebury is.

All this is very bad, and all this must be drastically remedied, if we want to keep the crowd of Inglishmen—or the inhabitants of Glancebury for that matter—healthy enough, and if we don't want to have a further weakening of our peoples by means of physical vulnerabilities that will become even more common in their biological systems as the years go by, and that will eventually affect even larger numbers of the Inglish demographic…

I therefore appeal to all the soil researchers out there to test the groundwater in—and around this mine. I call on the government to finally drain the mine of its water and to get rid of all the remaining coal, no matter how much effort or money this may cost.

And then it may very well be that the white death and all of its frightening side stories will disappear like snow before the sun…

My name is the anonymous whistleblower.

And this here, dear readers, is what I call: the deception of Glancebury. I thank you sincerely for reading…

People put their newspapers away again, many trumpets were blown, and many a week, this ill was still talked about. Both among the paupers in the dilapidated backstreets of Light town, as well in the upper echelons and even in The House of Commons - there where the Inglish parliament resided.

Who was this new emerging talent? Who was this bold news reporter who had already caused a small schism within the nation and fatherland? Almost all newspapers wanted to bring in this new talent by now. Even newspapers of the surrounding provinces; province names that Marcus had only heard of before but where he had never set foot in once. Marcus was now fully praised, but at the same time also fully condemned for his revelations. The Pritchard family was looked down upon even more by their fellow villagers, and Marcus' behavior also started to change because of this. Partly thanks to the wrath of his father because all of this had been brought about by his own rebellious scion. And the man, as always, never said it aloud, but Marcus could simply read the words from his look; a look that the man had shown him so often in the last couple of years. An angry, somewhat annoyed look, which had begun to mark his face at the time of Marcus' theses; at the time of his personal statements that he, with a certain pleasure, had nailed to the sturdy wooden gate of the abattoir so many years ago.

One day, Bertus approached his son, and it didn't even take an intervention from his mother's side or for a meeting within the small side room...

'Is this what you wanted so badly, Marcus?!' the man shouted in a desperate tone.

'A preferred fame over that of your own family?! Above that of your own flesh and blood?! Above our so precious, and also much needed, livelihood?! I...' And even though the man didn't say his last words, Marcus could still read them from his piercing eyes:

I... I am deeply ashamed to call you my son... His mother had also joined him in the meantime. She had already heard Bertus' words in the far distance. She looked at her son pitifully for a moment, after which she followed her husband Bertus in his footsteps...

A lot had changed in the quiet village of Glancebury, and that seemed to have a certain hold on Marcus because his behavior began to change even more.

Marcus began to withdraw himself even further, he became even quieter than before, and he kept his thoughts even more to himself, even more than he had always done so before.

Marcus was now finally a great reporter. His dream had

finally been achieved. And his life's task was now finally fulfilled. Many newspapers now wanted to employ him. Even the newspapers from the far corners of the country; from provinces, cities, and also places, that Marcus had never heard of before but where he might always have wanted to live. However, there was still one little problem lying around the corner; just one petite tricky point of discussion, a very small dilemma within this beautifully sketched picture of Marcus' near future: because… Where was that beautiful dreamer from Glancebury anyways? Where had that young, vibrant Marcus actually gone...

Epilogue

Marcus had disappeared one day and no one knew where he exactly was, where he could've been, or whether he was actually alive at all.

The years passed by with time. His parental home was eventually sold. And the family tree, which bore the name Pritchard, was increasingly forgotten. The village of Glancebury was still a peaceful community, within quotation marks, and it still thrived entirely on agriculture, on the dairy trade, and some other small crafts.

The years flew by, and Marcus' revealing article in the newspaper had long since become old news; almost forgotten news from an unknown reporter who was popularly known as the anonymous whistleblower. A person who had managed to address something very important but who, together with all his revelations, had also vanished into thin air. Even the government was eventually forgiven, simply because the majority of people also understood that, in the long run, the masses had a greater interest than a number of civilians.

A genius from the Lower Countries invented a more effective pump not long after Marcus' disappearance; a pump with which the problem around Glancebury could be solved very quickly, very easily, and also very coincidentally, and the mine could thus actually be drained. A very strange turn of events indeed, and it was almost as if fate itself managed to make a funny game out of all of this. More and more social developments were being implemented in everyday life and in the environment.

Even life itself became easier, because more and more discoveries and also inventions came to light, and thus less effort was required for the same amount of labor and for the same amount of production. This allowed even more time to be freed up for scientific thinking, which literally changed the social landscape. The transport revolution also began a spectacular advancement. And while in the past, a lot of transport took place over waterways, now more and more railways appeared, and the quality of vehicles was also improved, which reduced travel times unprecedentedly. Travelling was not only faster by now, it also cost less money, and the same was true for the transport of goods.

With all this, important conditions were fulfilled for the essential industrial revolution, which had already largely begun in Ingland, even in Marcus' time, and which soon would spread to other parts of the continent.

As a result of increased population growth and falling prices of agricultural products, an incentive was formed for the development of more intensive and also more cost-effective methods on the already existing agricultural land.

The import of new crops, and the export of domestic grain, for example, formed new trade relations that made the economy of Ingland flourish even more; new capital was released, so to speak. Various cities could thus be embellished with parliamentary authorization more often. Dilapidated centers were increasingly cleaned up, and more and more theaters, banquet halls, and also public gardens, appeared in the blooming streetscapes.

Four developments played a key role in this industrial revolution: the trade, agriculture, transport and finally, the production of goods. The share of the traditional Inglish export product cloth decreased more and more over time, but that of other domestic products, on the other hand, seemed to be rising again. It had often been said that thanks to this growth of trade, sufficient capital at a low interest rate became available for the industrial revolution.

On the other hand, this was, of course also made possible by colonization and by the shameless exploitation of other countries that, in the fields of their own development, could have used some extra help… Although that kind of delicate information was often withheld from the avid newspaper reader of course.

New crops increasingly enriched the fields of Ingland due to an agricultural revolution. These new vegetables, which of course, could also serve as animal feed, ensured that more and more cattle could get through the winter, and that in turn not only resulted in more meat, it also ensured that large parts of agricultural land no longer had to lay fallow.

Technical agricultural tools—again from the inventive Lower Countries—such as the threshing machine, were also of great importance. After all, one no longer had to take a swing with the flail against the harvested ears in order to free its grain.

This increased both production and speed, and it also prevented a somewhat clumsy farmhand—as Marcus had so often been described—from beating his colleagues over the head with this potentially life-threatening tool. Some of the families of Glancebury, who may have been somewhat small and insignificant before, had now suddenly become a lot larger, and they could now enjoy a certain prestige. Other families, on the other hand, that in earlier times were granted this form of recognition, had in the meanwhile, become a lot smaller or had even been driven out altogether by the rapid economic changes and now had to look elsewhere for their wages and salvation. The cloth weaver had gone back to his own Light Town, for example. His earlier missteps had now expired, and his slip ups in the field of his own craft had been largely forgiven him—perhaps partly by offering the right amount of compensation—and so he settled back in the city where he once came from.

He had also joined a guild again to his complete satisfaction, which was of course, a lot more beneficial for him, since the demand for high-quality cloth was decreasing more and more, although it was still in reasonable demand in the capitals. The down-to-earth John McAllister had improved significantly. A small business only had to be simple of course, without too much fuss behind it, but with an effective product or a simple service that was much needed in daily life, and McAllister's shuttle service was a great example of that. And so it came that, partly due to the small expansion of Glancebury itself and because of the now somewhat more modern inhabitants of it who - just like the young Marcus himself frequently had done in the past - tried to seek their refuge within the high city walls of the bigger cities further on. John's small business was also able to grow somewhat because of such a development. The man now had two real carriages at his disposal, four horses, and two servants working under him, although he still remained the good-natured, the always good-humored, but also the somewhat simple John McAllister…

The explanation for the national population growth was of course, mainly to be found in the increase of birthrate; an increase that in turn had everything to do with the lower prices of the available food. This increased the disposable income per household, which in turn resulted in a decrease in the age of marriage. Another consequence of the increase in income was a greater demand for products such as household goods: of cutlery, pottery, and clothing. And also of other haberdashery such as buttons and shoe buckles for example.

This expansion of the domestic market is now often seen as an important explanation for the development of a mechanized industry. In the past, the source of the capital required for this was sought in the commercial sector in the first place, but nevertheless, a large part of that capital also came from agriculture. It could therefore, be said that, partly due to the development of the agricultural sector, a certain aristocratism took place within the common bourgeoisie and that of the farmers.

This was therefore, rightly ironic since farmers had for long been seen as a form of lower class since the beginning of the Middle Ages, but were nevertheless largely the cause of this shift in classes. So it turned out once again that everything was ultimately connected with each other, that everything and everyone eventually influenced one another, directly or indirectly, and that this as a whole eventually seemed to complete the social circle again.

Many developments and inventions have since emerged

within Ingland. In 1825, the first railway line was opened over a greater distance, a year later, the first photo saw the light of day, and around 1832, the first cars were driving around - albeit still on steam power.

Around 1850, the rotary press was developed. Until then, books still had to be printed per sheet of sixteen pages, for example; when one sheet was ready the device had to be opened up to place a new sheet underneath, as was also the case with the platen press; a device that Marcus had worked with so many times, that he knew all too well about, and which he had despised so often.

In the rotary press, however, cylinders were used, and also rolls of paper instead of sheets. Newspapers and magazines could thus be produced very quickly, and also in large circulation, and the circulation of such copy was therefore practically unlimited.

There were also whispers among the common people about mechanical weaving; about a machine that could handle the work of up to a hundred people at the same time, but if this rumor was really true? The first bicycles, although still in rudimentary form, also saw the light of day, and people could see them more and more often riding through the streets and over the large paved squares of the capitals. At the same time, another technical tour de force took place: the flywheel was developed; an object that could generate kinetic energy and that could eventually even store it. This wheel had numerous mechanical applications, and it even seemed to be at the cradle of a future - almost a technocratic society - over which only a few dared to bend their heads; within a time of scientific progress that even seemed to be moving too slowly for these kinds of bright minds.

Foreign settlers wanted to take the land from the ancient Indians In the early 19th century. And so it came that the Imerican government forced fifteen thousand Cherokees to leave their homes in the year of 1818. The Cherokees had to move west, and they were accompanied on that obligatory journey by Imerican soldiers, as well as by their own people, who began to work for this government. Some of these Cherokees refused to leave their homes, and they decided to hide in the mountains. Thousands of Cherokees died of hunger along the way unfortunately, and this journey is popularly called the *Trail of Tears...*

Certain things were even implemented in the field of education, and there was a discussion going on whether corporal punishment of school children was still appropriate. The attention therefore, seemed to shift from a clear discipline to a more form of pampering; an approach that was mentally healthier for the child, so people thought, but also brought its own disadvantages. It was therefore, claimed by some that it made children weak, with softer characters, that it gave them a big mouth laced with rebellion, and they didn't develop a backbone as a result. One could be right about this, and a certain middle ground might have been ideal, but knowing human nature, it was often one way or the other, either black or white, and also within the field of education a certain shade of gray, an effective middle ground in this area, still wasn't completely found. However, this may come at a later date. After all... A fairly constructive path had already been taken...

Agricultural land was also reclassified. In the middle of the 19th century: the so-called 'allotment' had taken place. And around 1850 no one had the piece of land in family ownership anymore that they had once inherited from their ancestors. If Marcus had listened to his father, and if he had followed in his footsteps, then he would probably have had a very difficult life, and he'd perhaps never been able to become a real farmer at all. After all, Marcus had no business acumen whatsoever, the laws and regulations that came with this 'new farming' would probably have gone completely over his head, and he would eventually, and undoubtedly, have had to close down his farm or sell it for next to nothing. Then he would not only have been a pauper, but perhaps even a homeless beggar; smelling of sweet liquor, and wandering around aimlessly and deliriously within the filthy slums of Light Town or any other big city. The only warmth he then would have felt was the blood alcohol level of the bottle or that of a woman of pleasure who would sometimes grant him a free turn out of pity, although that would probably only happen when Easter and Pentecost fell on the same day. No, Marcus had clearly chosen a path in life for himself, and he finally seemed to be reaping the well-deserved fruits of it. That is...

That is, if someone knew where he had gone. Because where was that beautiful dreamer anyway? Where had that brave pioneer, that brave anonymous whistleblower of Glancebury, actually gone to...?

Sometimes, there was a brave young man from the town of Glancebury that dared to venture into the noisy excesses of metropolitan life. A now shorter journey to the now even larger capital of Light town, to try his luck there somewhere, sitting in the back of the carriage of a now old man who still bore the name of John McAllister. And very occasionally, this unsuspecting commuter would stick his head out of the side window of the carriage to shout a few words to the easygoing horse driver: 'Dear coachman!' the person in question would usually shout. 'What is that beautiful chateau that manages to shine over there in the distance?! And who is that pitiful pile of human being who sometimes, and almost always with his head bowed down, seems to shuffle around there in the vicinity?!' And the good old John McAllister would then often say the following; with his gaze still strongly fixed on the road in front of him; a road that still went straight on: 'Ah!' the good man would then often shout to his passenger:

'That one is nothing but an odd figure! Malevolent even! Someone who seems to have eternal life! You'd rather not have to deal with that sort! Believe the people! That's a wicked person...!'

It's always better to follow a dream, than to have never dreamt at all…

-    Marcus   -

About the Author

Rambaro Pellegrino was born and raised in the Netherlands to a Dutch mother and an Egyptian father. Pellegrino means 'traveler' in Italian, and that's exactly what he likes to do. Not necessarily in the physical form, but traveling within his own mind to come up with good stories in that way, to entertain the reader with, and mixed with some insights here and there. He has been writing since 2006. It hasn't always been an easy journey, and sometimes one could try and put away the pen, but it always seems to beckon again at some point.

It's funny that one can write many pages on a specific subject and still not finish writing. Writing is almost something magical; worlds are being created, and characters and creatures see the light of day, but these can just as easily be erased. However, the ink never runs out, the pen never wants to rest, and a good story, fueled by sufficient inspiration, actually writes itself. Always. Without concessions…